Bonus Daddy

The Dad Coms

Book 3

Daphne Elliot

Melody Publishing, LLC

Published by Melody Publishing, LLC

Editing by Beth Lawton at VB Edits

Cover Art by Elen Bushe Art

Cover Design by Mel D Book Cover Designs

 Formatted with Vellum

Dedication

To all the readers who fell in love with The Mom Coms.
Just try to resist our Daddies...

PLAYLIST

Dance Dance – Fall Out Boy

Still Into You – Paramore

I Was Made For You – River Cuomo

Begin Again – Taylor Swift

The Better of Me – Dashboard Confessional

I'd Do Anything – A Simple Plan

Back to You – Selena Gomez

Mr. Brightside – The Killers

You Missed My Heart – Phoebe Bridgers

Jersey Boys:

The Very Thought of You – Frank Sinatra

Love Her – The Jonas Brothers

Some Type of Love – Charlie Puth

CHAPTER 1

Jess

This couldn't be it. The dilapidated brick building with crumbling stairs, weeds in the alley, and a glowing neon sign advertising psychic readings could not be my new lawyer's office.

I walked further down the street, past a yummy-smelling kebab shop, and turned around to make sure I hadn't missed the correct building, finding no hidden structure.

With a sigh, I smoothed down my pink floral skirt, second-guessing the choice. The weather was glorious. The sun was shining and a light breeze blew the damp garbage smell of Jersey City toward the river and away from my nostrils.

I had a few black pieces left from my days as Kenneth's wife, but the thought of putting one on made my stomach ache. For the past few years, I'd been devoted to finding and reclaiming myself. So I'd reached for the pink dress and I hadn't looked back. Until now.

Since I didn't work at the hospital on Wednesdays, I typically walked the girls to school, then I'd run errands and clean the house before teaching an afternoon yoga class. And I always made a point to cook on Wednesday nights. This afternoon, I'd prepped a lasagna—Greta's favorite—and I couldn't wait to surprise her with it. If I made it home from this meeting...

I looked at the shabby buildings surrounding me, trying to figure out where I'd gotten lost. All the fancy high-rises, the banks and law firms and insurance companies, were near the Hudson River. This neighbor-hood was... not that.

Double checking my phone and confirming I was at the right place, I took a deep breath. Appearances could be deceiving, and my intuition was telling me this would be a good meeting.

I never imagined I'd find my legal representation in my yoga studio, yet here I was. As I took in the sights, enjoying the warm breeze, I real-ized how much I'd miss the city noises when we moved to Vermont. Getting rid of that dumb McMansion in the 'burbs was like having an enormous malignant tumor removed. Putting space between myself and those memories was healing, and now that we lived in Jersey City, I hardly needed to drive. Everything I needed was walkable, and on nice spring days, it was downright blissful.

Soon we'd have the Green Mountains in our backyard and we'd be inhaling air that smelled like maple syrup rather than hot garbage. My kids would run wild on the farm my siblings and I had. I could close the book on the heartache and strife of the past four years.

But first, I needed a good lawyer. I had to start the inevitably expen-sive and frustrating legal process of moving out of New Jersey.

The legal process was called relocation, but it was so much more complex than the single word made it seem. Already, several attorneys had turned me down, citing a low likelihood of success. But I was a posi-tive person, and I wholeheartedly believed that I'd be granted permission to move my children to my hometown.

Lo and her boyfriend had become regulars in my yoga classes over the last few months and had even begun to feel like friends. They were kind and helpful and intelligent. So when they told me one of the partners at their law firm handled complex relocation, I jumped at the chance to meet him.

As I shuffled up to the partially rusted steel door, I spied a small sign that read *Murphy and Machon.* I paused, hit by a warm familiarity. *Weird.*

I stepped inside, unsure of whether I'd find a fancy law firm or a crime scene and was a bit concerned when the space was, oddly enough, a bit of both.

Shiny leather chairs sat on top of vomit colored linoleum, and the cracks in the ceiling were too numerous to count.

Lo was so put together, so sharp and smart. Did she actually work here? This was the best family law firm in the city?

"Hello, Yoga Jess." I heard Cal's posh British accent before he came around the corner to greet me, his arms held wide. "Delighted to see you here."

He was wearing the kind of suit that cost more than my car, again making me question what the hell he was doing in a place like this.

Lo appeared a moment later, her gorgeous red hair pulled back into a braid. "Jess," she said cheerfully, her hands full of files, "let me put these down and I'll get you situated. Can I offer you a cup of coffee?"

I shook my head, still studying my surroundings. This simply didn't add up.

"This way," she said.

I followed her down a musty corridor, squinting against the flickering of the fluorescent lights.

Another tall, dark, and handsome man appeared in a doorway. "This is my brother Sully," Cal said brightly. "He could really use one of your restorative classes. Might help dislodge that stick up his bum."

His brother stared at me, his gray-blue eyes intense. It was a bit unnerving. While he was as good looking as Cal, he gave off a real serial killer vibe.

"Sullivan Murphy," he said gruffly, still studying me.

Lo tipped her head, signaling that we hadn't reached our destination yet, and I followed. Behind me, Sully stepped out into the hall. He spoke to his brother, his low words unintelligible, though it felt an awful lot like they were about me.

Lo stopped at a large door, where I couldn't help but notice a suspicious brown stain on the faded commercial carpet.

"Don't look at that," she said, waving me inside. "We can't tell if it was a leaky pipe or Sebastian's remains."

My heart lurched. What had I walked into?

Before I could turn and run, she herded me into the office. It was lined with floor-to-ceiling bookshelves and filing cabinets, and in the center, a massive mahogany desk that looked completely out of place in this dilapidated building.

Still trying to fit all the pieces of this strange puzzle together, I zeroed in on the man sitting behind the desk.

As I took in his auburn hair and the familiar features, recognition sank in. *No way.*

When he looked up from his computer screen, I wasn't sure if it was the beard or the sparkly tiara on his head that startled me the most. Pink and glittery, with turquoise jewels, it was almost as jarring as the face of the man wearing it.

Was it?

No.

"Brian," Lo said. "This is your new client, Jessica Mosely."

Between one blink and the next, he was standing and walking toward me, all broad shoulders and rolled-up shirtsleeves, with a serious expression on his face.

"Brian Machon," he said, holding out his hand.

I froze, studying him. Was I hallucinating, or was this really him?

When I took his hand, large, warm, and strong, I gasped.

"Brian," I breathed.

His eyes widened as recognition dawned.

But then he made a choked sound and dropped my hand. "Excuse me. I'll be right back."

He skirted around me with catlike movements and darted out of the room, slamming his shoulder into the doorframe and stumbling a bit down the hall. He almost plowed into Sully, who was wearing a look of horror, before he disappeared.

I looked at Lo, who was likewise shocked, then Cal, who looked amused. Had the boy I once loved just run away from me? While wearing a pink glitter tiara?

The four of us stood silently as the man who's taken off like a criminal on the run thundered up what sounded like a flight of stairs.

"Okay," Lo said with a sigh, smoothing down her dark green pants. "That was weird. Have a seat, and I'll grab the rest of your files."

She walked away quickly, leaving me in this run-down office with more questions than I could handle. This man, who, although painfully handsome, had run at the sight of me was my best hope?

At this rate, I'd never get out of Jersey.

CHAPTER 2
Brian

With a long breath out, I shuffled to the sink, where I splashed cold water on my face.

Focus, Brian. Focus.

Why the hell was I having a breakdown over my college girlfriend showing up in my office?

Cal had added the meeting to my calendar as "Yoga Jess." I had no clue it would be her.

It had been years—no, it had been literal decades—since we'd broken up. Since I'd last seen her.

My body buzzed with adrenaline as I tried to corral my racing thoughts. I was a lawyer. One of the best family law attorneys in the state of New York—and Jersey now too. And she was a client who needed help.

The shock to my system was enough to clear away some of the spiraling thoughts, and the gasp that escaped me when the temperature of the water registered was enough to reset my breathing, allowing me to inhale deeply for the first time in the last two minutes.

Water dripped from my beard as I snagged a paper towel from the dispenser, muttering to myself.

"Get it together," I said, surveying my reflection in the mirror and noting my aching shoulder from where I'd slammed into the doorframe.

Only then did I realize I still had a fucking tiara on my head.

God dammit. I'd forgotten about the bet I'd lost to Murphy and T. J. I probably looked like an escapee from a psyche ward, not a competent attorney.

"Get it together."

Lo appeared in the doorway, her expression murderous. "You're acting ridiculous. You scared that poor woman and almost maimed Sully. Be a professional." She paused, a slow smile spreading across her face. "And the tiara really brings out your eyes."

I could be a dick and lash out. Make some mention of her relationship with Cal, which was a walking HR nightmare. But regardless of Lo's judgment when it came to dating her boss, I couldn't do this job without her. She was my right hand, and even now that I had to share her with Sully and Cal, she was the most efficient paralegal I'd ever worked with. Even stuck out here in Jersey City, in this hellhole of an office, with its musty gold carpet and peeling paint, she ran a tight ship, allowing us to keep things moving at the same pace we had back in the city. I couldn't lose her, so I kept my thoughts about her office romance to myself. And while Cal was like a brother to me, I would seriously break his kneecaps if he fucked this up.

Luckily, he followed her around like a damn lost puppy. He was obsessed. He knew he'd won the girlfriend lottery, so for now, I pushed any concern about them to the back of my mind.

Currently, I chose to focus on how close we were to getting the fuck out of this state. We'd survived almost nine months in Jersey purgatory so far, meaning we'd be back in the city by the end of the summer. In a few short months, I'd be back in my corner office, where I could once again watch the fish tank to calm my nerves. And I'd be back in my own brownstone. Alone. Where I didn't have to share a locker room–style bathroom with my two best friends, their women, and two seven-year-old boys.

I stomped out of the bathroom, tossed the plastic tiara onto the ping-pong table, and jogged down the stairs.

Faced with the choice between ripping off the band aid and telling Lo the whole story, or going downstairs and doing my job, I chose the latter, giving her a firm nod before jogging down the stairs. It was time to be a fucking adult.

"Has the motion been filed?" I asked with a professional smile, trying to salvage this meeting.

I sat, my lungs constricting, as I took in the woman sitting across from me.

She was blond, and the pink floral dress she wore, though modest, accentuated every one of her curves. A wave of nostalgia washed over me with so much force it almost knocked me on my ass.

She was older, her expression more serious, but those eyes were the chocolate brown color I'd seen in my dreams for years. And that dimpled smile hadn't changed at all. What the hell was *she* doing in my office?

Jess flipped through the large Redweld folder she'd brought with her. "No. It hasn't. Will was supposed to have done it, but he kept delaying things. That's why I'm here. I can't afford to wait any longer. School will be out soon."

I nodded, attention drifting to my legal pad as I jotted down notes. Jessica was still beautiful. Long blond hair, full rosy cheeks, and dark brown eyes. The more I studied her, the more her features were familiar to me.

But regardless of her beauty, she was also unlikely to win this. "Relocation cases are notoriously difficult in New Jersey," I explained, keeping my tone firm.

She nodded. "I know it's a long shot. But I need this. My daughters need this." She sniffled.

As an uncomfortable sort of sensation unfurled in my chest, I pushed the box of tissues on my desk toward her.

"The kids need a fresh start," she said, wiping a tear from her cheek. "I need a fresh start. It's been four years since the divorce. My ex doesn't even live in the state anymore. He's engaged. Again. I think this is fiancée number three. He doesn't respect our visitation agreement and has no interest in his daughters."

I clenched my fist in my lap, my teeth gritted. That motherfucker. There was nothing worse than a deadbeat dad.

"I'm not sure if you remember, but I'm from Vermont," she explained, her lashes fluttering as she continued fighting back tears.

Oh, I remembered. I remembered every detail about her. Including the constellation of freckles on the top of her right thigh. Since the moment she walked in, memories had been hitting me at warp speed, like a highlight reel of my college days.

"The farm?" I asked. "How are your parents?"

Her face fell, and the tears she'd barely gotten under control welled once again. "They passed." She dabbed beneath one eye, then the other. "Dad a few years after his heart attack and Mom last fall. My brother Josh runs the farm now, with help from Jasper. And Jenn lives in town with her wife and kids."

I smiled at the mention of her siblings. They were good people. Memories of Jenn, especially, stuck out to me. The first time I met her, she'd sat me down and grilled me about my intentions, looking me in the eye, her shoulders pulled back the whole time.

That sensation was quickly followed by one of sympathy as the comment about her parents sank in. "I'm so sorry for your loss."

She nodded, her shoulders sagging. "I can provide my kids with a much better quality of life up there. I'm exhausted, and I miss my family and my community."

Lips pressed together, I searched for the right words. As a lawyer, I knew this was a tough case. But as a man? I felt a bit breathless at the thought of her leaving.

In the twenty minutes I'd been in her company, so many memories and emotions had come back. The calm that washed over me when she was close. The joy I felt when we carried on a conversation.

She'd once had the innate ability to make even the most mundane things joyful, and already, it was clear to me she still did.

"Will probably mentioned how difficult cases like this are to win. Especially if your ex-husband is actively opposing the move." I scanned the papers she'd handed me. "And because he's represented by Burns and Glenn." They were among the most elite and expensive firms in Manhattan. We did pretty well for ourselves, but those jerks lit their celebratory cigars with hundred-dollar bills.

"Will thought it was doable, especially since my ex has moved out of state," she hedged. "And my prior firm spent months working on this." She pushed another folder at me.

I flipped this one open, impressed with how organized she was, even if I gritted my teeth knowing Will Fucking Higgins had probably gleefully taken this woman's money, then dragged his feet. I hated that fucker, and it didn't look like he'd done anything substantive.

"New Jersey is notorious for this," I explained. "Even if he's moved, the legal system will still want the child support payments flowing through the state."

Her lips tipped down. "That's so unfair."

"It's how things work here." I smoothed out the corner of one page. "But in this county, there is a chance. And his disinterest in seeing your children during his allotted visitation will work in your favor." I flipped to the next document and scanned it quickly. "We need to show you have a plan in place. A home for the kids, school choices, and sufficient income to support them."

She nodded. "He's only fighting to mess with me. He gets some sick satisfaction out of knowing that I'm stuck here, away from my family, miserable, while he's off gallivanting with his twenty-six-year-old fiancée in Palm Beach."

I knew nothing about the asshole she'd married. We'd lost touch after college, when life had thrown us curveballs and we'd gone our separate ways. But from the multi-year divorce battle and this bullshit, I knew in my bones he was nowhere near worthy of her.

"What does your ex do for a living?"

"He's a principal at Excel Enterprise Capital. He's obsessed with his job, his watch collection, and his boat," she said, her voice shaking with underlying rage. "His kids don't even make the top ten on his list of priorities."

I figured the guy was rich when I discovered who represented him, but this confirmed it. The asshole was loaded. I flipped through the pages, looking at the marital settlement agreement. The child support was adequate, but given his income, she could have easily gotten more, and honestly, she should have.

"No alimony?" I asked, looking up again.

She shook her head. "I waived it."

It took all the strength I had to school my features. Never in a million years would I have let her do that if she'd been my client from the beginning.

"Okay." I scratched at my beard. "In our petition, we need to make it clear that you have the means to provide for the children in Vermont. Home, job, schools, social support. Is that feasible?"

"Yes. I'm a social worker," she explained.

"Oh, sorry." I sat straighter. "I thought you taught yoga."

"I do." Her face lit up. "That's my second job. But I have a master's in social work and have been at Brooklyn hospital for the last few years. I've already filed the paperwork to have my social work license transferred to Vermont and have put feelers out. There aren't a ton of job prospects, but I've got a few leads, and the owner of the yoga studio in my hometown is willing to let me take on a few classes if I need the income."

Pen in hand, I tapped the glossy surface of my desk. "And a home for the kids?"

"My brother took over the farm. He lives in my parents' house and insists the girls and I move into a cottage on the property. It used to be a rental, but when the last tenants moved out, he kept it vacant with the hope that this would work out for us."

"Schools?" I asked, scribbling notes again.

"Maplewood has award-winning schools," she explained.

Ah, that was it. *Maplewood.* I'd forgotten that her hometown had a funny name.

"As soon as my motion is granted, I'll get them enrolled."

I put my pen down and studied her. Her expression was hopeful, though she fidgeted a little, like she was keyed up. Her nails were short and bare, like maybe she still bit them when she was nervous.

She should be nervous, unfortunately. These cases were pains in the ass, and depending on the judge, this could be a total nightmare.

But I'd always been a sucker for an underdog. And as we silently surveyed one another, all I could think about was making her happy.

I wanted it.

More than that, I needed it.

I had no life of my own.

No wife.

No kids.

No pets. Except the damn cat. I'd tried my hardest to stay away, but since the day Cal brought him home, the menace had decided that I was his human servant.

My entire existence revolved around my job. I'd long ago given up on having more than this. But I could make her life a little better. Even if it would be an uphill battle.

"Can you take the case?" With her head lowered in uncertainty, she had to look at me through those long, dark lashes again.

The answer should have been no. My workload was barely manageable as it was. Relocation cases were time-consuming, and I couldn't in good conscience bill this single mom my usual rate. Especially when she'd already spent so much money on the parent coordinator and guardian ad litem.

But there was no universe in which I wouldn't help her. From the little information I had, it was clear she'd been in a bad marriage and then suffered through an even worse divorce.

"Yes."

The smile that spread slowly across her face was worth every late night I'd endure while prepping this motion.

Eyes crinkling and dimple appearing, she stood. "Thank you, Brian." Her voice wobbled on my name, and once again, her tears got the best of her.

"Happy to help," I said as I guided her to the door. "And I'm sorry about earlier. Seeing you was kind of a shock."

She smiled, and I felt warmth spread through my chest. "Don't worry about it. I gotta say, though, between this office and you running off, I was planning to climb out that window."

She gestured to the old metal-crank window on the side of my office.

"Joke's on you," I said. "That thing hasn't opened for twenty years."

She narrowed her eyes. "Isn't that a fire hazard?"

"This entire building is a fire hazard, and I'll save the story of why we're here for our next meeting. I want to call the court and see if I can file the notice of representation before it closes in an hour."

Her face brightened, and before I could realize what was happening, she threw her arms around me and crushed me in a hug. She was a lot shorter than me, but she was strong, her body toned in some places but soft in others. The feel of her lit up emotions I no longer thought I was capable of experiencing.

I froze, my breath held. I didn't hug my clients.

But the warmth of her body and the strange familiarity felt right. Maybe it was muscle memory. Maybe it was some strange response from my olfactory system as her scent washed over me.

But nothing had felt this right in a long, long time.

Wrapped in her arms, it felt like I was finally home after years and years away.

So I hugged her back, closing my eyes and inhaling deeply.

Knowing full well she would be my downfall.

CHAPTER 3

Jess

My meeting at the law office this morning was confusing, to say the least. I was still processing how my college boyfriend, who was, strangely, wearing a tiara with his Tom Ford suit, had run out of the room after seeing me for the first time in almost twenty years.

Maybe it would have been a hit to my ego if my ego hadn't long ago been destroyed by my ex-husband, along with my self-esteem, my confidence, and my financial future.

And if that wasn't bad enough, I'd had the strangest interaction when I walked out the door. Madame Esmeralda, who was a regular at my vinyasa classes, had appeared on the sidewalk. Instead of the brightly colored yoga sets she wore to my class, she was decked out in a long floral skirt, a knit scarf, and several pounds of jewelry. She returned my friendly wave by grabbing my forearm forcefully.

"You're finally here." She turned my hand over and gently stroked the lines of my open palm.

"Excellent love line. Just as I expected." Then, before I could extract myself, she patted my cheek and said, "He's been waiting for you. Keep the faith, Cricket."

I'd almost fainted on the spot. My dad had always called me Cricket, but I hadn't heard the nickname since he passed away. And while I'd met this woman before, we certainly weren't close enough for her to know that. Lo had told me she was some kind of psychic, but I had always assumed it was a joke.

After that run-in, I'd needed a long walk to calm myself down. I filled my stainless-steel mug with tea and headed to the studio. I'd get my own workout in, plan today's class, and then do a deep clean of the space.

The studio was small but gorgeous, with large windows along the street side. It had been a shoe store many lives ago, and Lana had kept the original woodwork, though she'd painted the walls in calming blue and green tones. Though it was not what one would expect to see in a place like this, the massive chandelier that hung from the ceiling added to the charm, and the large white cabinets along the back wall that housed mats, straps, and blocks meant it always looked tidy.

I lit the candles on the altar, then opened the windows and the door to let in the fresh spring air. Then I put on my favorite playlist.

My body itched to move, eager to find a natural flow. I'd always been a mover. My mom used to joke that I was "a bad sitter." She wasn't wrong. It wasn't until I found yoga that I could achieve stillness with any sort of success.

The techniques and meditation involved allowed me to still my brain and move my body. It was a foreign concept, but one that I quickly grew addicted to.

I stripped off my T-shirt and tossed it onto the counter. Then, in a sports bra and yoga pants, I rolled my shoulders. Quickly, heat built within me. Today was a day where I needed to sweat.

As I pushed myself through a long series of sun salutations, my heart rate accelerated and a euphoric feeling took root in my bones.

I continued, relishing my strength and flexibility.

There was no better cure for the postpartum body blues than yoga.

As women, our bodies evolved and created life.

The bullshit societal notion that we should be the same size we were as children was absurd. And yet, once in a while, a niggle of shame tugged at me.

I'd get self-conscious, remembering that my belly was no longer completely flat. That I had stretch marks and cellulite that no amount of yoga would destroy.

As I pushed myself from a three-legged dog into a standing split, I focused on breathing in confidence and breathing out negativity.

Despite my best efforts, my ex's voice would sometimes creep in, taunting me. Tormenting me like he had when he'd buy cocktail dresses a size too small for events, insisting it would "motivate me." Judging me the way he judged Kit when she once asked for a second popsicle after dinner.

Mentally blocking the memories of his denigration, I rolled into a headstand. I found inversions helped quiet the negative thoughts. From there, I rolled into upward-facing dog to get my back loose.

When my body told me I'd done enough, I reached for my water. Only then did I realize that I'd left it at the check-in desk by the windows.

So I stood and padded through the sun-drenched studio, rolling my shoulders as I went. As I got closer, a figure outside the window caught my eye, and my heart stuttered.

The sun was a bit blinding, so, shielding my eyes, I examined the person. It was definitely a man. He was tall and lean, but muscled, and he was staring through the window.

"Brian?" I gasped.

Eyes widening, he took a step back and dropped his attention to his feet.

His dress pants were gray, and the sleeves of his Oxford were rolled up, exposing his forearms. He hadn't changed since our meeting, but he'd ditched the coat and tie.

My heart lodged itself in my throat as I took a step closer. What was he doing here?

I waved awkwardly through the open window, anxiety coursing through me, undoing all the work I'd just accomplished.

Movement near his feet pulled my attention down to the oversized animal wearing a harness and a leash.

"Is that... a cat?"

He looked down at the feline, who flopped onto the sidewalk and stretched out like it was dying of boredom.

"Yeah." He let out a beleaguered sigh. "It's a damn cat. I walk him every day."

It took effort not to wrinkle my nose at him. That wasn't weird at all. Nope. Totally normal. Also normal? How red his cheeks were. Had he been watching me practice?

A fresh wave of mortification washed over me. I'd been facing the back wall, with my sizable ass in the air, and I'd spent the last thirty minutes falling out of handstands.

Heart thumping, feeling awkward, I took a big swig of water and shuffled toward the door I'd left propped open. I'd wanted to invite the breeze in, yet I'd also garnered confused stares from my new lawyer–slash–college sweetheart.

He ran a hand through his hair, discomfort radiating from him. Interesting. If anyone needed some time on the mat, it was Brian.

The tension in his shoulders flowed down his arms, past where his sleeves were rolled, the muscles in his forearms flexing. His skin was dotted with light freckles and brown hair with a reddish tint.

"Why?" I brought my water bottle to my mouth again, cringing at how unruly my hair must have looked.

He watched me with a confused frown.

I patted the messy bun on my head, certain the look had morphed from cute Instagram influencer to deranged raccoon over the course of my yoga practice.

"Why do you walk the cat?" I clarified.

"For exercise," he replied, like it was the most natural answer in the world.

"For you or the cat?"

"The cat," he said with an awkward laugh.

"It's a large cat."

"Comically large."

His eyes darted away, and he ran his hand through his hair again. If I remembered correctly, it was one of his nervous tics. He wore the façade of a polished lawyer well, but beneath it, the working-class kid from Brooklyn I'd known all those years ago still existed. The guy who loved boxing and greasy pizza.

His auburn hair was darker and shorter than it had been back in college, and his face was leaner, his cheekbones more angular.

He filled out that dress shirt well, like he wasn't the kind to skip a workout, no matter how heavy his caseload.

Shame flooded me, and on instinct, I laced my hands over my abdomen to hide the sliver of stomach between my sports bra and high-waisted pants. It was silly, really. He'd already seen my body. Dressed like this, all my curves and lumps were on full display. After giving birth to two kids, my hips were wider and my boobs way less perky. I'd worked hard to battle my insecurities these last few years, but standing in front of this gorgeous man, it was hard not to wish I still looked like the fresh-faced farm girl he'd met all those years ago. Before a toxic marriage and the loss of my parents had sucked the life out of me.

Back when I was young and wide-eyed and hopeful. When we'd walk around Castle Island eating one-dollar hot dogs and planning a beautiful future together.

He looked back down at the bored-looking cat. "I know. Getting out like this helps with the litter box situation. Plus it needs regular exercise or it gets depressed."

I nodded, lips pressed together. "Cat depression..."

"Is a thing, sadly," he explained. "Cal came home with this beast, and now it's my feline overlord. I'm the one who feeds him, so he's latched on to me."

The navy blue harness with matching leash was pretty adorable, especially against the creature's long gray and white fur.

"Is it a bobcat? I saw one at the Central Park Zoo when I took the girls there last year. That size and the super pointy ears are sus."

"He's a purebred Maine Coon," Brian said. "Cal has his papers and everything. But he behaves more like he's half dog, half face-eating leopard with a superiority complex."

The exasperated look he gave the cat was pretty adorable.

"What's its name?"

"Dammit," he replied and I shot him a look.

"His legal name is Fuzzy Wuzzy Murphy, but he terrorizes me, so I call him Dammit."

I gazed down at the cat, who, aside from enormous, looked harmful. "He looks like a Fuzzy," I declared with a smile.

"Anyway, I'm sorry I bothered you," Brian said. "We don't usually walk this way. But Madame Esmeralda suggested it." Frowning, he looked down the street. "Right after she told me that baked goods are the love language of the unworthy."

I blinked, not sure what he was referring to.

"I'd been thinking about sending you some muffins, to apologize for my behavior earlier."

I nodded.

"And then she said I'd find what I was looking for on 8th Street."

"Esmeralda strikes again," I whispered. "Is she really psychic?"

"Yes." His face was stony. "She's our psychic. Okay, not my personal psychic. Except she says weird stuff to me all the time. But she's a tenant in our building. Cryptic old lady. Has been telling me to join her for yoga for the last six months. I thought she was either hitting on me or subtly trying to tell me I'm out of shape."

I laughed. No one could ever accuse Brian of being out of shape. "She's a regular in some of my classes."

"So you get it."

"I did not know of her talents until this morning when she called me Cricket."

His eyes widened. "Isn't that what your dad—"

I nodded, already feeling emotional. "So," I said, changing the subject, "she sent you down 8th Street to creep on me while I was doing yoga?" I crossed my arms and bit back a grin.

Face reddening, he sputtered. "No. Of course not," he forced out, tugging the cat to his feet. "I happened to notice the studio as I passed. Cal and Lo rave about your classes."

"The studio isn't mine," I clarified. "My best friend owns it. The whole building, actually. She's the one who got me into yoga. She lived upstairs, but after she got married and had a baby, she moved to the 'burbs. So she hired me to teach a few classes and let me and the girls move in."

With a thoughtful nod, he wandered in, the cat willingly stalking along beside him.

As I led him back toward the office, he studied the murals on the walls keenly, and when we stepped into the large room used for group meetings and community organizing, he smiled. "Back in your punk days, I would have never guessed you'd be into this stuff. But I see it. You're very Zen."

"Far from it," I admitted with a laugh. "But I enjoy the pursuit of Zen."

"You've always had this calming, happy presence," he said earnestly. " I'd imagine that's a great quality in a yoga teacher."

Stomach fluttering, I crouched down and changed the subject. "If anyone is Zen, it's this bobcat." I ran my hand over its back, and it purred loudly.

"He's not chill. He's a menace."

The cat purred again, its eyes widening sweetly.

"This is not a menace. You are a sweet fluff ball," I cooed. "Sure, you're enormous, but this is an inclusive space. We don't body shame."

"The damn cat hates me," Brian huffed. "He goes out of his way to fuck up my days."

"That's how cats show their love."

"Lucky me," he mused. "I should get going. I've got meetings."

"Oh."

I moved for the door, and he did the same, awkwardly getting in one another's way.

"Sorry," I said, stumbling back. "And thank you. For your help."

"Just doing my job."

I pushed a strand of hair behind my ear. "Maybe, but you didn't have to take my case. I know relocations are hard to win. It's just..."

Emotion welled up inside me. Jeez, why couldn't I be one of those cool women who knew how to keep it together? Maybe on a better day, I'd have the energy to hide the pain, but this day had gone and kicked my ass. I was wiped after the meeting this morning. Then he had to show up here and throw me off-kilter.

"It all feels so overwhelming sometimes." I tipped my head back and stared at the ceiling, willing the tears back into my eye sockets. "I'm pushing a rock up a hill most days. The cost of living here is ridiculous. I'm trying to be a good mom and ensure my daughters feel loved and cared for. I want to give them everything they could ever wish for, but I'm just one person, and I'm fucking tired."

He placed a heavy hand on my shoulder. "You're doing a great job."

I snapped my head forward and glared. "You don't know that."

With a step back, he crossed his arms. The new position made him look authoritative and grumpy. With the beard and the forearms, it was, as my kids said, a vibe.

"I read through your case file after you left. I know all the bullshit your ex-husband pulled. Hiding funds, offshore accounts, bogus real estate transactions. I know he fought you for custody and that he questioned your fitness as a mother during trial. And I know that after all that warfare, he can't even be bothered to exercise his parenting rights."

My heart climbed up into my throat, making it hard to breathe, as he scrutinized me.

"So yes, Jess," he continued. "I know you're a good mom. I've got the records to show for it. Including affidavits from the guardian ad litem, the parenting coordinator, the social workers, and the kids' teachers."

The tears were back, threatening to spill over. "You read all that? It's only been a few hours since I left your office."

"I told you: I'm good at my job." His response was full of certainty, but without hubris, making it hard not to believe him.

Being a single mom was exhausting on a good day. Even on the days when I didn't let anyone down, didn't drop one of the dozens of balls I was juggling, I was overwhelmed.

In the blink of an eye, I'd gone from my Bergen County McMansion, cooking dinner and volunteering at the elementary school, to trying to piece a life back together.

It was my own damn fault. I was too trusting. Too optimistic. Too hopeful.

When Kenneth and I vowed to love and cherish one another, I really believed we meant forever. Sure, he was difficult to live with, but he was my husband, the father of my children, and he was doing his best.

Or so I thought. In reality, I was an idiot.

And for years, I'd been kicking myself for being as naïve as the rest of the world assumed I was. I'd proved Kenneth right. And that hurt more than anything else.

"Here's the thing," I hedged.

I wanted to trust Brian, and my gut told me he could help. But I'd learned to fight my instincts. To be harder and meaner and less hopeful than was my nature.

"I'm exhausted," I admitted. "I don't want to fight anymore. I want peace and a fresh start. I have to stand on my head just to get through the days, and I don't know how much longer I can do it."

"Didn't I just see you literally standing on your head?" He quirked a brow.

Amusement threaded its way through me, dampening the defeat that had become my constant companion. "You know what I mean."

He chuckled. "If anyone can do it all, it's you. And you've got me on your team now. The rest of my firm too. We'll fight for you." He moved closer, stepping around the cat, which was once again lying at his feet. "Do you want me to go after him for more child support? For school tuition? For some of the real estate holdings he hid from you?"

"No." I shook my head, my heart pinching. "I want nothing from him but peace and freedom. Maybe my low-conflict style of managing my co-parenting relationship seems silly to you. You're an attorney, after all. You argue for a living, right?" I force a smile. "But over the years, I've learned that I'd give up a lot of things to protect my peace. Anything he gives me comes with strings. And I want my girls to be free. I want them to have the opportunity to be who they want to be."

He dipped his chin. "I respect that."

"All I need is the relocation. The house is ready for us, and I swear, some days, when I close my eyes, I can feel the mountain air on my face. I miss the farm. The community too."

His face fell slightly, though he quickly evened out his features. "Of course. And we'll make it happen."

I walked him to the door and waved goodbye, and as he and the monstrosity of a cat strolled away, a sense of calm washed over me.

Brian was on my team. He'd promised to fight for me and the girls.

Though my last attorney had let me down and gone back on his promises, this felt different. And if the Brian I used to know was still inside this older, more mature, even better-looking man, then I could allow myself to hope.

CHAPTER 4

Brian

I woke up the next morning, as I always did, with the damn cat sprawled out across my chest. For the first few months, I'd dream that I was being suffocated. Over time, though, my subconscious caught on, understanding that it was just thirty pounds of cat on my sternum.

"Food, Dammit," I wheezed out.

It pushed off me, forcing the rest of the air from my lungs, and darted for my closed bedroom door.

"Figures." Wiping the sleep from my eyes, I squinted at the clock. It wasn't even six. Fuck. I flopped back down onto the mattress. Why the hell was I up so early? The damn cat hadn't even been kneading at me or poking me with his claws. Yet here I was, more alert than was natural.

A few inches from my head, inside the wall near my headboard, a rattling sound caught my attention.

I roughed a hand down my face and groaned.

"Fuck you, Sebastian," I grumbled to our resident ghost. He had a habit of making weird noises just to mess with us.

Fuzzy hissed, reminding me that I'd promised the demon his food, so I heaved myself to my feet. Now that we were up, he'd also need a walk, so there was no chance of going back to sleep.

The damn cat was the epitome of high maintenance. The only cat food Sully had found that he wouldn't turn his whiskers up at was an organic brand we had to drive to the Whole Foods in Hoboken to pick up. He'd gone on a mini hunger strike not long after Cal had first brought him home, along with a standard bag of kibble. I, being an absolute dumbass, had felt bad for the oversized feline, so I'd given him a can of tuna. Now he expected Michelin-starred kitty chow on the regular.

Most days, I wasn't sure whether he was a beloved pet or an overgrown gremlin with delusions of grandeur.

Since Tia's birth, I'd taken over feeding duties for Sully, so with a sigh, I fed the damn cat and filled his water fountain. Yes, a bubbling fountain, because the damn cat would not deign to drink from a common bowl.

While he ate, I chugged my protein shake. My mind immediately went to Jess. The conversation in the yoga studio had inspired me. I had to help her. In fact, how I was going to help her and why I felt so compelled to do so had consumed all of my waking thoughts since she'd walked into my office.

The girl I used to know was tough, but this woman? She had a quiet, determined strength I was in awe of, and from what I'd read, she worked hard.

And she was gorgeous. She was bright and kind too. Though there was a weariness in her, creeping around the edges, that concerned me.

I was drawn to her the moment I saw her again. We were practically strangers after all these years, and our lives were moving in different directions, but there was a tiny spot inside my brain that lit up every time I thought about her. Her dimples, her smile, how graceful and sexy she looked doing yoga in that damn sports bra.

It inspired a want I'd only ever felt for her. It was a general ache. A phantom emotional limb. But the want that had plagued me in my thirties was back.

It was the desire for more.

More than my career and my brownstone. More than fun trips and a nice car.

A partner. A person.

It was bound to happen. I could only bury my feelings for so long, even if, like most Irish Catholic men, I was excellent at it.

First Cal and Lo fell in love. Watching their journey tugged at my heartstrings, but I'd become adept at ignoring those types of feelings.

It was trickier to deny the sensation when Sloane and Sully found their way back to each other. I witnessed their love story play out from the beginning, when the three of us were in law school, and nothing had ever been as satisfying as knowing they'd made it full circle. My best friends, happy and thriving and growing their family.

That's when the lock I'd put on the desire to one day find that for myself had been irrevocably damaged.

When I'd begun to think about finding a person to share my life with.

Yet in the last twenty years, I hadn't dated a single woman who turned me into a simp the way Lo does for Cal. And I hadn't once had the need to reevaluate my life and become the best version of myself the way Sully did with Sloane.

And maybe I'd chosen those women for that reason.

But when I looked at Jess?

A rightness I hadn't ever felt before consumed me.

I couldn't date my client. And I couldn't date a struggling single mom who needed my help. But I could learn from this experience. Instead of continuing to shut down these feelings, I could let them out and explore them.

Shit. That probably meant I'd have to do the thing I dreaded most.

Therapy.

"Did you find the Phillips trust file?" Lo said, her voice crackly through the walkie-talkie.

"Yes," I hollered back, my hands too busy knotting my tie to respond using what we'd dubbed the Jersey intercom system. With a final adjustment, I debated running upstairs to make a protein shake but realized I was already behind schedule. So I scooped the files up and headed toward the door. I had a meeting with Cliff Phillips today, and I would not keep him waiting.

When I stepped out onto the sidewalk, Dominic, Cliff's driver, was waiting out front with a smile and a black coffee for me.

Cliff Phillips had become a friend over the many years I'd worked for him. When Terry had hired me straight out of law school, he'd brought me to a meeting with him, and the old man had taken a liking to me.

Eventually, Terry handed the man's estate over to me. Not only did I work with him regarding his personal estate but also another two dozen family and corporate trusts. He was kind and down-to-earth, unlike just about any billionaire I'd ever met, with the exception of my sister's family and closest friends.

He was so down-to-earth, in fact, that the moment he saw me, he called me out on my shit. Just like he did every time we met.

"You look tired," he said as I sat at the conference table. "You're young. Gotta take better care of yourself."

I glared at him. "I'm not young, Cliff, and I'm feeling my age every day."

He leaned back in his chair, making the leather cushion creak. "I'm in my eighties, you ass. Trust me, I know what old feels like. And you're not old. You're in your prime, son. And as someone at the end of their journey—"

"Don't say that," I interrupted. "You're sharp as a tack."

He chuckled. "Yes. My mind is solid, but the docs said the cancer's bad this time."

"You beat it before."

"I did. But I had my Betty then." He let out a long sigh. "Now that she's gone, I'm not really living. Which is why I need you on your A game. I don't want any bullshit after I'm gone."

Straightening, I nodded. "Yes, sir."

"I mean it. Yes, I busted my ass for decades for what I have. The companies, the real estate, all the money, and I'm grateful for it all. But my proudest achievement is my family, my daughter, my grandchildren and my great grandchild. My priority is ensuring everything is set up correctly for them."

I nodded. His estate plan was complex and had been several decades in the making. A man didn't go from selling peanuts at Metros games to owning the stadium without planning ahead.

We spent more than an hour going through the new trust paperwork and the updates I'd made. And at every turn, Cliff asked clarifying questions and made suggestions. For someone with very little formal education, he missed nothing.

I'd have hours of work ahead of me to make all the requested changes, but I admired a man who knew what he wanted. So often, my high-net-worth clients dithered and struggled to make decisions, making the process miserable. No one wanted to confront their mortality, but rich people especially liked to pretend death would never come for them.

Cliff rang for coffee and sat back in his chair, surveying the field and the skyline behind it. Every time I came here, it was like I was ten again, attending my first game with my dad. He'd saved for months to purchase the tickets, and the day had been the best of the short life I'd lived up until then. I'd been to dozens of games as an adult, and I'd brought him into the owner's box a few times, but none of those experiences would ever compare to that sunny day in July when the two of us sat in the outfield bleachers.

"Anyway." He waved a hand. "When are you gonna get married? Best thing you'll ever do."

I kept my attention on my notes, not wanting to get baited into this conversation again.

"I mean it," he insisted, his voice loud in the large room. "Partnership is beautiful. Raising kids? God, it's the hardest and most rewarding thing you'll ever do. And I should know. Not only did I raise Charlotte, but then Landon and Lennon too. And now we've got Amelia in the mix."

The emptiness I typically kept at bay wormed its way through me. "Not sure that's in my future."

"Nope." He shook his head like he was rejecting my answer. "Work less and you'll see. There's a woman out there who's perfect for you. Someone who will make you want to cut out early and live a little."

I sat back, glaring at him. "Really? You're my biggest client, and you're condoning poor work ethic? If I start skipping out early, who's gonna pay the bills?"

He scoffed. "Don't I pay you enough? The offer still stands. Come work for me. You could have a nice office here. Plenty of vacation. Handle the nonprofit and all the trusts."

He'd been trying to poach me for years. But Murphy and Machon was my home. Terry had been like a second father to me since Sully and I met that first month of law school. And I'd never give up the client relationships I'd spent years building.

"We've talked about this. I can't be your personal lawyer."

"Is it because those Berkshires won't give you up? I'll call Henry."

There was no way Henry Berkshire would ever let me go. He'd also repeatedly offered me a position with his company. It was overwhelming, though I couldn't deny it boosted my ego when billionaires fought over me.

"What I'm trying to say is that you only have one life to live," he goes on. "So you better get living. There's got to be a girl out there for you."

I smiled politely, pretending his words didn't sting a bit. Because there was a woman. A woman who'd ruined me for all others twenty years ago. A woman I'd never stopped thinking about, who now consumed my every waking moment. Who was making me question things I'd long ago accepted as fact.

But she wasn't perfect for me, and I sure as hell wasn't perfect for her.

She was beautiful and fun, and somehow, I'd transformed into a curmudgeon. I was nowhere near good enough. But maybe I could be?

"There is someone," I admitted.

His graying brows rose with curiosity.

"The problem is..." I cleared my throat. "She's a client."

"So?" he practically shouted. "Get Cal or Sully to take her case."

"Can't. Out of the three of us, I've got the most experience, by far, with her particular situation, and it's a tricky one."

"Okay." He nodded slowly, rubbing at his chin. "But she doesn't have to be a client forever. Do the work, and when it's all wrapped up, ask her out. If she's the right girl, the timing will work out. It always does."

My chest tightened as I leaned forward. "How can you be sure?"

"Because I was once a twenty-four-year-old college dropout who walked out of a diner on 51st Street with seven dollars in my pocket and met the love of my life." He rested his forearms on the table. "And together, the two of us built a life and a family and an empire." His eyes began to mist. "She never missed a home game. And now her seat is empty."

"I'm so sorry," I said, feeling choked up myself. Betty had been a firecracker and a lot of fun. Her presence was missed everywhere. As if she had been his life force, and now he was surviving without it, he'd aged significantly since she passed.

"If I did one thing right in my life, it was this: I got the girl and I held on with everything I had."

A strange combination of anticipation and fear swirled inside me. "You did."

"Remember that. Because when you're my age, staring down death, you'll discover that your family was your greatest achievement."

I nodded, though I didn't respond. He made it all seem so easy, yet my situation was anything but.

When I finished Jess's case, the best-case scenario would be that she'd move to Vermont. Worst-case scenario? I'd fail and she'd be devastated. Hell, she'd probably hate me. So asking her to dinner after we'd wrapped up in court was far less simple than it seemed.

And I wasn't sure I could even survive that long. I'd spent less than two hours in her presence this week, and already, my brain cells were rearranging themselves.

"You're good at what you do, Brian. Because you're strategic and precise," Cliff said. "Ever think about applying those skills to situations beyond billable hours?"

I cringed. "Dating and lawyering are not the same."

He swatted a hand at me. "Jesus, don't tell me you lied when you said you graduated at the top of your class in law school. A man that smart surely couldn't be this dense."

Tipping back in my chair, I rolled my eyes. Second in the class, technically, thanks to Sloane, but I didn't bother correcting him.

"Be patient, lay the groundwork, play the long game."

I sighed, my body deflating. "I'll try."

"Don't screw it up." He gave me a wry grin. "Take it from me. I got the girl, and she made every day worth living. Now I just want to move on to the next life so I can be with her again, because the world is a hell of a lot less fun without her in it."

He stood, and relying more heavily on his cane than he had the last time I saw him, he headed for the door.

As I followed him out, he turned and held out his arms.

I gave in and hugged him. For the second time this week, I'd hugged a client.

He patted my cheek affectionately. "I mean it. Bring her to the owner's box. You know there are always seats for you."

CHAPTER 5

Jess

"**Y**ou sound tired."

"I am tired," I replied quietly. Our apartment was tiny, with thin walls, and I didn't want to wake the girls.

Greta had conked out early, and Kit had been worried about a math test, so after an intense study session, she willingly turned in before her usual ten-p.m. bedtime.

I'd just checked on them and was getting supplies together so I could paint my toenails when my phone rang.

My brother Josh wasn't much of a talker, so my heart leaped into my throat when his name appeared on the screen, and instantly, every worst-case scenario flashed through my mind. Thankfully, he was just checking in.

"I've got a new lawyer," I admitted. "And I'm feeling good."

"What did they say about the relocation order? Is it doable?" I could almost picture him pacing around the farmhouse, his evening cup of tea in a mug one of us had painted in art class in 1996. Though he was a thirty-five-year-old Stanford MBA graduate, he lived like a Victorian recluse on the farm.

The tightness in my chest I'd been breathing through all day reappeared. "I hope he can. He's supposed to be the best."

Josh grunted in response. During the divorce proceedings, he'd pushed me to fight harder. More than once, his frustration had slipped through, despite how adamantly he supported me. But in the end, it was just money. My kids were all that mattered, and we weren't going to starve. I'd finished my master's and had gotten a decent job. And day by day, things were getting better.

After years of doubting myself—mostly because Kenneth constantly told me I was useless, dumb, and silly—I was making it on my own.

But I missed Josh, Jenn, and Jas. I missed Maplewood and my nephews. The tug to return home, to my roots, grew stronger every day. Sure, staying in Jersey wouldn't be the end of the world, but my girls deserved an epic childhood. Family and community and hikes and festivals. Picking wildflowers and tapping trees. Memories and tradition and vacations.

They deserved so much more than scraping by while living above a yoga studio in Jersey City.

I should ask about the farm. Get the local town gossip. But for some reason, my mouth kept moving.

"It's so funny, really. The lawyer is actually Brian Machon."

He was silent for a heartbeat, the only sound his footsteps on the hardwood floors. "Why does that name sound familiar?"

My stomach sank. I shouldn't have mentioned it. I shouldn't have opened this door. But there was a niggling feeling inside me that told me not to keep this from him.

"I dated him, back in college. Weird, right?"

He inhaled sharply. "Is this *the* Brian? The serious boyfriend? The one you brought home to the farm?"

My heart stumbled over itself. "Yes."

"I don't remember much about him, but I remember how obsessed you were."

"You were in high school, so I'm sure you had other stuff on your mind."

"This is not a good idea," he said, his tone firm. "Ethically or—"

"Yes, it is. It's fine," I interrupted. "We dated twenty years ago. I've lived a whole lifetime since then. And he's one of the best family law attorneys in the state. He's my best shot at winning this."

"Is it weird?"

"No," I lied. In fact, it was extremely weird. Though surreal was a better way to describe the situation. He was nice. Smart and competent. Professional.

He literally possessed every quality I'd want in a lawyer.

He was also handsome and sweet and a tiny bit awkward, just like the brilliant boy I'd fallen for during poli-sci study sessions.

"It's fine." Thinking about Brian was bad. I'd been working my hardest to avoid it. But he kept popping into my brain. Present-day handsome, confident lawyer Brian interspersed with long-forgotten memories of college Brian.

"Totally professional," I babbled, trying to convince myself as much as my brother, who, based on his silence, wasn't buying it.

"What have you been up to?" I asked, mentally kicking myself for even bringing up Brian.

"I've been working on the guest cottage. Put up crown molding to fancy things up a bit. Tore out the old porch and built a new one. And I ordered new appliances for the kitchen."

"Josh." I groaned. "We talked about this."

He ignored me, talking instead about his plan for putting up the giant tire swing Greta had requested during our visit at Christmas.

"I'm not even sure I can move yet," I reminded him. "And you work so hard already. Don't add to your never-ending list."

"You know I like projects," he said softly.

I did. Josh needed to keep his hands and his mind busy. It was the most effective way he'd found to manage the anxiety that had already stolen so much from him.

My brother didn't worry about money. He'd made a lot of it on Wall Street before our lives fell apart. Then he used his MBA and investment skills to turn the farm from failing to profitable. He worked from sunup to sundown, even though at this point in his life, he could probably afford to live on a beach on some island tax haven.

But that was not him. If there was a job to do, Josh was on it.

Even as a kid, he constantly tinkered, rooting out problems before we even realized they existed and fixing them with the type of skill only professionals typically possessed. Broken fences, leaky faucets, weeds in the vegetable garden. He had this sense about him. He knew where he was at all times and could sense the condition of each person, place, or thing around him. Of the four of us, it made the most sense for him to take over the farm. Jas helped between his shifts as a firefighter and EMT, but Josh ran the show.

"Seen Jenn recently?" I asked, eager to change the subject.

"'Course. I see her every morning, and she and Liz never let me skip Sunday dinner, no matter how hard I try to avoid it."

I let out a laugh. That tracked. Jenn had always possessed a heaping dose of firstborn energy. She'd bossed us all around as kids, and that hadn't changed once we migrated into adulthood.

"And Jas?"

"He gets out of dinner sometimes because of work. Or because he sweet-talks Jenn."

A soft smile crept over my face. "Still living in his childhood bedroom?"

"When he actually sleeps here, yes." Josh sighed. "But you know him. He's always moving, that kid."

Like Josh was one to talk.

And Jas wasn't actually a kid. He had recently turned thirty, but as the baby of the family and my parents' unabashed favorite, he had youngest-kid energy to spare. He had Jenn, who was twelve when he was born, wrapped around his finger. She'd always been like a second mom to him, going out of her way, even now, to take care of him. Leaving Josh and me to deal with the messes he made.

"So Jenn is actually taking Sundays off during the tourist season?" My sister and her wife, Mel, owned the coffee shop in town, Been There, Sipped That. And she was also in possession of the dominant family trait: an inability to slow down.

"Shockingly, yes. The college kids are home for the summer, so they've got all kinds of extra help. For the first time ever, she's actually been working reasonable hours."

I snorted. The Lawrence kids had never been known for their work-life balance.

"And Elijah is working there now."

"No." I gasped. "Not possible." Elijah, my oldest nephew, had definitely hit a growth spurt this year, but he was still a kid.

My brother chuckled lightly. "He's starting high school in the fall."

"Damn, we're old."

"You're old. I'm still on the right side of forty."

"Yeah, yeah, little brother, I remember. But middle age comes for us all. And I worry about you, working yourself so hard and all alone in that big house."

He scoffed. "I've got Bruce."

"Your horse dog doesn't count," I said a little too loudly. Cringing, I stepped into the kitchen, putting more distance between myself and the girls' room.

"He'd be offended by that statement. He's excellent company. Besides, I've got visitors coming soon, so I'm focused on that. Shame you girls can only stay a week."

I slumped against the counter. It was a shame, but I was thankful for the time I could take off to take the girls home for the Fourth of July. Maplewood did Independence Day right. And I'd been working so much that it had been months since we'd visited. The girls were already planning their hikes and arguing over which secret swimming holes they wanted to visit with their cousins.

I planned to use the week for job hunting and working out logistics. We weren't on the docket until mid-July, but I'd be ready when the time came.

"It's all the time I can get off. Trust me, once that motion is approved, we'll pack up the car and be out of here." I'd kill to spend the entire summer there so the kids could run wild and cleanse their lungs with fresh mountain air. But I'd settle for the month of freedom before school started.

"I miss you," he said softly. "And the girls."

"I miss you too."

My heart clenched. The loss of our parents hit each of us so differently.

Josh had thrown himself fully into the farm, preserving their legacy, while I often reached for my phone to call my mom, only to be hit with a fresh wave of grief.

I missed them, and I missed my siblings.

I'd given up so much during my marriage, and I'd lost so many parts of myself.

When we finally moved back to Vermont—*if* we moved—I was determined to find those parts again.

And to build a new version of myself.

CHAPTER 6
Brian

Every time I opened the case file, my hands shook with rage. She deserved so much more. Including better divorce lawyers years ago.

I'd been up half the night, making the changes Cliff and I discussed. And then this morning, Lo and I had sat down with Jess's paperwork and strategized, deciding to file the initial motion next Tuesday so we'd get on the docket quickly.

And while reviewing the documents Will had finally sent over, my blood pressure had skyrocketed.

When Lo went back to her own office, I googled Kenneth Mosely. Mostly so I'd know what I was up against, though part of me was curious too. To understand the kind of person Jess had married.

He was older. Probably in his early fifties, and handsome in that *I belong to a yacht club* kind of way. Medium height and build.

I could kick his ass. That was immediately apparent. Cracking my knuckles, I geared up to do a deeper dive into this motherfucker.

Kenneth Mosely. Venture capital. MBA from Wharton. Lots of credentials.

Reading his profile felt like taking an Ambien.

Another undeserving rich dude drunk on self-confidence and unearned privilege.

Also? Accomplished sailor. And golfer.

I could assume these were some of the activities he was busy with when he wasn't bothering to show up for visitation with his daughters.

I should have stopped once I'd read his professional bio.

That would have been the dignified thing to do.

But after the pain that had radiated from her in the yoga studio, the pain that had come with being on her own, with the knowledge that her ex was choosing not to have a relationship with his kids, the temptation to keep digging was overwhelming.

And the more I dug, the less I liked what I found.

Images of him at society functions, looking like a smug old prick with a series of duck-lipped girls on his arm. Most of whom looked young enough to be his daughters.

My stomach churned at those images.

The charity golf tournament images and galas for cancer research made me want to vomit. Because while he smiled and laughed like he didn't have a care in the world, his ex-wife and daughters were here, struggling to make ends meet.

With a frustrated grunt, I slammed my laptop closed. That fucker was in for a world of hurt.

Dylan and I had been raised by a single parent. I knew the struggles. After our mom passed away, our dad did a damn good job raising us, but even now, her loss haunts me.

It reminds me that every day matters. The people in our lives are gifts, and we never know how long we'll have them.

And here was this asshole, too busy schmoozing and gallivanting around the world to make time to see his children.

Instead, his only contribution was a monthly check, like they were a debt to be paid off.

I stood, hands balled into fists. I needed to punch something.

Carefully, forcing myself to breathe evenly, I unbuttoned my dress shirt and draped it over the back of my chair. Then I sprinted down the basement steps and flipped the lights and the fan on. I just needed a few minutes.

Rolling my shoulders, I donned a pair of gloves. I was short on time, so I didn't bother with hand wraps. Our firm in the city was equipped with a gym, where I worked out most mornings. This building had a spider-infested basement with cinder-block walls, but I made do. I didn't have time to make it to a local gym with the workload I'd brought to Jersey with me.

I'd been hitting the bag twice a day all week, yet it had done little to quiet the emotions rising up inside me.

When Jess had walked through my office door that first day, something in my chest had cracked wide open. Now, no matter how hard I tried, I couldn't close it up again.

I set a timer on my phone and gave myself ten minutes to work out my frustration and anger using jabs and crosses. As I shuffled around to get my heart rate up, I worked through it all in my head.

As a working-class kid in Brooklyn, trouble was easy to find, but I'd discovered boxing early and had poured myself into it to work off some of my teen angst and to keep from falling into the wrong crowd. Dad worked a lot, which meant I was responsible for Dylan often. Between caring for her and studying, I had little free time, but the old boxing gym was a place I could let go and just be a kid for a bit.

With each strike, clarity settled within me.

Reading about Kenneth Mosely had set me off. What a bastard. He'd had it all. Everything. And he'd thrown it away cruelly.

It offended me deep in my bones.

Because fatherhood was a precious gift.

One I'd wanted for a long time.

I'd grown up assuming I'd one day be a loving dad like my own. Then, for most of my adult life, I'd wanted nothing more than a loving marriage and kids.

But at every turn, life got in the way.

During law school and for those first few years after, I spent a lot of time at home, helping Dylan care for Liam after his birth father abandoned them. I was there when he lost his first tooth, and I had the honor of teaching him to ride a bike. It filled me up in the best ways.

That kid was amazing. My sister was amazing. I wouldn't trade those years for anything.

But they were brutal. Law school, the bar, then the beginning of my career. It took so much out of me.

I loved what I did, and I was proud of the career I'd built. But I was over forty now. I'd built a life, yet I'd missed some of the essentials along the way.

Memories and regrets and what-ifs raced through me as I thought about Jess and her daughters.

I'd ensure Jess was successful in court. But more than that, I wanted her and her daughters to soar, to have everything they'd ever wanted. Then I wanted to rub it in the face of the bastard who'd discarded them.

"Lo," I called over the walkie-talkie Cal had insisted we use when we needed our paralegal's assistance.

I'd cleaned up quickly, slipped back into my Oxford, and gotten back to work, and already, my frustration was growing again.

A moment later, she appeared in my doorway with Murphy at her side. Both looked at me with austere expressions, though it was difficult to take them seriously when Murphy's mouth was tinged blue.

"Slushy today?" I asked.

Murphy nodded. He looked just like Cal, with the same dark hair and blue eyes, but his personality couldn't be more different. His dad was the most easygoing person I knew. Life was all fun and games for my friend and business partner. Murphy, on the other hand, was more stoic than any seven-year-old had the right to be. Though he'd loosened up a bit in the nine months or so since he'd come to live with Cal.

"When are we going to finish the Dark Falcon?" he asked.

One of the benefits of our communal living arrangement was that T. J. and Murphy loved building with Legos as much as I did. Growing up, we'd never had money for them, but I'd found my love as an adult. If I was too tired to run or hit the bag, I'd sit at the ping-pong table and focus on a set to unwind.

"Soon." I grimaced. "I'm a bit swamped."

He nodded. "That will make it easy to finish before you. Then you'll have to wear the crown again."

I winced. The stupid tiara. The day Jess walked into my office, I'd been wearing it. For months, we'd had competitions. If the boys built a set faster than I did, they forced all sorts of ridiculous things on me. I'd worn reindeer antlers around the holidays, and honestly, I'd happily trade the tiara if I could have them back.

"How about this?" I asked. "If you and T. J. help me out and finish the *Star Wars* sets we've started, I'll go pick up the Infinity Gauntlet this weekend."

His eyes bulged, but the kid didn't make a sound. This was actually a pretty big display of excitement for the typically aloof boy. Without a word, he turned and ran out of my office at a speed that easily could have left holes in the gold carpet.

Lo shook her head as she watched him go, her blue-tinted lips twitching. When she turned back, though, her expression was serious. "When were you gonna tell us?"

I lifted one shoulder. "What was the point? Sully already told everyone." He and I were roommates in law school, and he'd been my best friend since. So, naturally, he knew about Jess. More than once, I'd confided in him over one-dollar beers, giving him far too much information about the one that got away. And he had been reminding me of it ever since.

"But I would have liked to hear it from you," she replied, her expression one of genuine disappointment.

Lo was by far the best paralegal the firm employed. It's why I'd literally begged her to move to Jersey with us. I couldn't imagine another person in her position taking on the work required to keep up with not only my caseload, but Sully's and Cal's. But more than that, over the years, she'd become a friend. And I trusted her with my life.

Yet here we stood, staring at one another, caught in a standoff I had no hope of winning.

"Ms. Mosely and I dated in college," I explained, going for casual. "I was a bit... surprised when she walked in."

She raised one eyebrow, silently urging me to get on with the full story.

"It never hit me that the yoga teacher you're always raving about—"

"Was your first love?" she interrupted.

My heart lurched. "Um. No," I sputtered.

"What are we talking about?" Cal appeared in the doorway, draping an arm around Lo's shoulders. "Brian's new client and how she's the college girlfriend he's been obsessed with forever?"

I glared at him. I was not obsessed. And just because my dating history had been less than stellar since didn't mean I'd been pining for decades.

As Lo smiled up at Cal with goddamn hearts in her eyes, I waved a hand to shoo them out of my office. I could deal with only so much today.

"I've been going through the details of this case. We've got to file quickly, but first, we need several pieces of information. Can you schedule another meeting with Ms. Mosely? We need to talk strategy."

She snorted. "Talk strategy? Is that what the kids are calling it these days?"

Cal practically melted into a puddle beside her. He was so smitten. It didn't matter what she said—every time she spoke, he was enraptured.

My blood pumped with frustration, but I ignored her comment. "Her ex-husband is a piece of shit."

"Most of them are," she said easily. "How are we going to bury him?" The gleam in her eye was what made her my most valuable employee.

"We're not," I gritted out. "We're going to do what she asked. We're going to file for relocation, and it'll be granted."

Her face fell. "But the child support order—"

I held up a hand. "Is bullshit. I agree. But this is what she hired us to do." It didn't surprise me that Lo had combed through the files as carefully as I had and had noted several injustices.

Lo crossed her arms, her brow creasing. She might be cool and detached most of the time, but the need for justice ran deep within her. It was why she was so damn good at her job.

"You gonna ask her out?" Cal waggled his eyebrows.

"Of course not," I snapped. "I'd be disbarred. Jesus, Cal."

His blue eyes flashed. "We could take her case."

Lo turned and glared at him. "You want a relo?"

"Hell no." Cringing, he ducked out and headed down the hall.

"I'll set that meeting up," Lo trilled, following him. "Better get yourself together before you see her again."

CHAPTER 7

Jess

"Sorry," I said, my pulse picking up. Nervous, I smoothed down my skirt. It was bright blue and covered with daisies. I'd felt compelled to dress up for this meeting, though I had no idea why. With all the time I'd spent in lawyers' offices over the past few years, the novelty had long worn off.

"It's no problem," Lo said. "The girls can hang here for as long as you need."

Kit and Greta sat at the conference table, pulling their homework from their backpacks. They'd gotten used to tagging along these days and were old enough to keep themselves busy.

Lo encouraged me to sit and handed me a stack of paperwork to fill out. It was interesting, seeing her in her natural environment rather than the yoga studio. While I was used to seeing her in athletic clothes and with her hair pulled up messily, today, she was dressed in a crisp button-down shirt and a black pencil skirt, with her deep red hair pulled back in a tight braid.

I had just started to fill out the paperwork when a figure appeared in the doorway and boomed, "Yoga Jess!" Though his voice was deep, Callahan Murphy's eyes were lit up and his smile was huge as he darted toward me like an overexcited puppy and swept me into a hug, lifting me off my feet.

Initially, I'd been deceived by the posh British accent and expensive athletic wear. Though it didn't take long to realize that this man was the antithesis of the stuck-up prick I assumed he was when we were introduced.

"I'm so glad you're here."

He'd just set me on my feet when the sound of a throat clearing caused us all to turn to the doorway again.

Cal was handsome, sure, but the man standing in the doorway, his auburn hair just a shade lighter than his trimmed beard, stole my breath. Brian was tall, with broad shoulders. Though he typically wore a stern expression, on occasion, when a person had really earned it, a dimple in his right cheek would appear.

Initially, I couldn't see how Cal and Lo were compatible. They were opposites in every way. But by the time they'd left that first yoga class, I understood. The two of them were more in sync than any couple I'd ever met, and they couldn't keep their eyes off one another.

"Yoga Jess saved my life," Cal explained, pulling me into his side protectively.

Brian frowned.

"She single-handedly fixed my back pain. You know"—he squinted— "because you make me sit at a desk all day."

Eyes closed, Brian sighed. "You're a lawyer, Cal. It's what we do."

The golden retriever who still hadn't let me go smiled down at me, his energy infectious. "We don't wanna lose her. But I can't blame her. Vermont sounds amazing."

It was. And his comment was a good reminder. I was fighting this battle, pushing to move to Vermont, so I could give my kids something different. So they'd have community and family and the kind of support they didn't even know existed.

Yes, leaving would be hard. But staying felt impossible.

I'd had more than my fair share of meetings with lawyers over the past few years, but none of them could hold a candle to Brian. I'd only recently come here for his help, and already, he'd done more work than Will did in the weeks he swore he was prepping for the request.

They'd recently received the files I'd consented to having sent over from Higgins, Smith and Dodge, and because, as Brian explained, sending emails back and forth could get costly, since he billed by the hour, I came in equipped with a list of questions, hoping this would be the most efficient way to move forward.

"You can send the girls upstairs," Brian said. "The boys are playing and Sloane is with the baby."

Apprehension blossomed in my chest. "I couldn't..."

"Nah," he said with a dismissive wave. "Girls, follow me. You hungry?"

My daughters lit up, as if I hadn't fed them a snack on the way over, and were all smiles as they packed up their homework and followed him up the back stairs. I shuffled behind them, suspicious. They weren't usually this compliant. Though I could see how the promise of snacks and an escape from law office boredom could be tempting.

Lo had warned me of their unconventional living arrangement, but I wasn't quite prepared for what we found on the second floor.

The living space was large, with a ping-pong table set up in the middle, and there were plants *everywhere.*

Two small boys sat on top of the ping-pong table, heads down and intent on their Lego creations. Sloane, I assumed—since she'd been rushed to the hospital before our first meeting at Higgins, Smith and Dodge and we hadn't actually met—was dressed in loungewear, with a newborn curled up on her chest.

"T. J., Murphy," Brian said. "How's the X-wing fighter coming along?"

The boys looked up in unison. The one with slightly lighter hair bounced in place and held up a half-built plane, wearing a toothless grin. "So awesome. Can you help us with the last part?"

"After my meeting, bud." Brian's face softened in a way that reminded me of the guy I'd known so well twenty years ago. "These are my friends Kit and Greta. They're gonna hang here and play for a while, okay?"

Greta had already approached the table, thoughtfully studying the

Lego set the boys were working on. Kit was at my side, silently taking in the scene.

"Do you need to start your homework?" I asked gently.

With a nod, she slid her backpack off her shoulders.

Sloane stood from an oversized chair and approached. "It's nice to meet you, Jess. I'm so glad you're working with Brian. Sorry I missed the meeting. This happened."

I peered down at the tiny baby dressed in shades of pink. "She is beautiful. Congratulations."

Sloane ducked, inspecting the infant, and broke into the most joyous of smiles. "Thank you."

As I checked on both girls, that apprehension returned. "Are you sure it's okay if I leave them?"

"Of course. Didn't you know? We're running an unofficial daycare up here." She laughed lightly. "After school, the boys hang out with Tia and me."

"We interviewed a couple of nannies," Brian said, sliding his hands into his pockets.

"Yeah, but none were good enough for Cal's standards. That man is the definition of a helicopter parent." Sloane's eyes twinkled with affection.

I huffed a laugh. "I get it, but now that it's just the three of us, it's nearly impossible to get by without hiring a sitter here and there. Though my girls can be prickly about new people, so I only use it as a last resort."

"They seem fine here." Brian arched his brows, looking around the room.

Greta had climbed up onto the ping-pong table alongside the boys and was fully engaged in building. Kit had made her way to the kitchen island and was already working on her math homework.

Swallowing thickly, I took in the scene. The slightly shabby but clean space, my kids hanging out in a strange location, with kids they'd never met, like it was no big deal, and my attorney-slash-ex-boyfriend tilting his head, silently signaling that I should follow him back down the stairs.

Had I fallen through some kind of wormhole?

By the time we were sitting across from one another in Brian's office, me holding a cup of herbal tea he insisted on making for me, I was mildly recovered. It was a shock to my system, how easy that transition had been. Nothing in my life had gone according to plan in years, and apparently, I'd forgotten what it felt like.

I was used to endless fuck-ups, bad luck, and constantly triaging the problems that popped up so we could move on to the basics.

My normal consisted of showing up at work with dirty hair because the hot water heater had died. And it often included forgetting the cookies I'd promised for the bake sale and calming Kit as she had a meltdown because she couldn't find her favorite scrunchie.

Brian settled with his forearms on his desk, a crease between his brows. "Is the tea okay?"

"Yes," I said, bringing myself back to the moment. "It's delicious."

We sat there, sort of staring at one another, the air between us growing just a tad bit awkward. Though it wasn't uncomfortable.

Sipping from my mug, I took the opportunity to admire Brian's suit. This one was dark gray with a faint pinstripe. His black tie was thin, and the crisp white shirt accentuated his tanned, freckled skin and his beard.

His auburn facial hair was threaded with just a hint of silver, which only made him look more serious and distinguished.

Ostensibly we were here for my legal case. But I couldn't stop my mind from wandering. Was he single? He didn't wear a ring.

A quick scan of his desk revealed no family photos.

Not that I'd have a snowball's chance in hell. Brian surely dated worldly, sophisticated women with impressive careers and long legs. They probably went to the opera and talked about their favorite caviar.

For most of my life, I'd been pretty confident and comfortable in my own skin. Like all humans, I had my flaws, but I was a good person and took care of myself and others. But since relatively early on in my marriage, I'd felt less and less like the confident, sunny woman who had dated Brian all those years ago.

I was a hot mess single mom now. With wide hips, ex-husband drama, and no time to myself. What I had to offer wasn't exactly enticing.

I looked down at the mug I was holding. It was navy blue, with the scales of justice etched into the ceramic, along with World's Okayest Lawyer.

"Cal gave it to me when I became a named partner in the firm," he explained.

Dragging my focus away from it, I smiled. "I think you're a lot better than okay."

Two pink patches appeared on his cheeks above his beard as he smoothed down his tie and cleared his throat. "We should get to work."

If I'd had a choice in how to spend this time with Brian, I wouldn't have picked reliving all my past choices and the absolute hell that was my divorce.

But he put me at ease immediately. He was so smart, asking insightful questions, his expression and tone genuine, like he actually cared.

I found myself getting emotional. The guilt that pervaded every single day of my life reared up and made its way to the forefront of my mind.

Each morning when I woke, it was there, an almost physical entity. I could practically see the depression it made on the pillow beside mine. It was my constant companion, accompanying me through all life's moments and dragging me down when I approached any sort of victory.

Guilt that I hadn't been enough for Kenneth. That I couldn't make my marriage work.

Guilt that my kids came from a broken family.

Guilt that I could not provide for them the way I wanted to.

"You okay?"

I nodded, sniffling slightly.

He leaned in closer. "Tell me how I can help." It wasn't a statement. It was a command.

"I'm just overwhelmed," I admitted. "I like my work at the hospital, but I don't get home until at least six. The girls have after-school activities some days, but on the days they don't, it's a struggle to find care for them. They can't be home alone. Greta would burn the building down and Kit would be too busy playing her keyboard to notice. I've tried babysitters. Both quit after the first day."

Brian gently pushed a box of tissues across the desk.

I took one. I had no idea why I was spilling my guts like this, but now that I'd started, I couldn't stop. "And the endless juggling of it all." I blew my nose. God, I was pathetic. "Sorry. I don't mean to dump on you."

He stared at me, those intense dark eyes wide with understanding. The man was gorgeous; why did he have to be easy to talk to as well? I felt like a blubbering mess.

Standing abruptly, he offered me his hand. "Let's go upstairs for a minute."

When we stepped into the apartment, Sloane, who was on the floor doing tummy time with Tia on a playmat, gave me a big smile and a thumbs-up.

"The girls can come here," Brian said as he shuffled toward Sloane.

My stomach lurched. "No."

"This may look like a law office from the outside," he said, giving me a wry smile, "but we're really running a daycare."

Sloane sat up and scooped Tia into her arms. She and Brian exchanged a silent look I couldn't decipher.

"He's not wrong," she said, patting the baby gently. "T. J. and Murphy are here every day after school. And two seven-year-old boys with a lot of energy is a lot some days."

"My girls," I hedged, lowering my voice. "They can be difficult. And they don't have the greatest track record with babysitters."

Sloane nodded. "I get it. But what if I hired them to help us?" Her brows rose in question. "The boys need playmates. The girls could keep them entertained and supervise until you're back from work. Kit seems like she could keep everyone in line and make sure homework gets done."

Affection for my daughter bloomed in my chest, along with a little amusement. "She does love being in charge."

In fact, right now, she was returning from the kitchen with a water bottle for one of the boys. She stopped at the ping-pong table, where

Greta and the boys were hard at work, and plucked a tiny Lego from a pile and held it out to them.

"They always wanted a little brother," I sighed.

Greta held up her X-wing fighter and made *pew* noises, firing at the Iron Man armor T. J. was building.

The boys giggled happily.

Sloane looked down, stroking the baby's soft cheek. "Murphy's easy. Mostly quiet and listens well, but my T. J." She nodded at the boy with slightly lighter hair. "He's a handful. I could really use the help. After those initial nanny interviews, we decided against it. For now, at least. I want to spend as much time with the kids as I can while I'm on maternity leave, and Cal wasn't keen on hiring a stranger to watch Murphy."

I took in the space, considering their proposal. The walls were covered in art projects, and there was a potted plant on almost every surface. Amid the clutter were four smiling, busy kids, plus one adorable baby.

Yes, it appeared that Sloane was up here with them all on her own, but downstairs, there were a handful of responsible adults who could jump in if there was an emergency.

I'd left work early too many times. And while the girls had done well hanging out at the yoga studio, it wasn't a long-term solution.

"Can I pay you?" I asked.

Sloane's mouth opened in surprise, and Brian scowled, as if I'd offended him.

"Please," I said. "I'd feel terrible. Let me do something. I can cook. Buy groceries? Maybe clean Fuzzy's litter box?"

Brian pulled up to his full height and slid his hands into his pockets. "Not necessary."

"It's really okay," Sloane said. "They're good kids, and in the hour they've been here, they've already been a big help."

"Free yoga?" I suggested.

"Fine," Brian huffed. "Cal and Lo will love that."

"Me too," Sloane added.

"And friendship?" Brian asked, his eyes pinning me to the spot.

"I'd like that."

CHAPTER 8

Brian

The sight of her was jarring.

She was dressed in a black skirt suit with sky-high black heels. Her hair was pulled back severely, showing off a pair of large pearl earrings.

The woman in front of me barely resembled the Jess I'd been spending time with over the past couple of weeks.

She was pale and nervous instead of sunny and confident. Dampened and dull when she was typically vibrant.

"I've never seen you in black." I rested a hand on her lower back and directed her through the door.

She shrugged stiffly. "Kenneth always insisted I dress like this. It was easier just to appease him. Today will go more smoothly if he has one less thing to criticize me about. He despised when I wore color. Especially pink."

"I like your pink." I frowned. "You don't look like yourself."

"I'm not myself. When I have to interact with him, I can't be. It took me years to find my way back, and now, this is an uncomfortable costume I wear for a few hours to keep the peace."

I gritted my teeth, keeping the rest of my thoughts to myself. How dare this fucker make her feel anything less than incredible? Normally I went into these kinds of meetings cool and collected, but my fingers were already itching, and the need to punch something was already welling up. I rubbed my bruised knuckles and focused on remaining calm as we rode the elevator up to the office.

Our New York office was state-of-the-art. We could be considered fancy, but it had nothing on Kenneth's lawyers. Though being fancy didn't mean a lawyer was good at their job. It had more to do with how much they charged and what types of cases they took on. Usually those involving corporate bullshit rather than helping actual people.

This place was famous for doing private equity transactions, so it made little sense for Kenneth to hire them to help him with his divorce. Yet here we were.

His attorney, a woman in her forties with a severe gray bob, did her best to maintain a calm, confident façade as we ran through the custody status, but I saw through the bullshit. She was completely out of her element, seemingly unable to even recognize the New Jersey statutes.

Good. I'd take every advantage I could get.

I crossed my arms and stared down Jess's ex.

Gray hair, perma-tan, the unlined forehead of a man who took his Botox regimen seriously. Then there was the "I don't give a fuck" attitude. Even though the mother of his children was sitting across from him.

He was even more repulsive than I'd anticipated after I'd read the case files and done my own research online.

"There is no need for your client to oppose our motion to relocate," I said to the attorney, though I didn't look away from the asshat across from me.

He didn't react in the slightest.

"We will oppose," the attorney said crisply. "He is the children's father."

"Kenneth," Jess said, her voice strained. "We've talked about this. The girls would be so much happier in Vermont. I did what you asked. I didn't force visitation, and I've been flexible. I would never keep them from you."

The impassive expression he continued to wear made me want to choke him with his thousand-dollar Hermes tie.

"Okay, then." I shuffled my files and got to work, laying out exactly what would happen, when he would be expected to appear in court, and how we'd use his opposition to this request to reopen the child support calculation.

His eyes widened when I dropped that truth bomb.

"And given that you exercise no visitation rights and have moved out of state yourself, I can't imagine a judge being sympathetic."

"We'll see," he said.

"It won't be a Manhattan courtroom," I replied. "It's Jersey, and if I know one thing about the Jersey legal system, it's that they really hate deadbeat dads."

His face paled, even as he kept his expression flat.

As his lawyer took her turn, asking me questions about basic procedure she should already understand, tension radiated off Jess, making the air thicker.

If the woman across the table worked for me, I'd have fired her. Lo would wipe the floor with this woman in court, and she hadn't even sat for the bar.

"They'd love to see you," Jess said to her ex, somehow maintaining a kind tone.

Her ability to treat this fucker with any respect whatsoever only proved she was a much better person than I was.

"Kit is playing at the Brooklyn Academy of Music next Friday. She's the youngest musician invited to showcase." Her lips tipped up in a barely there smile. "She's been working so hard on this very difficult Bach piece."

My chest squeezed. I had no idea Kit was so talented.

Kenneth's face softened for an instant, though the look was quickly replaced with a scowl. "I can't. I'll be at the Miller Foundation gala. I bought a table."

Jess stiffened, the smallest sound of defeat escaping her.

This motherfucker. Poor Kit. She deserved support at such a significant event. If I thought it would do any good, I'd grab him by the hair plugs and drag him there myself.

I slid my phone out of my pocket and quickly typed out a text.

Like I hoped, I received a response immediately.

"You're not, actually," I said, placing the phone on the table.

He puffed up, his eyes narrowing. "Excuse me?"

"You're not attending." This time, I plastered on a smile.

"Evelyn Miller is a friend. I've attended every year for the last decade."

"Sorry." I rubbed a hand over my bearded jaw. "You've been disinvited."

As if on cue, his phone buzzed on top of the walnut conference table.

He picked up the device and unlocked it. When his pompous expression morphed into a furious scowl, satisfaction washed over me.

"Who the hell do you think you are?" He slammed the phone onto the table. "Jess, what kind of two-bit con man of a lawyer did you get?"

I stood, sweeping up my files and offering Jess a hand. "Great news. Turns out you're free the night of Kit's event after all. Now there's no reason you can't show up for your child. You need a ride? I can pick you up."

His face turned red, and I swore steam billowed from his ears.

I wanted to shake Jess and ask her what she'd ever seen in this guy, but my anger was replaced with heartache when I remembered that, when we entered this room, she physically shrank. Fuck. She was afraid of him.

There was certainly no love there.

I'd been doing this long enough to know when the hurt a person wore was really a mask for all the love they'd shared.

Jess's pain? It was caused by fear and resignation.

She was resigning herself to the knowledge that he would once again get his way.

But now more than ever, I was determined to fuck with this guy. And I would relish it.

As we stepped out into the sunshine, I grasped her hand and gave it a quick squeeze. It was cool and soft and so much smaller than mine. And the contact felt incredible.

When that thought registered, I released her. Fuck. I was her lawyer. She was my client. "Sorry."

She looked up at me, her eyes shining in the sunlight.

"This may be a weird request from a client, but can I have a hug?"

When we'd stepped into the shade of one of the many skyscrapers of lower Manhattan, I turned to face her.

She immediately looked at her feet, avoiding my gaze. "I shouldn't have asked."

I set my briefcase on the sidewalk, then cupped her chin, tipping it up toward me.

"At Murphy and Machon, we provide full service for our clients," I said in a serious voice. "That includes hugs."

Without hesitation, I pulled her to my chest. Like it was second nature, she wove her arms around my waist and hugged me tight.

She fit perfectly against me. In her sky-high heels, she was just the right height to tuck her head under my chin.

Eyes closed, I relished this moment. The joy that overwhelmed me was more potent than I'd felt after any courtroom victory.

Now more than ever, I wanted to help her. To ensure she felt safe and protected. To give her and her kids anything they wanted.

"Thank you for getting him uninvited from the gala," she said into my chest. "That's going to bruise his ego so much."

A rumble of a laugh worked its way out of me. "It was my absolute pleasure."

She stepped away, eyes shining. "How did you do it so quickly?"

"My sister," I said.

"Dylan?" She broke into a smile, the fear that had consumed her finally abating. "I remember her."

"Yeah. She's a Miller." I smirked. "Her husband, Cortney, is the son of Craig and Evelyn Miller. The retired baseball player. There is nothing Dylan hates more than a bully, so I shot her a quick text. And now Kenneth is officially blacklisted from all Miller Foundation events."

Jess's jaw dropped. "That is diabolical, Brian Machon. But I appreciate it."

"And now he can go to the concert."

She shook her head. "He still won't go."

"For Kit's sake, I hope he does." I picked up my briefcase. "And if he doesn't, it will only strengthen our case. So either way, it's a win."

"I don't remember you having such a vindictive streak," she said as I led her into the parking garage.

I didn't. At least until recently. I'd always prided myself on being a cool, calm, strategic professional. I didn't take things personally or get caught up in petty bullshit.

But apparently, that wasn't the case when it came to her. For her, with her, I would burn shit down and enjoy every second of it.

I hummed, wishing I could hold her hand again. "Only once in a while, when it really counts." As we turned down the aisle where I'd parked, another thought came to me, and a plan formed in my mind. "I overheard him talking to his lawyer about the Metros."

"Yes." She nodded once. "He has season tickets, a luxury box. He's obsessed."

A wicked excitement coursed through me. "Oh, really?"

"Yes. Greta is a huge fan and has begged him to take her to a game, but he won't. His excuse is that it's only for 'business.'" She used air quotes on the last word.

Ooh, this would be fun. "Here, hold this." I handed her my briefcase and pulled my phone out of my pocket.

She sucked in a breath. "What are you doing now?"

"Do you have any idea how long the wait list is for Metros season tickets?" I asked as I pulled up the contact I needed.

"I've heard it takes years."

"Yup. And today is someone's lucky day, because Kenneth Mosely is no longer a season-ticket holder."

I typed furiously, wishing I could see her ex's face when he found out.

Her responding laugh lit up my nerve endings. Damn. I would burn the world down just to hear that sound. "How is this possible? Do you have superpowers?"

"The Phillips family," I explained. "I've worked for them for more than fifteen years. They are the best kind of people. There are hundreds of people who would take that luxury box in a heartbeat, and I'm just gonna let Cliff Phillips know that he should give it to more, ahem, deserving fans. And if Greta is a fan," I continued, scratching at my beard, "I'd be happy to take her, and you. Let me know which games. I have an open invitation to the owner's box."

The way she beamed up at me, like I was her hero, made my heart stutter in my chest.

I averted my attention, taking my briefcase from her, and headed for the car. I could feel my stomach rumbling. A protein shake was definitely not going to cut it today.

"C'mon." I strode quickly, hoping the speed would help me avoid the complicated feelings brewing inside me. "Do you like ramen?"

"Yes," she said, her tone unaffected. "Everyone likes ramen."

I clawed at my tie, tugging a little too violently to loosen it. "Great. Then let's go. Fucking with ex-husbands makes me hungry."

CHAPTER 9
Jess

"I'm sorry we're late." I handed the bag of bagels to Max as I kissed Lana's cheek.

Max grinned at me. "You got onion?"

I smiled. "Of course. Shira saves a few for me on Fridays. You're still her favorite customer, and she knows I come in to refill your stock."

"Thanks for that." Lana passed the baby over, then scooped my girls into hugs.

Kit and Greta had buzzed with excitement all day. More than just about anything, they looked forward to our monthly dinner with my best friend and her family.

Lana and I had worked together as assistants at a PR firm in our early twenties in New York, climbing the corporate ladder together, and had become fast friends. While I married Kenneth, moved to New Jersey, and had babies, Lana went to India to study yoga and transcendental meditation. She came back, traded in her Jimmy Choos for a nose ring, and started teaching.

She started in the Upper East Side, working in luxurious studios, where the money was good, but she got tired of the drama and the ass-kissing quickly. So she used her trust fund to buy a building in Jersey City and transform it into a yoga and meditation center where she could offer sliding scale pricing to make yoga more accessible to the local community.

It was part yoga studio, part community activism hub.

She organized food drives and park cleanups and provided space to community organizations. By the time I'd filed for divorce, she was a mainstay in the area. During the hardest years of my life, she introduced me to yoga, and when I fell in love with it, she not only helped me train as a teacher, but she took care of me and the girls.

She was tall and lean, with smooth dark skin, sparkling eyes, and waist-length braids. Today they were twisted into one massive braid that hung down her back.

The woman always wore athleisure. Today's outfit consisted of mint-green high-waisted leggings with a matching sports bra with thin straps that crisscrossed in the back, along with a matching slouchy sweater tied around her shoulders.

I envied her ability to show her stomach only six months after giving birth.

My tummy only made an appearance when I was doing yoga on my own, and even then, only with my highest-waisted pants.

Lana had often brought in guest instructors so she could continue traveling the world, but then she met Max, a physicist who was a few inches shorter than she was. While she was the definition of new-agey and wild, he was nerdy and straitlaced. They fell madly in love, and when baby Marie Curie came along, they moved to the suburbs.

The girls loved visiting. The house was massive, with a large yard, a pool, and a swing set. Marie was too young to enjoy much of it, but my girls immediately changed into the suits we kept here so they could swim while Max fired up the grill on the patio. Along with the swimsuits, we kept toothbrushes and pajamas as we'd spent a lot of time here over the past year.

While the house was magnificent, the local bagels, according to Max, were not. So I kept him stocked with Jersey City's finest, and in return, he cooked feasts for us when we came over.

With wine in hand, Lana and I sat on the deck, watching the girls splash, while Marie sat on a playmat, banging her toy giraffe against the ground.

My heart squeezed as I cataloged all the ways she'd changed in the seven short days since I'd last seen her. "I can't believe she's already sitting up."

"I know." Lana sighed. "Max is convinced she's a baby genius."

"Obviously she is," I cooed, waving at her.

My best friend let out a light huff. "I'm trying to have reasonable expectations for my daughter here, Jess."

I shrugged. "Reasonable expectations are lame. Be delusional about your kids. This baby here will probably split atoms during her free time between walking high-fashion runways and qualifying for the Olympic fencing team." I held up my wineglass. "And compose a few iconic symphonies when she's bored. Let the girl live."

Lana giggled into her glass. "I'd never have survived the newborn stage without you."

"I wouldn't have survived the past five years without you," I countered, seriousness edging into my tone.

Lana had pulled me out of the depressive swamp and had helped me rebuild my life, giving me a job and childcare while I finished my master's in social work. She'd done homework with the girls so I could study and she'd lent me clothes for job interviews. She'd been the most solid of rocks when I needed her.

As I slid to the ground, playing peek-a-boo with her beautiful baby, a wave of shame hit me. I should have been doing more for her. I should have been visiting this sweet girl more often, building the kind of bond Lana had created with my children.

"You've been busy lately," she said. "Any movement on the legal front?"

"Yes. I've got a new lawyer," I explained as the girls came running out of the pool to devour the snacks Max had laid out.

Greta snatched a carrot from the tray. "He's our babysitter too," she said, her mouth full. Without further explanation, she inhaled a piece of cheese and darted back to the pool.

"Babysitter?" Lana raised an eyebrow.

"Not quite," I said, a strange, protective sensation settling over me.

Lana was my best friend. I could tell her anything. But our current situation felt too complex to even explain.

"I found my new lawyer through some friends at the studio," I explained. "He's great and can help me."

Lana nibbled on a cracker, eyes narrowing. "What aren't you telling me?"

"It's Brian," I said, wincing.

She straightened, her mouth dropping open. "*Brian* Brian?"

I grimaced.

"College Brian? First love Brian? The boy you lost your virginity to Brian?"

I nodded. "Yes. His firm. He and his partners are temporarily working in Jersey. They and their families live in the apartment above their office, so they've got a whole after-school-program situation happening. The girls love it. They've made new friends, and it's been a big help to me, since we can't keep a damn babysitter."

Lana nodded. "They hate babysitters because no one could ever measure up to me."

"Correct." I grinned. "So I was in need of after-school coverage, and Sloane—the attorney I was supposed to work with at Higgins, Smith and Dodge, actually—happens to be part of this family. She's on maternity leave, so she's home with her newborn, her seven-year-old son, and her nephew."

"So you're crowdsourcing childcare from your law firm?"

I cringed. "When you say it like that, it sounds sketchy."

Lana pinched the bridge of her nose. "It is sketchy, sweetie. Do you know these people? Have you vetted them?"

"Of course," I said. "Obviously, I know Brian. Lo has become a friend and I trust her, plus she is an emergency guardian in the court system. Their place is chock-full of Legos and art supplies, and the girls spend a couple of hours after school doing homework and playing."

"You can always call me. Marie and I can jump in the car and come to the city."

I leaned forward, careful not to squish the baby, and squeezed her hand. "Of course I know that. And I love you. But I promise this is working. And we're so close to getting approval to move. I just need to get to the finish line."

"You think Vermont's gonna happen?"

I did. I was a positive person at my core. Kenneth may have drained a lot of that energy, but over the last few years, with distance from him, it had begun building up again. Things were finally coming together. And I knew in my bones that Brian would win this for me.

We'd head to Vermont. It was only a matter of time. "I know it," I said. "We had a meeting today. Brian stood up to Kenneth and scared the shit out of him."

Lana clasped her hands. "Okay, tell me everything."

Her smile grew wider as I gave more and more detail. "He did that? The precious Metros tickets?"

"Yes. So, for the first time, I feel hopeful that Vermont will happen. That we can get our fresh start."

She scooted around so we were knee to knee and put her head on my shoulder.

"I'm all for you and those kids. Whatever is best for you. I want you to live the brightest, happiest, and most fulfilling life possible, my love." She sniffed lightly. "And if I have to lose you to the maple farm and those damn green mountains, then I'll have to be okay with it. But there are good things here. Don't forget that."

Tears filled my eyes. This woman had lifted me up and carried me through some of my darkest moments. "I could never forget."

"Who wants ribs?" Max called, saving us before the moment could get any heavier.

After dinner, Max gave Marie a bath while Lana and I cleaned up. As usual, he'd made way too much food. He'd get no complaints from me. I'd gladly eat these incredible ribs for breakfast tomorrow.

"Don't think I've forgotten about Brian," Lana whispered.

I didn't dare look up from the dish I was scrubbing.

"How does he look?" she asked.

I sighed, and a snapshot of him appeared in my mind. "Amazing."

"Single?"

I hesitated, knowing exactly where her brain was going. Since falling for Max, Lana had transformed from one of those "men are unnecessary" types to a hopeless romantic.

"This is fate. Out of all the lawyers you could have been referred to, you end up in Brian's office?"

"Yes. Fate that I'd finally get a good lawyer."

"Sure." She chuckled. "Because the universe is deeply concerned with the quality of your legal representation." She whipped me gently with her dishtowel. "Obviously the universe knows you need to get some."

"Can we not talk about this, please?" I said through gritted teeth. "He's my lawyer."

"He fucked with your ex-husband for sport, hitting him where it hurts the most—his social standing. For that alone, he deserves a blowjob."

"*Stop*," I hissed, peering over to where the girls were playing in the living room.

"All I'm saying is that you've been through hell, and you deserve a break. You deserve all the good things. And finding an amazing lawyer worthy of fantasizing about? Seems like a good thing to me." She lifted a shoulder. "Are you attracted to him?"

I looked at her with wide eyes. "Brian? Of course I am. I'd have to be dead not to be. Between the rumbling deep voice and those golden eyes? Jesus."

Her smile was almost diabolical.

"He was cute in college," I said. "More than that. He was handsome." I set the dish I'd been rinsing in the dish rack beside the sink. "But now? I can't explain it." My cheeks heated just thinking about him. "He's older, more serious. And he's grown into his whole protector role. He was like that when we were younger, but it mostly consisted of walking between me and the road and making sure I got into my apartment safely. Now? He's fucking with Kenneth's life to protect us. It's impossible not to be attracted to him after all that."

She fanned herself. "Halleluiah. I want this for you. I am going to manifest the shit out of this."

My stomach twisted. "It's not like that." It couldn't be. No matter how much I wanted to kiss him.

She grinned widely and clapped her hands. "No, seriously. I'll be on Canva making the vision board tonight. This is such good news. I bet he's amazing in bed. The serious, focused types always are."

"It's not. It's confusing. And we have this..." I sighed, drying my hands. "This connection. Like what we had so long ago never went away. The chemistry, the intensity, every time I'm around him I can feel it crackling in the air."

"Oh shit. He's the *one*," Lana said, clasping her hands together.

"But there's no way he's into me. He's gorgeous and successful and I'm..." I trailed off. "Short and stumpy and—"

"*Nope*." Lana clutched my shoulders and gave me a little shake. "Don't do that. Don't talk negatively about your body. We've healed those generational wounds and we do better now, remember?"

My chest ached. I'd come so far, but... "I'm not doing it in front of my daughters."

"Doesn't matter," she insisted. "They will know. I'm half convinced Kit has telepathy."

I let out a breath of a laugh. "That would explain a lot."

"Jessica Mosely, you are an absolute bombshell. A pocket Venus, if you will. Tiny but with plenty of curves."

Cheeks warming, I turned away, draping the towel on the oven handle to distract myself.

She waited patiently until I was finished, then turned me around and tipped my chin up so I was forced to look at her. "The boobs, you were born with. But that ass? I take credit for that."

Frowning, I twisted, checking out my butt in my stretchy black yoga pants. It was bigger than I would like, but she was right: it was defined, thanks to years of yoga.

"True," I admitted.

"Thank you." She crossed her arms. "No one talks about yoga ass, but it's a thing, I swear it."

"Girl, I know."

"Anyway," she went on. "You are beautiful. And more importantly, you're fucking awesome. Funny and interesting. No matter how hard Ken tried, he did not drain the life force from you. You're just as energetic, glowing, and hopeful as ever."

"I don't want to be hopeful. I want to be a badass."

"You are. You can be both, you know. Badass comes in many flavors."

Sighing, I leaned against the counter. Deep down, I wanted to believe that. I wanted to have the kind of confidence that Lana oozed.

But I'd been hurt too many times.

She'd been pushing me to date since my divorce. But I had yet to feel ready for that step.

I didn't have time, working multiple jobs and raising my kids on my own while dodging legal issues Kenneth threw my way and then losing both my parents.

The few times I'd downloaded dating apps, I'd ended up deleting them within hours. There were so many creepy dudes out there, and the thought of getting all dolled up so I could attempt to convince a stranger I was worth spending time with made me queasy.

Head hung, I toed at the fancy tile beneath me. "I'm not sure I can do this all again."

"I think you should try," she said, taking a step closer. "Brian was one of the good ones. The best. Sounds like he still is."

"I'm not sure yet," I hedged.

She hummed. "The evidence is solid. And if he's interested and wants a chance, why not give him one?"

"Who said he wants a chance? I don't have a good picker," I reminded her.

"Kenneth wasn't a bad pick. You got two amazing kids out of the deal."

"Yes." My chest warmed at the thought of my girls. At the sound of their laughter from the next room. "But," I argued, "I don't have good instincts. I let him walk all over me. And it took me way too long to realize he'd been cheating."

She cupped my cheek. "Because you're trusting and hopeful. Because you want to see the best in people. That's not a flaw. It's a wonderful asset. You are wonderful." Her dark eyes were intense. "Shitty people have taken advantage of your kind and generous nature. And yes, that's awful, but you've learned and grown and are healing."

Her words hit me square in the heart. She was right. I might have been older and squishier and more jaded these days, but I'd fought hard to heal and grow.

"You deserve good things." She wrapped her arms around me. "It's time you started believing it."

CHAPTER 10

Jess

"I made you something. To say thank you." My words were stilted as I forced them out. This was dumb. I should have walked straight upstairs and collected my kids. But as if pulled by an invisible string, I found myself here instead, drawn in, and not by the massive cat curled up on the file cabinet.

Brian stood. "You don't have to do that."

"I do." I fidgeted with my phone. "I thought about sending flowers. Or whatever the guy equivalent of flowers is. Fruit? A beef jerky gift box? But I'm broke, so I made you a playlist."

His eyes lit up as he rounded his desk. "A playlist?"

The boyish smirk that brightened his face made my heart melt a little. The beard, the deep golden-brown eyes, and the rolled-up shirtsleeves had a slightly different effect on me. One that wasn't appropriate for a client to have for her lawyer.

"Yup. I would have made you a mix CD, but I doubt you have a CD player."

"Does that mean you still have a CD burner after all these years?" he teased. "You were the music girl. The mix CDs you made for me are probably in a box somewhere in my dad's garage."

I chuckled to myself. I'd made him so many CDs back then. It was my love language. "No." For a minute, I wished I had. "Instead, I made you a Spotify playlist."

I held up my phone. "Here, I'll text you the link."

When his phone chimed in his pocket, he pulled it out, and with a smile, he scrolled through.

Nerves skittered through me, and my face heated. "You might hate it."

"I do not hate it at all." He peered at me through his lashes. "These are our songs."

A giggle escaped me. "Early aughts grunge and punk. All our faves from college."

He ran his hands through his hair and chuckled. "The Offspring? Amazing."

My body relaxed as he continued scrolling, a sense of ease washing over me. All those years ago, just being in his presence calmed me, and apparently, it still did.

"Just Breathe." He stopped, and this time, when he looked at me, he straightened and made pointed eye contact.

Instantly, I was transported back to that night in Fenwick Hall. We'd been hanging out for a couple of weeks, and I had a major crush on him. We sat side by side on the twin bed in his dorm room, a giant tapestry covering the cinder block wall across from us.

When this song came on, we talked nervously about how much we loved Pearl Jam. Before the music ended, he got bold. He leaned in, tucked a strand of hair behind my ear, and kissed me.

Our first kiss.

That song was the soundtrack to a lot of our firsts.

My warm cheeks now burned. I should not have included it. Stupid Jess. But I'd been so deep in nostalgia as I made my choices that I hadn't thought of how awkward this moment would be.

"It was our song," he said.

It was. How had I forgotten? So many nights, we lay wedged into that tiny twin, snuggled under his baseball-themed comforter, planning for the future.

A nebulous concept. Adulthood was something we talked about as if we had any idea what it might bring.

"I'm sorry." I shook my head. This was a terrible idea. I had been shooting for a kind gesture, something fun. Instead, I'd sent us straight into an awkward trip down memory lane.

Internally, I cursed myself. Why couldn't I just act like a normal human being around him?

He'd been my first love, yes, but it was that young, consuming kind of love many find in college and move on from. We'd parted amicably and gone our separate ways into adulthood. And since then, he'd been a fond memory. He hadn't broken my heart; the situation had. We'd been heading in different directions, and at the time, each of our families needed us.

He smiled intermittently as he scrolled, and eventually, he looked up, his golden eyes shining. "Thank you. This means a lot to me."

"Pfft." I waved a hand. "Please. What you did to Kenneth means a lot. And like I said, I'm broke," I said, my words coming out quickly, nervously. "This is the best I can do. Unless you accept payment for legal services in sexual favors?"

His eyes widened comically at the rate my stomach plummeted.

Stupid Jess and my stupid mouth. I could feel my face turn purple, and I looked down at the sad gold carpet and willed a hellmouth to open and swallow me whole. I'd rather face down Satan and his hellhounds than look Brian in the eye right now.

"No. Not like that," I said, waving frantically, wishing I could bat the absurd statement away. "I will pay your bills with real money, of course. That I make, you know. At my job. I don't know why I said that. Please ignore me."

He only blinked in response.

"God, you must be so insulted." My entire body was on fire, my armpits suddenly sweaty. "Here you are, a serious professional, then there's me. I'll show myself out."

I turned on my heel, but before I made it to the door, his strong hand landed on my arm.

"Jess, no," he rasped. "You don't have to go. You were making a silly joke. I get it. You don't have to censor yourself around me. Yeah, I may be your lawyer, but we're also friends. I like your awkward jokes."

My heart seized up. "You do?"

"Yes. There's nowhere near enough humor in this office. Other than when Cal pelts Sully with his mini basketballs and when Lo thinks she's seen a mouse." He winced. "I promise there aren't any rodents. We got that taken care of quickly after we moved in. And Fuzzy provides extra insurance."

I barely heard a word he said as I focused on breathing. I'd come in here, excited to see him, eager to make a kind gesture. Then I'd gone and made a big old mess out of everything.

"I'm doing my job. No gifts necessary. And trust me, it was truly my pleasure to fuck with Kenneth. This..." He held up his phone. "This makes me happy. You used your precious free time to come up with an idea and to create something I'd enjoy. That means a lot. I'll listen to it on my run tomorrow. It'll motivate me to keep working hard for you and the rest of my clients."

My nose stung and my eyes got hot. That was the sweetest thing he could have said. And it only made me want to kiss him more. Why couldn't the best relocation lawyer in the state be a crotchety old man? Or maybe a hyper-competent woman who intimidated me?

Either would have been preferable to this. Because I wasn't sure I'd survive working with this handsome, competent, thoughtful man whose presence always brought back the best memories.

"I'll get out of your hair," I said awkwardly, taking a step back. "I've got to grab the girls."

With a nod, he padded back to his desk. "Thank you again."

I gave him a goofy grin and a double thumbs-up before closing the door behind me.

Double thumbs-up? God, I was a disgrace. I knew I was rusty after the whole traumatizing marriage and divorce, but my God in heaven, it would have been better to trip and fall on my ass. This man was my literal savior. He was managing my legal issue, no doubt at a reduced hourly rate, and had thrown in messing with my ex-husband for free. And I had a raging, inappropriate crush.

Edna, my hypothetical therapist, whom I could not actually afford, would have a field day. I was definitely buying ice cream on the way home.

CHAPTER 11
Brian

"Where are you going?" Lo called as I passed her office. "It's not time to walk Fuzzy."

I backtracked, stopping in her doorway. "I have an appointment."

She pulled up my calendar on her computer, wearing a studious frown. "Who is Doctor Johnson?"

Cal's laughter echoed down the hall. "Good man," he said as he ambled closer. "It's time you got that checked out. It happens to a lot of blokes. There are a lot of medication options these days."

I yanked the small basketball from his hand and tossed it at his forehead. "What's a guy gotta do to get a little privacy around here?"

"I'm your assistant," Lo said, chin lifted. "You don't get privacy from me." She looked over at Cal, whose blue eyes were shining with curiosity. "Are you gonna tell him, or should I?" she asked, eyeing me. "You know he has ways of getting information from me."

"Fine." I huffed. "And I could do without the mention of how he gets information from you, thank you very much." I shuddered. "Therapy."

Cal took a step back, as if receiving a physical push, and a second later, Sully darted out of his office.

"You?" Cal gaped. "You're going to therapy? I thought you were going to the penis doctor."

"It's called a urologist," Sully explained.

"Since I'm much younger, I have no need to know such details," he said, giving Lo a wink.

I shuddered. "Not that it's any of your business, but yes, I am going to therapy. Why? Have you been?"

"I'm British. Stiff upper lip and all that."

"I have," Sully admitted. "For T. J. and Sloane. And it helped. A lot. Good for you, mate." He clapped me on the shoulder, and then he was gone, ducking back into his office.

I appreciated it. Sully had done nothing but grunt and snarl for months after Sloane had asked him to move out. These days, I caught him smiling more than he had since law school, when he fell head-over-heels for his wife, and too often, I'd accidentally walked in on the two of them dancing in the kitchen.

"I go to the gym to take care of my body," I explained. "Why not go to therapy and take care of my mind?"

"Oh, look at who's drinking the self-improvement Kool-Aid." Lo rubbed her hands together, her green eyes dancing. "This is an excellent development."

"Eh," Cal said, crossing his ankles and leaning against the doorframe. "I think it's because he fancies a certain blond client."

I glared at him. "I'm a forty-two-year-old single guy who lives with you two idiots, your wonderful women, and three children—two of whom I think I might relate to better than anyone else in my life at the moment —I've got a lot of improvements to make."

"Amen." He dipped his chin. "Go get fixed."

"Fuck off," I said, pushing past him. I strode through the office, ignoring Amy, the moronic intern Cal brought in to help, as she called my name and waved like a maniac from the conference room, grumbling about the complete lack of privacy in my life.

But as I stepped out into the sunshine, a smile broke free. Our little Jersey family was loud, disruptive, and ridiculous, but these people had become my family. Sully and Cal had been like brothers for decades, and Sloane and I had been friends since before she and Sully got together.

Lo? She and I had worked well together from the moment Terry had hired her, and we'd developed a friendship too. But living together the way we'd all been doing for the last several months had forced us all to grow and evolve.

Until now, my changes had been the least drastic, but it was finally my turn. In Manhattan, my life had been so structured and organized that I'd never gotten a chance to really take stock. Now, I was seeing the world through a new set of eyes, experiencing life with a newfound appreciation.

This living situation had definitely been a jolt to my nervous system.

It woke me up and made me realize that many aspects of my life were lacking. It made me wonder if I'd been wrong when I'd settled for just being that guy. The lawyer in the expensive suit. The man who had such a sad, empty life that he spent hours walking his damn cat around Jersey City.

Now that the seed had been planted, it was time to do something about it. So off to Doctor Johnson I'd go.

He was in his seventies and saw patients in the office inside his large brownstone in Hoboken, which was probably worth a small fortune. And had a pipe.

"Don't worry. I don't smoke anymore," he said, ushering me into a room stuffed with leather chairs and wall-to-wall books.

"Gave it up a decade ago. That shit will kill you. But never got out of the habit of holding it between my teeth."

As I settled into a leather armchair, I couldn't help but think this situation felt strange but also right.

Once he was settled as well, Dr. Johnson bit his pipe and looked me up and down.

"So, Brian, what's her name?"

I frowned and leaned forward, the cushion creaking beneath me. "Come again?"

"The woman who knocked you on your ass and motivated you to finally come to therapy." He arched a brow. "You're nowhere near my first forty-something overachiever, never-been-married kind of patient. So let's just put the cards on the table now. What's her name?"

Embarrassed about being called out so easily, I shrank back.

But I was here to grow, dammit, and I'd do my best. So I straightened again and said, "Her name is Jess."

THERE WAS NOTHING MORE SOBERING THAN BEING PICKED APART BY a person I'd never met, then having all my deeply held bullshit unwrapped and presented to me on a silver platter.

And that's precisely what Dr. Johnson had done.

Asshole.

That man had cut me open and made me bleed. And I'd paid him for the privilege.

And I'd be back next week to do it all over again.

But I couldn't deny how much lighter I felt as I walked back to the office. Already, I was certain I'd taken a small step in the right direction.

And after years of bottling up my emotions and working until exhaustion, this was a novel feeling. At Dr. Johnson's instruction, I was not allowed to check my phone until I got back to the office.

My mission was to experience the world around me.

What a strange sensation. It wasn't a tranquil country stroll, but walking down the streets of Jersey City without distraction was eye-opening.

It gave me time to ponder all the shit I'd have to figure out. Who I was and what I wanted and how to open myself up to more.

Dr. Johnson had forced me to say out loud the truths I'd been hiding from myself for years.

That I wanted a partner.

That I wanted to build a life with someone.

And that I wanted to be a father.

Facts I'd never dared to admit to anyone.

Now that I'd put them out into the universe, there was no denying them. Already, I could see how stubborn and closed off I'd been. Giving everything I had to my work, never even stopping to feed myself. I needed to do better. I would do better.

So I walked, soaking in the beautiful day, just existing in this world before I got sucked back into the vortex of work and the never-ending tasks awaiting me. Lo was probably foaming at the mouth, waiting with a stack of filings for me to review.

I'd review them happily. The girls wouldn't be dropped off at our place after school, since Jess didn't work on Wednesdays, so I'd bury myself in work, put in some time in the basement gym, and think about the strange turn this day had taken. The more I accomplished today, the earlier I could finish up tomorrow, when Jess would be stopping by to pick up Kit and Greta.

By the time I reached the office, it was after lunch, and I'd fought the urge to check my phone only about nine hundred times.

"Brian," a familiar voice trilled. "Haven't seen you in ages. Have you been avoiding me?"

I smiled at Madame E as she sashayed toward me on the sidewalk. Today, she was wearing an orange caftan covered with jewels. It looked like it weighed more than she did.

"Why don't you come up?" she suggested. "I have time for a quick reading."

I looked at my watch, not actually registering the time. "I'm so sorry. I have a client call in a few minutes."

She arched a brow, those nearly purple eyes pinning me to the spot, making it impossible to look away. "I've been seeing a lot lately."

My heart skipped, and I reconsidered her offer. For months, even after Cal and Lo swore she had psychic abilities and Sully, of all people, began to believe in her foretelling abilities, I was sure Madame E was full of shit. Now? I had to admit she had some eerily accurate predictions.

"Genaro's," she said, tapping her chin. "I can smell it."

I grunted. What the hell was she talking about? Genaro's? I thought she wanted to do a reading.

"Give me your hands."

I offered them to her, and she closed her eyes, humming softly to herself, making her large, beaded earrings vibrate in her ears.

"I'm feeling music, beautiful music. And passion. And a barn with big ceiling beams and the faint smell of manure."

I had no earthly idea what she was talking about. "Let's go upstairs. I'll get my tarot cards."

"Thank you, Madame E," I said politely as I stepped around her to get into the building. "But I have a client call in five minutes."

She shrugged. "Tomorrow. Come up and see me." I wasn't sure how my friends had fallen under her spell. Granted, she'd been pretty helpful in managing Sebastian.

Jesus, I was thinking about the ghost like another roommate again. I ran my hands through my hair. I definitely needed to sleep more.

"I'm proud of you for going to therapy," she said as I walked away. "We're never too old to grow."

I froze, suddenly curious about just how powerful her sight was. "Did you see that when you held my hands?" Maybe I had underestimated her.

"No." She laughed. "Cal told me. We go to Katz's for Reubens on Wednesdays."

Fucking Cal, sharing my personal business.

"I'd need my crystal ball to go that deep. But I've got a busy afternoon. That CEO kid is coming back to talk about his crypto investments. I keep telling him the bubble's gonna burst."

I walked away, shaking my head and trying to make sense of that interaction.

"How was the shrink?" Cal appeared in the doorway of my office before I could even sit down. "Does your dick work now?"

"My dick has always worked, thank you," I replied, shucking my suit jacket. "And you told Madame E? What the hell?"

"She'd figure it out anyway, and she's worried about you. She says since she fixed Sully and me, she would help you, but you're so difficult. I think the words she used were 'cosmically constipated.' You may wanna call the penis doctor after all to deal with that."

"It's a urologist. You're a grown man, for fuck's sake. And I've got work to do."

"Okay." He rapped his knuckles on the doorframe and backed up a step. "Just wanted to let you know that Jess called Sloane."

I froze, my jacket held out in front of me.

"She was called into work, so the girls will be here after school."

I let out the breath I was holding. Jess was coming today. The news lightened this already weightless sensation in my chest.

"Looks like you get to see your girl today."

Stomach twisting, I glowered at him. "She's not my girl."

"Yet," Cal retorted. "She's not your girl *yet*. Trust me, Brian, I know a thing about manifesting true love. You want pointers, I'm your man. In fact, grab a stack of Post-its. I can start now. It's all about affirmations and positive thought loops."

"Do you ever work?" I snarled.

"Don't hate on my efficiency." He bounced his basketball off the wall and caught it with one hand. "Now where's Lo? I need a kiss."

CHAPTER 12

Brian

All day my heart had been racing. Though I felt bad that Jess had been called in on her day off, I wasn't angry that I might catch a glimpse of her. Maybe it was pathetic, but I looked forward to the few minutes we'd spend together on the days she picked up the girls.

A call from the courthouse came in not long after I'd returned, and we discovered that Amy hadn't provided proof of service or the signed CLIS to the court. A deficiency notice was not how I wanted to start this day.

My heart sank, but without hesitation, I slipped into my suit jacket and headed out, hoping like hell Judge Gordon's clerk would accept a late filing. Cal had offered to go over in his orange suit, and while he and that hideous thing had a 100-percent success rate, this was my case; it was my responsibility.

By the time I got home, it was almost seven, and I was a disheveled, cranky mess. It killed me to know I'd missed Jess. Especially after such a breakthrough of a day. But I'd spent over an hour at the courthouse, and then traffic had been terrible.

Music played upstairs as I stopped into my office to drop off files, the thump of the bass making the whole place vibrate. It was a bit loud for the boys' video games, and Sloane had been cracking down on T. J.'s screen time lately. Maybe she'd pulled out the karaoke machine Sully'd brought home for her. She'd been obsessed with karaoke in college, and she had already introduced the boys to the art of singing along with songs while getting just about every word wrong.

At the top of the stairs, I opened the door and came face to face with a sight I hadn't expected.

Pop music played from a Bluetooth speaker that had been set up in the middle of the ping-pong table. In the center of the living room, Jess was swaying and jumping and laughing with total abandon. Even in her work clothes after a long day, her joy was infectious. Kit was dancing beside her, her moves much more complicated. And Greta and T. J. were holding hands and spinning in circles.

Sloane and Sully were slow dancing in the kitchen, the baby strapped to Sully's chest between them. With every revolution, he'd lean down and kiss the baby's head. Lo and Cal were doing a robot-type dance, and though Murphy was sitting on the couch, being his usual reserved self, he was grinning at them.

"What's going on?"

Jess came to an abrupt stop and gave me a warm, wide smile that instantly sent a wave of relief through me. "It's dance party Wednesday," she declared with a spin. "DJ Kit, we need a new song. And no more Lake Paige."

With a roll of her eyes, Kit dragged herself over to the ping-pong table and picked up the tablet set on its edge.

"Can you play 'The Gummy Bear Song'?" T. J. asked.

Kit smirked, and Greta giggled, and a moment later, the most obnoxious sounds I'd ever heard filled the apartment. Ridiculous lyrics blasted loud enough to damage eardrums, and I swear I could feel the walls vibrating with every *Pop* in the song.

Murphy finally stood and joined in, jumping alongside T. J., a two-child mosh pit in front of the couch, losing their ever-loving minds over this nonsense.

As I watched, I couldn't help but feel a little bit silly too.

"You have to dance," Greta said, grabbing my arm.

Jess approached me, her swaying hips holding my attention. Despite the words "gummy bear" being repeated endlessly, all I could think about was gripping her there and digging my fingers into her soft flesh.

"Come on," she said, pulling me from my stupor.

I had a lot of work to do, and I was not the kind to join in when Sloane did break out the karaoke machine. In fact, I typically volunteered to babysit the boys when the rest of our group wanted to head out to the Grasshopper on karaoke nights.

But with the look Jess was giving me? I'd have walked over hot coals if it meant seeing her smile.

So I loosened my tie, shed my jacket, and bopped around like the world's biggest idiot while the song played.

"Play 'It's Raining Tacos' next," T. J. yelled.

Nodding, Kit slid a finger over the screen of the device, and soon, we were dancing to a new beat and my face hurt from smiling. I hadn't felt this carefree and silly in I didn't know how long. And it hit me then that I'd been missing this kind of joy in my life for decades.

Sully and Sloane continued to stare at each other like no one existed, and Cal was swinging and twirling Lo around like he'd had professional dance lessons. The kids were yelling and laughing, and I was sweaty and red-faced and having the time of my damn life.

"Ooh," Jess said, plucking the iPad from Kit's hands. "This one is for Brian and me."

She set the device down, sauntered to me, and loosened my tie further, her face lit up in the brightest grin.

"Ready to dance?" she asked as the opening chords played.

It took half a second to recognize the song, and when I did, I'm certain my brows hit my hairline.

"You remembered," I said softly as "Dance, Dance" by Fallout Boy played.

She pulled my tie off with a flourish. "'Course I did. You were such a cute punk nerd." With her lip caught between her teeth, she spun and danced wildly. The girls joined in, yelling the lyrics. I guess she had remained a fan.

Soon T. J. was spinning around Sully, Sloane was swaying with Tia, and Cal and Lo were back to flirting as they danced. Lo's giggles were loud enough to be heard over the music, and Murphy joined in too.

Lo had worked for me for almost a decade, and I could count on one hand the number of times she'd giggled before Cal had finally worn her down and wooed her.

"Come on," Jess said, grabbing me by the arm and pulling me toward her.

Surrounded by kids, with my best friends in the world close and the only woman I'd ever loved in front of me, I wasn't sure I'd ever been happier.

After one more song, Sloane turned the speaker off. "It's bedtime," she said.

She was met with a round of groans from Greta and the boys and quickly gave in to the pleas for one more song.

Smiling, Kit tapped the iPad screen and put on another Lake Paige song. Then she broke out into an elaborate dance.

When it had ended and the music was turned off for good, the entire crew collapsed in a sweaty heap, some lounging on the couch, others on the chairs, and the kids sprawled out on the floor.

As Cal and Sully wrangled the boys so they could get ready for bed, Greta approached me. "Mom brought pizza. Want some?"

"So what were we celebrating?" I asked Kit when she handed me a slice of cheese on a paper plate. Jess was busy cleaning up the kitchen and chatting with Lo.

"It's dance party Wednesday."

"Our mom loves to make traditions," Greta said, popping up behind me with a full glass of water.

I took it from her with a nod of thanks and sipped from it so it'd be less likely to spill.

Kit sat on the couch. "Right after the divorce, things were rough. So Mom started doing all these silly things with us to cheer us up."

"Like Munchkin Mondays," Greta said, dropping onto the cushion beside her sister. "Every Monday morning, we get up early and stop at Dunkin' for Munchkins on the way to school. I eat the chocolate."

"I love the jelly kind," Kit added.

"What about your mom?" I peered at Jess, who had her back turned.

"She likes the butternut ones. But they're hard to find. Not every Dunkin' has them, and they don't make very many." She frowned.

"Oh, really?" I asked, my mind zeroing in on an idea.

Greta bobbed her head. "Yup."

"She's obsessed," Kit went on. "They remind her of when she was a kid and her grandpa would take her on special occasions."

"Before we moved here, it took forever," Greta complained. "We had to leave super early because there wasn't a Dunkin' near our house."

"Now it's easy because we walk by one on the way to our new school."

"Yeah." Greta bounced on the couch cushion. "And we know all the people who work there. It's cool."

"Do they sell butternut Munchkins?" I asked.

Greta shrugged, and Kit said, "Only sometimes."

"Okay. I'll keep an eye out for them for you," I said. "What other traditions do you celebrate?"

"Saturday is game night and charcuterie," Greta chirped. "We call it girl dinner because we don't have to cook anything. We get the fancy cheese from Trader Joes, and sometimes Aunt Lana and Uncle Max come over with their baby."

My heart warmed at the image of their Saturday nights that formed in my mind. "You have a great mom."

Greta grinned, but Kit eyed me warily. Tween girls terrified me for exactly this reason. She'd been happily chatting, filling me in, then suddenly, she was on guard. I had no clue what was happening in her head.

"We know." With that, she stood and walked into the kitchen without looking back.

Deciding our conversation had been a positive one, despite her change in temperament at the end, I stuffed my face. When I finished, I headed to the kitchen to feed the cat, finding Jess telling the girls to collect their things.

"Did you enjoy your first dance party Wednesday?" she asked.

I scanned the open space, noting that my friends had disappeared and the girls were occupied.

"The girls told me about your traditions." I took a step closer, maybe too close, but she didn't back away. "You're an incredible mom, Jess."

She crossed her arms and looked up at me, her glare reminiscent of the one her daughter had leveled me with only a few minutes ago.

"Brian," she said sharply. "Stop it."

"I'm being sincere," I promised. "You make every day magical for your kids, and they love you for it. They'll never have to wonder how much you love them. It's obvious. I see how hard you are on yourself, but you are doing an amazing job."

She squeezed the bridge of her nose and pinched her eyes shut like she was in pain.

"God damn you, Brian Machon," she said, shaking her head.

My heart lurched. *Shit. Had I said the wrong thing?*

"You had to grow up even more handsome than you were in college. And you're kind too?" She huffed. "Now you're telling me you see me and how hard I work? And you go out of your way to mess with my ex-husband?" She dropped her arm to her side with a *thwack*. "Shit on a brick. Why do you have to be so perfect? It's not fair how much you're making me want to like you when you're my damn lawyer."

Anticipation and hope swelled in my chest. She *liked* me? Part of me found that extremely interesting, and another part was throwing up red flags, shouting that I'd crossed a line. "Sorry," I said weakly as I took a step back.

"You should be." She moved forward, poking my chest with her finger. "It's not fair. I'm an exhausted single mom. You can't just look like that and speak like that and be so freaking nice all the time. It's torture on my poor hormones."

I had no clue what was happening, but I certainly enjoyed it. "Tell them I'm sorry."

"Mom," Greta called. "We're ready."

With a long sigh, Jess stepped away from me and snagged her purse off the counter.

"See you tomorrow," she said. "And behave."

CHAPTER 13

Brian

After Jess and the girls had left, I ran down to the basement for a punishing workout, my every cell buzzing with adrenaline.

The woman had all but come out and admitted to having feelings for me. She said I was handsome. Perfect, even.

Perfect. That was the farthest thing from the truth. This kind of thinking had to stop. It was dangerous. I had too many unresolved feelings when it came to Jess, and she was my client. I'd built this career over the past twenty years, and I'd never, ever crossed a line.

She was my client.

My punch landed hard, making my knuckles tingle. I shuffled and followed with some quick uppercuts, trying to let go of these complicated feelings.

She needed my help.

I had an ethical obligation to do all I could to get her relo request approved. To help her move to Vermont.

By the time I came back upstairs, it was after midnight and I was sweaty and exhausted.

I leaned against the sink, refilling my water glass and staring out at the dark city.

"You okay?"

I turned, discovering Sloane pacing in the dark with Tia in her arms.

I'd known this woman forever. She was another sister to me, and last year had been so brutal on her and Sully both.

In law school, I'd had a front-row seat to their love story. I'd been their third wheel then, and I'd remained that way until last year, when their marriage fell apart.

Now that they'd reconciled, they were better than ever, both more at peace with themselves and with one another. Even with a newborn keeping them up all night.

"She keeps growing." I padded closer and gently stroked the infant's soft little cheek.

"Babies do that. Remember how massive T. J. was?"

"His cheeks." I laughed. "They were the chubbiest."

Smiling, she pressed her lips to the top of Tia's head.

For a moment, we stood in the dark silence, cradled in the peace of the moment, watching Tia sleep. Memories of my nephew Liam at that age surfaced, and my heart tugged. I'd had many sleepless nights back then. Dad and I had taken nighttime shifts so Dylan could sleep. Her every waking moment had been focused on feeding him and caring for him, and she'd come close to running herself into the ground.

When Liam was born, I was a twenty-three-year-old dumbass who had never held a baby. But I'd figured it out quickly. As long as we were moving, he would sleep, so I'd walk circles around the living room in Dad's house for hours at night. Then I'd catch a little sleep before heading to class.

And now Liam was headed to college. Just the thought made heat gather at the backs of my eyes.

"Would you...?" Sloane held Tia out to me.

Without hesitation, I cradled her in my elbow, immediately falling into the swaying pattern she liked.

Sloane filled a glass with water, and after a long, slow sip, rolled her shoulders.

"What's got you up so late? And don't try to downplay it. For the twenty years I've known you, you've always stuck to a strict sleep schedule."

I huffed. "Not so strict."

"Please. How many times have you lectured me about sleep hygiene? Even in law school, you tortured me with it. And you'd set Sully's alarm to wake me up at the crack of dawn."

"You're a wild night owl who used to write briefs at one a.m. And it's critical to eat a good breakfast on important days. Like when you had exams," I argued. "You weren't complaining when you graduated at the top of our class."

She stuck her tongue out at me. "Yes. Beating your ass was deeply satisfying."

"Yeah, yeah," I teased, keeping my tone soft so as not to rouse the baby. "Spare me."

"So what's eating you?"

I avoided her eye, choosing instead to examine Tia's perfect little nose and eyelashes.

"Get it off your chest. There's no sense in hiding it. You're distracted, not sleeping, working out like a fiend and..." She opened the cabinet next to the fridge and pulled out a nearly empty package of cookies. "Back on the Oreos?"

Chin lifted, I turned, still swaying evenly. "I have no idea what you're talking about."

"You sneak Oreos the way a nicotine addict sneaks cigarettes. So spill it."

I groaned. It was annoying how well she knew me. And unlike Sully, who generally let me spiral in peace, she was not going to let this go.

"It's late," I hedged.

"I've got time." She put a hand on her hip. "She's gonna want to eat again in like twenty minutes."

Maybe it was because I was exhausted, or maybe holding this perfect little baby weakened my defenses, but I found myself giving in.

"It's Jess."

A wide smile spread across Sloane's face, and she bent at the knees, bouncing without lifting her feet from the floor. Then she whisper-squealed, "Brian likes *a girl*."

I snatched the Oreo bag from her and shoved one into my mouth while she did a celebratory dance around the kitchen.

"You *love* her."

"Stop that." I squeezed my eyes shut and exhaled loudly. "My world has been off-kilter since the day she walked into my office. Like my life isn't my life anymore. Everything has changed, and I'm thinking things and feeling things I don't understand."

Sloane came to a stop, her eyes wide. "This is awesome. Don't you see? You're growing." She patted my bearded cheek, her dark eyes twinkling in the moonlight. "For more than fifteen years, I've heard story after story about Jess, the one that got away. The blond goddess with the dimples you fell madly in love with in college."

That was an overstatement. Had I thought about her from time to time since our lives had diverged and we'd broken things off? Yes. But I hadn't spent the last two decades pining after her. I'd moved on.

"And you never went on more than a few dates with anyone. Though I can't blame you. Every one of them was a bore."

"Hey," I said. "You introduced me to Deborah."

"Yes. And immediately regretted it." She picked up her water again. "Cal tried to disown me when I brought her into our lives. Remember that time we all went to Montauk for the weekend?"

I flinched. That had been painful.

Deborah was a tax attorney. Sloane had met her at a law conference and invited her out with us a couple of times. She'd asked me to dinner, and because I admired her confidence, I said yes. She was intelligent and obsessed with her work, and so it made sense to date her.

Sadly, her idea of fun was debating the tax code, and pretty much nothing else.

"And Viola?"

I winced. After I'd broken it off with her, she'd broken into my apartment and stolen all my left shoes. That was weird.

"She collected stamps," Sloane hissed a little too loudly, making the baby stir in my arms. "*Stamps.* We should have known she had psychopathic tendencies."

I shuddered. She really was an odd woman.

"Anyway," she sighed. "What I'm trying to say is that despite being good-looking, successful, and kind, your track record with women is shit."

Amusement and incredulity twined through me. "Why, thank you."

She tipped her head and gave me a serious look. "I tell the truth because I love you. You're my brother, and I want to see you happy. You've been on autopilot for so long, so to know you're having feelings makes me disgustingly happy."

My heart sank. "It's unethical."

She waved her hand. "Of course it is. But she won't be your client forever."

"And she's leaving."

"Maybe." She crossed her arms. "If you're successful."

Head tilted, I glared at her. "You know I'm good at my job."

Tia stirred in my arms again, this time getting a little louder, so I handed her back to her mother.

"Honor your feelings," she said as she took the baby. "Explore them. Keep going to therapy and work through your shit."

A huff of air escaped me. "Does everyone know I'm going to therapy?"

She let out a quiet laugh. "As if you could keep a secret in this building. Of course we all know, and I'm proud of you. Do the work. Trust me, because I have firsthand experience here." She sobered, her tone going serious. "If the stars align and you're given a second chance with your first love? Then you'd better not blow it."

Her words hit me hard. "You think I'd blow it?"

"No. Not if you're determined to do it right. But you're a little emotionally unavailable. And you know me. I have a soft spot for emotionally unavailable men who do the work and learn to do better."

The beautiful baby in her arms was living proof of that statement. If Sully could win back his wife when they were on the brink of divorce, surely I could figure out how to manage my attraction to my client.

Tia let out the cutest little yawn and her eyes snapped open.

"Feeding time," Sloane said, padding down the hall toward the bathroom.

It may have seemed like a strange place to feed a baby, but when she moved in last year, she and Sully had converted the handicap stall into a sort of lounge for her, with a lava lamp, courtesy of T. J., a plush rug, and a rocking chair.

"You've got a heart of gold, Brian Machon, and a brain that's worth nine hundred dollars an hour. Put them to work and get your girl."

CHAPTER 14

Jess

No matter how many cleansing breaths I took, nerves overwhelmed me. If I hadn't already bitten off all my nails, I'd do it again. I was half tempted to take off my shoes and bite my damn toenails at this point.

Being a mom was joyful and amazing. Absolutely the greatest experience of my life. But at times, it was terrifying. Because I couldn't protect them from failure or disappointment or hurt, and I couldn't fix all of life's problems for them.

And this was a big stage. The Brooklyn Academy of Music was one of New York's most prestigious performing arts centers. Being invited to play in a showcase here was a very big deal, and Kit had been obsessing for months over her piece.

The space was something out of a movie, with crystal chandeliers, velvet curtains, and art déco architecture. The scent of expensive perfume wafted around like a floral cloud, and the high-society alpha parents working the room around me only made me feel more out of place.

Most days, I was proud of the life my girls and I were creating for ourselves. But in a place like this, surrounded by Julliard prodigies, private tutors, and world-class teachers, I couldn't help but doubt myself.

Kit had fallen in love with the piano when she was four.

The white marble foyer of our house in Bergen County was bigger than the apartment the girls and I inhabited now, and Kenneth had insisted on placing a grand piano in the middle of it. The instrument was beautiful and cost more than most luxury cars, but neither of us played. It was a showpiece the designer thought would add to the ambiance, I guess.

Then preschool-age Kit discovered the sounds it made. She lifted the cover off the keys, sat on the bench, and played. She didn't plunk randomly, with too much force, like one would expect a four-year-old would do. She didn't bang on it but played, stretching her fingers and experimenting with notes and rhythms, her smile growing wider by the second.

I put her in lessons soon after, and since then, nothing had made her as happy as playing. At her first recital, when she played an amazing rendition of "When the Saints Go Marching In," I wept with pride.

Her teacher had pushed for her to be included in tonight's showcase. Some of the best musicians in the tri-state area were here, many a lot older, but Kit belonged here.

She worked hard and practiced nonstop, even though we no longer had a piano. My mom guilt surged each time I thought about it. I'd found a hand-me-down keyboard, though, and my sweet girl hadn't batted an eye at it. Every night, she'd plug her headphones in and practice. I'd also been able to speak with the administration at her school, and they'd agreed that instead of study hall, she would go to the music room and practice every afternoon on a real piano. It had made the transition to a new school a little less painful, and it had given her plenty of practice time.

She was naturally talented, sure, but she was also passionate. She was dedicated and she was invested, sometimes crying when she couldn't get a part of the piece right, then beaming with joy when it clicked.

I'd spent my life searching for a passion, yet she'd figured it out before middle school. I was in awe of her.

Tonight, I was in awe, yes, but I was also on the verge of throwing up. This was a big freaking deal. Everyone who was anyone in the classical music world in our area was here to scope out future stars. And I couldn't imagine handling that kind of pressure at only twelve.

Greta sat next to me in her ruffly blue dress, one of Kit's hand-me-downs, smoothing the French braids I'd struggled to get right this afternoon. Lana and Max, who'd hired a babysitter for the night, sat on her other side.

"Stop twitching," Greta scolded, like she was the parent and I was the child. "She's gonna be amazing."

I smiled softly at her. I admired her certainty and her faith in her sister.

"She's practiced so many times. At this point I could play it."

Tipping closer, I kissed her forehead.

She gave me an annoyed look, pulling back. Then, eyes widening, she tapped my shoulder. "Mom, look."

I whipped around, and when I caught sight of the three devastatingly handsome men marching down our row with two smaller but just as handsome boys behind them, I gasped.

Brian.

"What are you doing here?" I asked as I stood, causing the cushion of my seat to fly up and bounce against its back.

He shrugged. "I mentioned that I wanted to come cheer Kit on, and they asked if they could tag along."

"Kit's our cousin now. We gotta cheer for her." T. J., grinning a toothless grin, bounced on his toes.

He and Murphy wore navy suits that brought out the blue eyes they'd definitely inherited from their dads. And the four of them together? Sully and Cal looking properly British in their bespoke suits? The sight was devastating.

I swore I could hear swooning in the seats behind us.

"T. J., Murphy," Greta said. "Come sit by me. My mom let me bring fidgets and snacks."

"Sweet," T. J shouted, plowing past me.

Murphy skirted around me with a quiet "excuse me," and Lana and Max moved down so the kids could sit together.

I made introductions, and after Lana shook Brian's hand, she turned to me, her eyes bulging. I could only imagine the unhinged texts she'd send later tonight.

Brian shuffled to my side. His beard was trimmed and his suit looked custom. God, he was so good-looking. Just having him here made me feel steadier. He looked powerful and confident as he homed in on me completely.

My stomach, already churning with nerves, flipped.

"Is this seat taken?" he asked shyly.

Sully and Cal had moved to my other side so they could sit next to the boys and were busy chatting with Max about the Metros.

"No," I said, my cheeks heating. "You didn't have to come."

He paused, still standing over me, his face lowered. The intensity in his golden eyes sent a shiver down my spine. "I wouldn't miss it for the world."

Once he'd settled beside me, he stretched his legs out and looked around. "This is a swanky place. I'm glad it's worthy of Kit. I can't wait to see her up there on stage."

I blinked repeatedly, focusing on the stage, trying not to burst into tears. The combination of nerves, excitement, and Brian's presence overwhelmed my senses.

"I'm sure you have better things to do on a Friday night," I said, still unable to look at him. If I did, I was certain I'd fall into some kind of handsome man vortex.

He chuckled. "As it turns out, I do not. Most Friday nights, I work late, work out, and then fall asleep watching baseball. This is a glamorous night out for me."

Within minutes, the seats around us were full and the lights had dimmed.

And suddenly, my nerves had ratcheted up again.

"Your hands are shaking," Brian whispered, leaning close.

"This is a big deal, and I'm worried about Kit. That she'll feel like she doesn't belong here."

Brian reached over, his large, steady hand engulfing mine. "She belongs here," he said firmly. "Because of you. Because you see her and you believe in her. Because you taught her to be brave and bold."

Finally, I forced myself to look at him, even as tears welled in my eyes.

"I know you're nervous," he whispered. We were so close now that I could feel the heat radiating from him. "But she's gonna be fine. That girl's got a spine of steel, just like her mom."

The tears were getting closer to falling. Dammit. How did he always know the right thing to say? With a cleansing breath, I dragged my attention to the stage, though I couldn't help but get caught up in the warmth of his hand and his cool, masculine smell.

In the silence, anxiety immediately clawed its way back in. Looking for a distraction, I checked on Greta, who was whispering to the boys, smiling and fidgeting a whole lot less with the dress she'd begrudgingly agreed to wear.

"You look beautiful, by the way," Brian whispered, the feel of his hot breath on my neck sending another shiver down my spine.

I bit down on my lip hard to keep from grinning. He was being polite. That was all there was to it. Yes, I'd dressed up, but I was wearing a simple, inexpensive bright blue dress. Hardly haute couture. I had no doubt his suit cost ten times more.

But I liked the fabric and felt comfortable in it. It was A-line, which flattered my hips, and had a swishy skirt.

Exactly the kind of thing Kenneth hated.

He'd have chastised me. He always wanted me in tight black dresses, boring as hell and god-awfully restrictive, along with sky-high heels. Serious, expensive outfits. The sort of thing a woman wore when she, or in our case, *her husband*, wanted everyone to know they had money.

Reclaiming my wardrobe had felt like an act of rebellion, and these days, it was second nature to wear pretty things that made me feel good. I didn't dress for men; I dressed for myself. But his compliment wormed its way into my heart anyway.

The lights dimmed further as a string quartet set up on the stage, and

I settled into my seat to enjoy the show. One after another—with some in groups—the most talented kids I'd ever seen wowed us with their skills.

My mother had been a pianist. She'd tried to teach me, but it had never stuck. My chest pinched at the thought of her. I'd give anything to have her here today. I missed her fiercely every day, but especially in these moments. She would have been bursting with pride.

After several impressive performances, it was Kit's turn.

"And now on the piano," the emcee said. "Katherine Mosely, playing *Adagio in D Minor* composed by Johann Sebastian Bach."

Kit walked onto the stage slowly, her face lifted, her attention completely focused on the piano. Once she'd settled on the bench, she ran her fingers over the keys. Then she took a deep breath and began to play.

The piece began slowly, delicate and melancholy, before building into something more emotional.

I sat, rapt, watching every movement of her hands, the sway of her shoulders. The way she flowed with the music was mesmerizing. She felt every note with her entire body and soul. And although her face was serious, joy radiated off her as she played.

Awe. I was filled with awe. And pride. Because this scrappy little twelve-year-old, who'd been through so much heartache and disappointment the last couple of years, was up on that stage, fearlessly sharing her gifts with the world. Halfway through the piece, there was no point in trying to stanch my tears, so I let them roll freely down my face.

When she finished, she turned on the bench, searching for me in the audience. So I stood, clapping my heart out, my cheeks tearstained but my smile wide. Greta stood too, clapping and jumping up and down. Kit spotted us and gave a small smile before bowing and exiting the stage.

I sat and immediately fished a tissue out of my bag. My makeup was probably a mess, but that was the last thing I cared about tonight. My girl, my brave, talented girl, had accomplished big things, and this was only the start.

Brian put his hand on mine on my lap and squeezed. "She is extraordinary," he said as the next performers set up. "Just like her mom."

The rest of the concert was a happy blur. I was on cloud nine, barely conscious of who was performing what. Not only had my daughter performed beautifully, but she'd had a whole cheering section here to support her.

Granted, T. J. had been fidgeting so much he got his foot caught between the seat cushion, and Sully and Cal had to do an emergency extraction while a harpist performed, but it was otherwise a smooth night.

When it was over, the whole group stayed to congratulate her, wrapping her in hugs and demanding photos. So often, I doubted my ability to do this job. To raise these girls on my own. But tonight, I was reminded that the most important thing I could do was surround them with love.

It was bittersweet, knowing that if all went as planned, we'd be gone before the end of the summer. We'd lose this support system. Though we'd gain another in Vermont.

Though in my hometown, we'd also find fewer music opportunities for Kit, and nowhere on earth could compare to the endless excitement of the city. It was for the best. I knew it in my bones. But it was moments like these that made the hard years we'd spent in Jersey almost worth it.

On the way out, I was still coming down from the excitement, a little stunned, so Brian steered me toward the door, his hand on my lower back.

As we neared the exit, my heart plummeted. Kenneth stood to one side, wearing one of his signature dark suits with no tie, his graying hair slicked back in his usual style.

It shouldn't have surprised me that he was here, but I'd been so nervous and distracted that I'd forgotten to even look for him. It was such a large venue, and I assumed that if he deigned to appear, I wouldn't even see him.

Beside him, hanging from his arm, was a young woman with her face buried in her phone. She was wearing what I can only describe as a scrap of fabric and texting furiously.

"Jessica," Kenneth said.

His voice alone, that tone he'd used for so long when he was angry with me, made my spine snap straight.

"And you," he said, sneering at Brian. "The lawyer."

"Hi, Dad," Greta said with a small wave.

Kenneth had the good sense to give his daughter a smile, if nothing else. "Margaret. So good to see you." The words were spoken as if she were a professional acquaintance instead of his nine-year-old flesh and blood.

He looked around Greta, eyeing Kit, who was chatting with Lana.

"Katherine," he boomed. "Excellent job. I would have thought the Bach piece was too challenging for you, but you seemed to make it work."

Seemed? I could feel my blood pressure spike. "She was spectacular," I corrected, bristling at his passive aggression.

"Thank you, Dad," Kit replied, her voice and her expression equally stony.

"Good to see you all," he said, looking at his watch. "Must run. We've got reservations."

The woman, who had only now looked up from her phone, was suddenly keen to participate in the conversation. "Kenny's taking me to Le Bain," she said with a smirk. "Bottle service. You know how it is." She flipped her waist-length hair over one shoulder and went back to texting.

I held back a scoff. He was taking this practical child to a club? He was a fifty-three-year-old father.

Greta's face fell, but Kit's expression only hardened, her eyes locking on her father. For a moment, she let her sassy tween glare burn a hole in his forehead. Then she grabbed her sister's arm and turned her back, focusing on the boys.

Kenneth stepped closer to Brian, jaw clenched. "Happy now?" he asked. "I know what you did. How my Metros seats were suddenly no longer available. And I'm sure the bar association will be thrilled when they find out you're fucking a client."

I gasped, stumbling back a step at the vitriol in his tone.

"You are out of line," Brian said, his voice steely.

Cal and Sully stepped closer, both pulling up to their full height, which was, honestly, intimidating.

"Did I get it wrong?" Kenneth asked me. "You want me to believe you dragged your lawyer here just for fun? Or so you'd have backup when you saw me? I didn't realize you could afford to pay someone to pretend to care."

Bile rose in my throat, and the instinct to run washed over me. But I couldn't. I wouldn't let my girls see me back down.

Kenneth looked me up and down, sneering in disgust, and a wave of shame nearly knocked me over. In this moment, I was reliving every criticism and nasty comment he'd ever made.

I closed my eyes, wishing the floor would open up and swallow me.

"I'm here to support Kit and Jess." Brian stepped in front of me, only an inch or two, in a protective way before looking to make sure the kids weren't listening.

He leaned close to Kenneth and whispered, "I can see why you'd be confused, since you had to be forced to show up for your own child. Seems like being a deadbeat dad really suits you."

The moment hung like a gavel strike. And I checked to make sure none of the kids had overheard that verbal smackdown.

Kenneth, his face now beet red, grabbed the woman at his side with a shaking hand and walked away without even saying goodbye to the girls, who'd migrated to the area set up for pictures and were taking selfies with my phone.

"You okay?" Brian's voice startled me.

Peering up at him, I nodded woodenly. He'd stood up for me. And more importantly, he'd stood up for my kids.

As he led me out of the lobby, it dawned on me that no one had ever done that for me before.

CHAPTER 15

Brian

"You are so talented," Cal gushed.

Kit lit up, the joy on her face making her look uncannily like her mother.

"Someday," Cal went on, "we'll be buying tickets to see you at Lincoln Center."

I couldn't help but stare at Jess, who had her arm around her daughter, beaming with pride.

I'd known the kid was good, but she'd blown my socks off, playing with passion and precision beyond her age.

And fuck if I hadn't almost teared up when the guys and the boys insisted on coming. Even T. J. and Murphy had enjoyed it. Though Murphy was rarely effusive, he'd been grinning all night, and a few feet down the sidewalk, T. J. was waving wildly, surely telling a tale.

"We need to celebrate this monumental achievement," I said, rubbing my hands together. "How about ice cream?"

The four kids shrieked so loudly it probably woke up half of Park Slope.

I grinned. "I know a very special place."

We walked along Sackett Street, the kids bouncing around ahead of us, with Cal acting just as rowdy and Sully policing the situation. Jess and I hung back a little, walking side by side. Every minute or so, I stole a look at her. I so desperately wanted to focus on the excitement of the night and how good this all felt. But instead, I kept going back to Kenneth's smug face and his cruelty. How long had he treated her like this? If I could, I'd reverse time and go back just so I could represent her in their divorce. I would have made that man bleed in court. We would have sucked every penny from him and the marrow from his bones for good measure.

My jaw was tight as I mentally cataloged all the ways I could destroy him in court, and I was deep in a legal-based revenge fantasy when Jess bumped my arm.

"You okay over there?" she asked.

I looked down at her concerned face and forced my shoulders to lower from my ears. "I am now."

She threaded her arm through my elbow, instantly scaring away another layer of tension. "Good, because you need to know. I really love ice cream, so this place better deliver."

"Oh, it will," I replied, eyeing Kit and Greta, who were now pirouetting down the sidewalk. "He doesn't deserve them," I blurted out.

Her body stiffened beside me, and she stumbled a step.

"Sorry." I winced. "It's not my place."

Squeezing my arm, Jess pulled me to a stop. "You're right. He doesn't deserve them. And it helps to hear you say that."

I gave her a soft smile and brushed a strand of hair from her face. For a moment, I was lost in her, her fathomless brown eyes making it hard for me to find my way out.

Ahead, T. J. screeched, and finally, I took a step back and huffed a breath. Then I grasped Jess's hand, and the two of us jogged to catch up with the group.

"What is this place?" Greta gushed, looking in the window.

"The Farmacy," Kit read. "What's that?"

"A uniquely Brooklyn institution," I explained as I stepped past Sully, who held the door for us. "At the turn of the century, this was an apothecary."

"What's that?"

"An old-fashioned drugstore, where people went to get medicine and other health-related stuff," Jess explained.

The place was now a vintage ice cream parlor and soda fountain. "I hope you're hungry," I said, "because the sundaes here are the size of Fuzzy."

"*Yes*," T. J. hissed, jumping up and down.

We all piled into a large pink booth, the kids clamoring to look at the ornate menus.

Jess smiled at me from across the table, where Murphy was quietly telling her a story about *Minecraft*, and my heart clenched.

That smile.

I wanted to earn it every day. I wanted all her smiles.

And that was a terrifying thought.

But this felt easy. Kids, chaos, ice cream. I wasn't sure what I'd been so afraid of for so long.

"What are you getting?" Greta asked me.

Before I could open my mouth, Cal jumped in. "Brian doesn't like ice cream."

Every person at the table looked at me in shock.

"No," I corrected, smoothing down my tie. "I like ice cream. I just don't eat it often."

"Sus," Kit declared, once again perusing her menu.

"Super sus," Greta echoed, giving me a dubious look.

"Do you want to share with me?" Jess asked. "I'm salivating over the Ninety-Nine Problems, but I can't eat the whole thing."

I tilted closer to Greta and scanned her menu. I didn't actually care what the Ninety-Nine Problems consisted of. I was too damn giddy about sharing ice cream with the beautiful woman across from me, but I figured I should pretend to confirm that it sounded palatable.

"Yes. Sounds awesome." I straightened. "I love chocolate."

Sully's lips tugged down, but I ignored the look, busying myself with listening to the kids while they debated the merits of the choices on the very extensive menu.

After we'd placed our order, Greta propped her elbows up. "Why is Brian the only one who ever walks Fuzzy?"

"Because Lo told him to," Cal said. "And we do what she says."

"When Fuzzy came to live with us, Brian started the walking routine. None of us had any interest, so we let him," Sully added.

"But Lo told us that he's your cat," Kit added, scrutinizing Cal.

He threw his hands up. "Fuzzy Wuzzy loves him. No one can explain it. I bought him organic cat treats and so many toys, but from the start, he chose Brian to be his bit—oops." He winced, then turned on the charming smile that always got him out of trouble. "Sorry. I mean butler. He wanted Brian to be his human butler, and who are we to say no to a cat who has made up his mind?"

The girls giggled. T. J. did too. Murphy gave Cal a soft look that resembled one a parent would give their child, not the other way around. But that was the kind of relationship the two of them had.

"So you got stuck with the cat," Jess said softly.

I shrugged. "I could do without the litter box, but I don't mind the walks. They help me clear my head. Though he's a pain in the ahh—butt at night. He likes to sleep on my chest. And he drives me crazy, knocking things off my desk for fun."

"He's a cat," Cal said. "It's what they do." He said this as if he'd taken care of the cat a single day since he'd brought him home. Lo had asked me to chip in, and I'd been happy to do it, especially since I'd escaped both the plant and fish maintenance.

Cal had gone through several caretaking phases when Murphy first came to live with him. Lo had secretly gone behind him and taken care of his plants and fish to help in order to build up his parenting confidence. Murphy had even gotten in on it. And together he and Lo had stashed a couple of fish in bowls in Murphy's room so they could replace the dead ones before Cal noticed. Bubbles the Ninth was still doing well so far. According to Madame E, ten was the lucky number, so before long, the charade would end.

After eating his weight in ice cream and ordering a milkshake to wash it down, Cal threw Jess a devious grin. "So, Jess. Now that we have you, I want all the dirt on College Brian. Tell us everything. Has he always been an uptight wanker?"

Sully barked a laugh, the loud sound startling Murphy, then ruffled his nephew's hair.

I glared at my best friends. Traitors.

"Brian is not uptight," Jess corrected in her mom voice. "But he was... intense. Focused. Didn't matter what it was. We'd go to concerts as often as we could. Really, any live music we could find. Brian was always great at making the plans, remembering the tickets, and knowing the T schedule so we could all get home safely. That sort of thing."

Her smile grew, her dark eyes warm with affection, or so I liked to think.

"And he was super helpful back then too." She gave me a wink.

My face heated ridiculously.

"He tutored friends who were struggling. And, oh my God." She put her hand over her mouth and giggled. "My junior year, my friends and I were living in the most horrid off-campus apartment. A basement with bars on the windows, no hot water, and lots of suspicious smells coming from the closets."

I had an instant flashback to that place and shuddered, already knowing which story she was about to tell.

"We'd come back from a party or concert or something, and I was complaining about how the washing machine was broken and had eaten my quarters. So Brian decided he'd fix it."

"Was he pissed?" Cal whispered, eyeing the kids to ensure they were distracted by their own conversation.

"Drunk?" Jess asked, brows lifted. "Tipsy, maybe. But my dad had sent me to college with a pink toolbox so I could take care of myself. So Brian got the pink tools, marched in there, and started taking it apart. But..." Her eyes flashed with amusement. "There was one problem. The door to the laundry room was this big steel thing, and it always got stuck, so we all kept it propped open with a large rock."

"Oh no." Cal ran his hands through his hair, grinning, not the least bit concerned for College Brian's well-being.

Jess nodded. "When Brian pulled the washer out of the wall, he quickly discovered why it wasn't working."

Both guys were leaning forward on their elbows, their attention darting from Jess to me and back again.

She bit her lip, like that could stop her from smiling. "There was a raccoon back there."

Cal straightened. "Bollocks."

I nodded.

"And my sweet Brian, thinking he was saving us from a feral animal, kicked the rock and shut the door to contain it. Except he was still inside, and like it always did, the door stuck, and he couldn't get out."

"And that's how Brian got rabies," Sully deadpanned.

"Not quite," Jess said, folding her napkin in half, then quarters. "We panicked. The windows were barred, so we couldn't get him out that way, and I was convinced he was being mauled by a raccoon inside. One of my roommates called 911, but this was Boston at two a.m. on a Saturday night. They had bigger issues to deal with than rescuing a drunk college kid who was trapped in a laundry room with a raccoon."

"They showed up eventually," I chimed in. "And got the door off its hinges."

"And?" Sully and Cal were still rapt, their blue eyes—Sully's more gray; Cal's more ocean-like—bright.

Jess's smile was blinding now, her cheeks pink. "Brian tamed the raccoon with a protein bar he pulled out of his pocket. And once he was sure it wouldn't bite him, he fixed the washing machine. Not only that, but he tampered with it so that when you put quarters in, you could start the cycle, but it would spit the money back out to you. We enjoyed free laundry for the rest of the year."

"No way."

"There wasn't a scratch on him," Jess said proudly. "It was so Brian. He didn't waste time panicking. Instead, he gave the wild animal a snack and got back to work."

"Man," Cal said, shaking his head. "You really were born this way, weren't you?"

"No wonder Fuzzy chose him," Sully said with reverence. "He knew he was an animal whisperer."

Jess ducked her head, averting her gaze. "I'm so glad he's still a knight in shining armor."

I watched her, silently begging for her attention, and when she locked eyes with me, that tug returned, the need to touch her and be closer to her.

But she was my client. That thought was like a bucket of ice water. So I broke the connection and used my napkin to wipe at the table.

I'd missed this. The ease I felt around her, the way she made every moment feel more fun and vibrant. I'd missed her.

But for now, at least, I couldn't do anything about it.

"You must have some good law school stories," she urged Sully.

"So many." He grunted a sound that might have been a laugh. "Including during our first year of law school, when he got a parking ticket, then wrote an eleven-page legal brief and showed up to traffic court to defend himself."

I smiled at the memory. I had been high on justice back then.

"He got up and gave this sweeping argument, citing a precedent that dated back to the eighteen hundreds, before cars were even invented, and argued his constitutional rights were being infringed. Dude thought he was Clarence Darrow."

"Classic Brian," Cal said, shaking his head.

"Did you get out of the ticket?" Jess asked.

I shook my head. "Judge still made me pay, but he offered me an internship."

After we'd paid the tab—Cal stealing the check off the table and insisting he'd cover it—we wandered back down to the parking ramp, our group a little less boisterous than before. Cal and Sully carried their sleepy sons, and Jess and I lagged behind with her daughters.

The night was warm, but the breeze was cool. It was the kind of evening that made me miss the city. In a few months, we'd be back here, our Jersey City experiment concluded. Since the moment we'd been given the details of Terry's trust and understood that we'd have to rough it in the rundown building where he'd started the firm, I'd been desperate to get back, but suddenly, the thought made my chest constrict.

Coming back meant returning to my home and my office with the incredible view of Manhattan. My oversized fish tank, which I'd been assured was being well-maintained by associates.

But suddenly, when I considered leaving Jersey, apprehension slithered through my veins. In the last nine months or so, Cal and Lo had found one another, and Sully and Sloane had worked things out and were more in love than ever. The firm was thriving, both in Jersey and in the city. I didn't want to lose a moment of the closeness this family of mine had gained. Or the little time I had with Jess.

Come August, we'd be moving back to the city, and the hope was that she'd be headed to Vermont.

The thought made me want to throw up.

When we reached her car. Kit threw her arms around me, startling me. "Thank you, Brian."

Jess stood behind her, beaming.

"You were incredible, kid," I said as I hugged her in return. "Can't wait for your next performance."

I waited until the three of them had loaded up and were heading toward the exit before dragging myself to Sully's SUV. In the passenger seat, I stared out at the world passing by, trying to process all that had happened tonight.

I'd come here to support Kit and Jess. But now, at the end of the night, I felt like I'd been accepted into the fold. Like I suddenly belonged to something I didn't even know I was missing.

CHAPTER 16

Jess

"Do you have a minute?" I asked, peeking my head around the door. Brian was at his desk, collar unbuttoned and sleeves rolled up, looking delicious, typing furiously with a pencil clenched between his teeth.

The pure focus in his eyes was *hot*.

"I was hoping we could walk through the documents you sent me," I hedged.

He nodded, and I quietly settled in a guest chair, admiring the achievement that was this office. Despite the ancient, dingy gold carpet and the flickering fluorescent lights, it was so organized it was practically sterile. Shelves full of law books with spines perfectly aligned dominated one wall, and the small window let in a decent amount of sunlight. His desk was bare, save for the two computer monitors and a small leather cup that held pens. On the wall behind his chair hung fancy diplomas in museum-quality frames. It smelled like printer toner and coffee. Only Brian could elevate a decaying seventies-style office in Jersey to his Manhattan standards.

As I flipped through the stack of papers, he stood and stretched, looking more disheveled than I'd seen him since our college days. He was just as adorable like this as he'd been back then. Though even now, disheveled may have been a strong term. For him, it meant an open collar and rolled-up sleeves, his hair a bit messy, like he'd run his fingers through it. Even like this, he could have been on a Times Square billboard selling fancy watches.

Brian had emailed me drafts of the motion and the memorandum to support it, but I didn't understand much of it, so he'd suggested I come in so we could discuss it.

After all the experience I'd had with the legal system, I should have been a pro at reading and understanding these documents. But I tended to zone out when they started citing precedent from the 1960s.

He walked around his massive desk and stood behind me, pointing at the papers.

"Here's where I lay out the arguments. Since we pulled Judge Gordon, I spelled out the logic."

He leaned over me as I read, with one hand on the back of my chair and the other on the table, essentially caging me between his arms.

His breath skated over my neck, causing goose bumps to erupt as he walked me through the elements of our case.

"And this." He leaned closer, circling something on the page, his warmth soaking into me.

I tried to focus on the section he was pointing out, but the words were blurry. I was better off trying to decipher the documents myself. At this rate, I'd have no clue what I was even doing in court. My heart pounded in my ears, my whole being hyperaware of his presence.

Words.

Read the words on the page, Jess.

But he smelled good, and he was speaking in his smooth, deep voice.

Focus, Jess.

This information was critically important for my kids' future. For my future. And Brian was my attorney, working hard on my behalf.

I wanted to understand. I really did.

But how could I when he was so close and smelled so good?

Warm and spicy and maybe a little woodsy, like a forest.

"What's that smell?" I blurted out, tipping my head up. "Cedar?"

Instantly, my face burned, and I wished with everything I had that I could take it back. Instead, I dropped my gaze to the document again, pretending to be fascinated by a paragraph about visitation.

"My beard oil," he said, raking his fingers through it. "It's cedar something."

The movement drew my focus. It was simple yet intoxicating. I'd never had a thing for facial hair, but on Brian, it served to make him look more manly and capable. Like he could start the day by filing my legal motion and follow it up by changing the oil in my car, then end the day by whipping up a gourmet meal.

In many ways, he was still the gangly boy I'd fallen for in college. Yet he was somehow also a completely new, fully grown man. He was smart and capable, with a soothing voice that made me believe that maybe I could win this and get the fresh start I'd been dreaming of for years.

He backed off a fraction, and the distance allowed me to find the wherewithal to read through the rest of the papers. I even came up with a few clarifying questions before I signed off on filing.

When I'd set my pen down, he gathered up the papers and jotted a few notes at the top.

"I'll get these edits done, and Lo will file at the court tomorrow morning."

I stood, smoothing the skirt of my sundress, a sense of relief twining through me. "I don't know how you got all this done so quickly, but I am so grateful."

He picked up the stack of documents and tapped them on the desk to straighten them. "It's what I do. I'd work night and day to help you, Jess."

My stomach flipped in response to his words. Or, more accurately, the tone with which he spoke. Like I wasn't just a regular client.

Rather than fan myself, which was my first instinct, I clutched my hands together and gave him a firm smile. I could swoon on my own time. This was business, and I had to at least pretend I was a grown woman who had her shit together.

He stood beside me, watching me. Not backing away, not returning to work, but just staring.

Close.

Too close, really.

In this tiny office, it was virtually impossible to put an appropriate amount of space between us. Like this, I was only a few inches from the hard planes of his chest. Like this, I could still feel the heat of his strong body. His golden eyes blazed as he assessed me in return. They kept me pinned to the spot. I couldn't move. I didn't want to move. I wanted to lean in closer, to pull his face down to mine.

A muscle in his jaw pulsed, and of its own accord, my body swayed closer. Wanting—needing—something I couldn't name or understand.

He reached out, his fingers brushing a strand of my hair behind my ear. "Jess." My name on his lips was a plea.

His eyes, still locked on me, darkened to amber as he flattened a palm on the desk and grazed my hip with the long fingers of his free hand.

My heart hammered, pounding against my rib cage. I was going to kiss Brian Machon. My first love and my lawyer. There was no other outcome.

"Yes?" I said, placing my hand on his chest and angling in.

He tilted his head closer, and in response, my eyes fluttered closed. I held my breath in anticipation of—

A snarl followed by a crash made my heart jump. Brian and I stumbled apart, eyes darting around the room. It took a moment to understand what was going on.

Fuzzy tore across the room like a furry missile. He jumped and bounded from the bookshelf onto the desk, sending the cup of pens flying. He padded over the top of Brian's keyboard, then jumped toward us, causing me to step back and get out of the way.

Without slowing, he leaped to the ground and took off again. He crashed headfirst into the bookshelf, causing a stack of documents to drop to the floor.

"*Dammit*," Brian roared, but the cat didn't slow.

As if they'd attacked him, Fuzzy shredded the papers with his claws. Once he'd laid waste to them, he circled, made eye contact with Brian, and bolted out of the room with a guttural *mrow* battle cry.

Laughter bubbled up inside me, an uncontrollable effervescent sensation. "What just happened?"

Brian ran his hands through his hair, surveying the mess. "T. J. and Murphy call it the zoomies of doom. Personally, I believe it's demonic possession."

His lips twitched, and when he made eye contact with me, he barked a laugh.

Before I knew it, we were both howling with laughter. I clutched the arm of the chair as tears ran down my cheeks.

It felt as though we'd just witnessed the rampage of a wild animal.

Brian rubbed his eyes and shook his head, collecting himself. "I want to sue that fucking cat for intentional infliction of emotional distress."

That sent me into another fit of giggles.

The romantic tension was gone, but watching Brian cackle while cursing out a dog-sized cat brought me a strange sense of happiness.

As we cleaned up the books and pens, we couldn't stop laughing, and God, was he handsome when he laughed. The sound triggered so many college memories, reminding me of all the fun we'd had. Once upon a time, we'd laughed our way through Boston together. He'd been my safe place, so familiar and so comforting.

Life sure had changed in the last twenty years.

"I'd better get my kids," I said as I handed him a stack of papers.

He took them from me, and as our fingers brushed, an electric charge rushed up my arm. The sensation urged me to step closer, to touch him more.

Clearing my throat, I fought the desire. I needed to get myself out of this office before I did something stupid like jump on top of him and kiss his handsome face off.

"We're gonna win this," he said, his serious lawyer face firmly in place once more.

"I hope so." I picked up my bag and shuffled to the door, trying to calm my racing heart.

Brian Machon had almost kissed me.

And I'd been more than eager to kiss him back.

CHAPTER 17

Brian

Upstairs, I found the usual mayhem. Sully stood at the kitchen counter with Tia cradled in one arm, using his free hand to type furiously on his laptop while Sloane played Monopoly with Greta, Murphy, and T. J. Jess smiled while chatting with Lo while Kit quietly read a book on the couch. Cal sat on the couch behind Murphy, holding that damn cat while he coached Murphy on his Monopoly real estate acquisition strategy.

"Brian," Jess trilled, giving me the kind of smile that made my heart skip a beat. "Did you hear? The Grasshopper is having karaoke night on Saturday."

Teeth gritted, I narrowed my eyes on Sully. He'd done this. He'd bought a machine and bribed Gunner, the owner, to put on karaoke nights in his quest to win back Sloane.

He swayed, shushing Tia, who stirred in his hold, and lifted one shoulder. "My wife needs a night out."

Sloane beamed at him.

I was not quite so elated, and my reply was automatic. "Great idea. I'll babysit."

"Awesome," T. J. said. "Will you buy us new Legos, Uncle Brian?"

"Yes," I said with a smile. I would have bought that kid a Lego factory to get out of karaoke.

Still glaring at my friend, I scooped his daughter from his arms. "What do you think, gorgeous?" I cooed at her perfect little face. "Wanna hang out with Uncle Brian? I can't buy you Legos yet, but when you're old enough, how about a pony?"

Sloane hissed. "Stop offering to buy her a pony."

"Brian," Cal said sharply. "Don't be a wanker. You babysat last time. Lo and I would love a night with the boys and the little princess."

I shot him a look. The last thing I wanted was to get roped into karaoke night. I'd done my time back in law school, but back then I tolerated it for the cheap drinks and the chance to blow off steam after long study sessions. I didn't have money or time for much else, so when Sloane dragged us, we usually went along.

But the last thing I needed was a night of bad singing and ear-splitting noise.

"Brian." A gentle hand landed on my bicep, though quickly, the sensation was joined by that of nails digging into my skin. Lo tilted her head over to where Jess was happily chatting with Sloane. "You should go. With Jess."

I blinked rapidly. On second thought, the thought of a night out with Jess, even as friends, made even my most hated activity palatable.

She glanced over at me, her smile wide and her eyes swimming with excitement. And suddenly, I realized I'd willingly walk over hot coals to make her happy. I'd been riding a high since our almost-kiss in my office and would take any excuse to spend time with her.

"It's been years since I did karaoke," Jess said.

Cal sat back on the couch, rubbing his hands together.

"We should go too," I found myself saying. Had I been possessed? Potentially, but the prospect of a night with Jess, even with Sloane shrieking her way through Def Leppard songs, was too good to pass up.

"The girls were planning a sleepover at my friend Lana's," she said.

Cal clapped. "It's a date. The lovely Lola and I will be on babysitting duty. You four get out and have fun. So much fun. Get knackered and get Brian to do his John Mayer impression."

All the blood drained from my face. I had wiped that from my memory. And I thought we'd had a gentleman's agreement never to speak of it again.

But Cal was already going. "He's got that raspy voice, you know. And he never sings. But when we all went out after Sloane and Sully tied the knot, Brian got very drunk and sang 'Your Body is a Wonderland.' Every lass in the building was throwing their panties at him."

Sully barked out a laugh. "I was so pissed, but even I remember. That was when your hair was floppy and you were more depressed than usual."

"He's got a good voice," Sloane said. "We never knew because he refused to sing."

Jess's eyes widened. "Why, Brian Machon, you are full of surprises."

"I'm not singing," I said firmly as I broke out in a sweat.

Sully barked a rough laugh. "Sure thing, mate."

THE GRASSHOPPER, THE BAR ACROSS THE STREET, WAS A DIVE similar to the one we frequented in law school. Creaky barstools and old vinyl booths. The cheap, strong drinks made up for the poor lighting.

The place was packed. Karaoke night was turning out to be great for business. And, of course, Sloane got priority song choices because Sully had bought the damn machine, and he and Gunner, as well as Neal, the bartender, had entered into some kind of blood oath regarding karaoke nights. I didn't pretend to understand, but my friend had gotten his wife back, and he was not going to risk losing her again.

Sloane would sing karaoke in an empty parking lot, so the crowd made her extra excited. She wasn't a terrible singer, though she rarely got the lyrics right, but that only added to her enthusiasm.

"What are you singing tonight, sweetheart?" Sully nodded to the emcee near the small stage.

Neal delivered all of our usuals. Guinness for Sully, red wine for Sloane, Jameson neat for me.

"And what can I get this beautiful lady?" Neal asked with a smile.

"I'd love a glass of sauvignon blanc." Smiling, Jess scooted in close, her arm brushing mine.

"And Neal?" Sloane said, leaning forward to get his attention. "A round of redheaded sluts to get things going."

She looked at the rest of us and raised her wineglass. "I'm pumping and dumping tonight. May as well do it right."

I did not take shots. It wasn't responsible. But my skin was starting to itch.

Jess looked so pretty tonight, wearing a dark pink dress with these bow strap things. I desperately wanted to untie one, but that would have been deeply inappropriate.

Even so, the urge to touch her was burning me up. After the moment we'd shared in my office, I could think of nothing else. I could not remember ever wanting anything this badly. I didn't think I'd ever needed to be near someone like I needed Jess.

It was like I hadn't taken a full breath in twenty years. Only now, when she was in the room, could I fully inhale.

Even in this stuffy dive bar while people butchered top-forty hits.

So when Neal brought the shots, I downed one immediately and asked for another round.

The alcohol was alcoholing, depressing my central nervous system. It was the only thing keeping me from running out of here screaming. Sloane had sung once, a painful yet enthusiastic version of "Dancing Queen," and Jess was in her element. She glowed under the neon lights, making friends with regulars and belting out "Wannabe" by the Spice Girls like she was auditioning for *The Voice*. It was adorable.

"Having fun?" Sully asked.

"I feel like I'm being audibly waterboarded by synth pop," I replied.

He just grinned at Sloane, completely ignoring me, as she and Jess wandered back to our booth. It was still jarring, the way his perma-scowl could so quickly transform into a bright smile when he spotted his wife. He might be my oldest friend, but he was a complete mystery to me some days.

"I signed us up for a duet," Jess said, plopping onto the bench and almost landing in my lap.

"No," I said.

She patted my arm and gazed up at me with the kind of look that scrambled my brain cells, making me incapable of decent judgment.

"Good thing I asked for more shots," she teased.

"I can't sing," I said.

"We know that's not true. And even if it was, when it's karaoke, you sing with your heart, Brian. Not your voice."

I had no idea what the hell that was supposed to mean, so I dutifully downed another shot and prayed they wouldn't call my name.

But luck was not on my side tonight. By the way Sully was smiling when the emcee said my name into the microphone, I had to wonder if he'd tipped the guy to call me next.

"And now, welcome to the stage, Brian and Jess."

Jess grabbed me by the front of the shirt and forcefully pulled me out of the booth.

Damn. Until this moment, I hadn't realized how strong she was. Must have been from all that yoga.

Guiding me toward the stage, she waved to her adoring fans.

"What are we singing?" My hands were shaking. No, this was not happening. I wanted to dissociate. To hide. But Jess's warm grip kept me grounded, and my feet kept moving as she pulled me on stage.

We stood in front of the monitor, and as the opening chords began to play, I recognized the song. Even so, the monitor looked blurry. Disney?

She nudged me hard, and on autopilot, I held up the microphone. "I. *Can*. Show you. The—"

She looked at me in horror. "Read the words," she whispered. Eyes bulging, she took over for me and sang Aladdin's part flawlessly.

I struggled to focus on the monitor, but when Jess reached down and squeezed my hand, it was like the haze engulfing me dissipated and I was free.

My vision cleared and the words came.

The crowd faded away, and the two of us faced one another, our hands clenched, as we sang. I couldn't take my eyes off her face. She was so beautiful, and in this moment, we were the only people in this building, in this city.

When the music stopped, the room erupted in cheers, startling me from my stupor.

Every eye was on us, and Sully and Sloane were on their feet screaming.

My face flamed and my collar was suddenly too tight. What had just happened?

I was drunk and I'd made a fool of myself, that's what.

Halfway back to the table, I realized we were still holding hands.

"Water," Jess mouthed, pulling me toward the bar.

Thank fuck. My body temperature rivaled that of the sun right now.

At the bar, Jess looked up at me, her body practically plastered to mine in the crowded space. "Thank you for doing that for me."

I should have said something charming. Or I should have smiled and kept my mouth shut. But drunk Brian was not quiet, contemplative Brian. So instead, I chose to say, "You're so pretty."

Her eyes widened. "What did you say?"

"I said you are good at karaoke," I mumbled, fooling no one.

She elbowed me in the ribs. "That's *not* what you said."

I should have run away. Maybe jumped behind the bar and hidden under the ice maker. At the very least, I should have kept my mouth shut. But did I? Nope. I kept going.

"Fine." I huffed. "You are pretty. Beautiful, actually. And your smile is infectious. It makes me want to be near you. At this rate, I'd follow you into battle anywhere, anytime."

Did I stop there? Oh no, I did not. My stupid mouth, fueled by Jägermeister and lust, kept going.

"I can't stop thinking about the other day in my office. When I was going to kiss you."

My brain was a swirl of alcohol and song lyrics and need. Because kissing her seemed like a wise choice. The decision was simple and so damn smart. At least in this moment. Both then and now, I knew I'd do anything to touch her, to taste her. Even if it meant blowing up everything else in my life.

With her bottom lip pressed between her teeth, she looked up at me, her dark eyes wide and her hand fisting the front of my shirt again. Like this, I swore I'd gone back in time several decades to the days when we would stare at one another across crowded dive bars before running back to one of our rooms to snuggle in a twin-size bed. To the nights we spent walking around Boston, eating dollar pizza slices and dreaming about where life would take us.

The same kind of heady euphoria that washed over me back then returned. Because when I was with Jess, things were right. I was right. And anything was possible.

"Bri—" She snapped her mouth shut, her eyes widening.

"Well done, mate." Sully clapped me on the shoulder, causing Jess to take a step back. "You really nailed it."

I stared at him for a moment, my brain struggling to catch up.

On the one hand, he had just saved me from doing something really fucking stupid. On the other, I wanted to punch him for interrupting my moment with Jess.

Mind still muddled, I picked up the bottle of water Neal had placed in front of me. I needed to get sober and get it together.

"Thanks. It's because I had a great partner." I winked at Jess.

She gave us a thumbs-up while chugging her bottle of water.

My heart sank. A thumbs up? After what we had just shared? The hand-holding, the singing, the shirt-clutching?

Shoulders slumped, I followed Sully back to the table. Fuck, it was time to sober up and stop lusting after my client.

CHAPTER 18

Brian

"It'll be so much fun." With a grin, Cal tucked his electric blue mat under his arm. He and Lo had really gotten into the yoga thing lately. So much so that they had matching mats. It was both sweet and a bit disturbing.

I had nothing against yoga, though I knew little about it and always assumed it wasn't a good use of time for someone as busy as I was. Want exercise? I preferred to run or hit something.

Needed to chill out? Great. Sleep or watch TV.

Combining a workout with relaxation seemed contradictory.

Sully lumbered quietly beside me, smiling at his phone. Probably at a photo Sloane had texted of Tia. That baby got cuter every day.

I punched him in the shoulder. "Thanks for coming."

He grunted. "I'm open to trying something new," he said nonchalantly. As if it wasn't the least Sully thing that had ever come from his mouth. He truly was a changed man.

"I hope you're ready." Lo smirked over her shoulder. "Jess doesn't mess around. This isn't nap time with candles. You're gonna work."

I gave her a nod. I could handle it. I ran miles and worked with a heavy bag until I dripped with sweat. How hard could yoga be?

Even if I hated it, I'd still finish the session having spent time with

Jess. Since creeping on her that day on the sidewalk, I'd been curious about this part of her life. Now I'd get to see her in her natural element.

Though today might not have been the most ideal day to try this out. It had been brutally long and exhausting. So much so that I worried I might fall asleep and insult her.

Cal held the door open, his blue eyes playful but challenging. "You guys ready?"

The second I stepped into the studio, I was hit with heat.

A dozen people, each equipped with a massive water bottle, were laying mats out and chatting happily.

Cal and Lo took spots in the front row and covered their own mats with super-thin towels.

"Come up here." Cal waved wildly. "It'll be easier to see the moves."

Already sweating, I frowned. Maybe it was the heat, but I was confused.

"Why's it so hot?" I asked.

"This is a heated vinyasa flow," Lo explained as if I should understand what the hell any of that meant.

"I thought we were gonna meditate." Sully roughed a hand through his dark hair.

"Restorative is on Thursday nights," Lo said, laying a mat out for him. "This is more athletic. I figured you boys would love it."

Cal, who'd set me up, pointed, gesturing for me to sit, then nodded, beaming at his girlfriend. "Yes. Get ready. Jess puts us through one hell of a workout."

As if on cue, she walked out of the back room, wearing light blue leggings and a matching sports bra with thin straps that crisscrossed in the back. Her hair was pulled back in a ponytail, and she wore a headset.

I couldn't help but drink in the sight of her. She was strong and curvy in all the right places. Her body had changed since college, but my reaction to her hadn't. Just looking at her made my already warm blood heat.

"Namaste," she said, putting her hands together and bowing her head. "And welcome, new friends."

I shifted in my cross-legged position, my Metros T-shirt already sticking to my back.

She walked softly around the room as candles flickered and soft piano music played. "Just as a reminder," she said in a calming tone, "yoga is an exploration of the self. I'll be offering modifications and alternatives throughout the practice. Go at your own pace and ease into it."

The breathing exercises felt great, and before long, my body adjusted to the heat of the room. Mostly, I couldn't keep my eyes off Jess.

She was glowing, focused and 100 percent in her element. "Now," she said, her breath gusting over the microphone just a little, "shift into child's pose."

I followed Cal's and Lo's lead, reaching forward. This wasn't bad at all. In fact, I could see how this could be relaxing after a hard day.

Jess moved us into some seated twists, and before long, my muscles were loose.

"Okay," she said. "Now that we've finished our warmup, it's time to move into sun salutations, some standing postures, and then arm balances. If you do not have some of these poses in your practice right now or you'd like a break, you can move into child's pose at any time."

Eyes darting from her to the mirror to Cal and Lo, I worked to keep pace with all the poses she called.

Warrior one, humble warrior, chair, swan dive, tabletop. What the hell was happening?

When we moved to a plank and then some kind of pushup, sweat dripped from my face onto the mat below me. Fuck.

Jess stepped onto her mat, which was bright pink, and brought her arms out and up. "Now reach to the sky."

We followed. While her head was tilted back, I checked my watch and nearly scoffed. How had it only been eight minutes? Sweat still poured down my face and back and chest, and already, my mat was slippery. My heart thudded against my chest with so much force I worried I'd explode.

Jess started the grouping of poses over again, calling them out. This time, though, she walked around the studio, correcting the posture of her students and giving gentle encouragement. Here and there, she'd wander back to her mat and do the sequences, being sure to show us modifications, which, naturally, I refused to do.

To make things worse? Every minute or two, she'd focus on me, giving me encouraging looks.

God, this was embarrassing.

How many more times would she make us do that swoopy thing from a plank to upward dog and into a downward dog? The move had a name. Chatter-something...

"And Chaturanga," she said, as if reading my mind.

The people around me moved smoothly through the postures. Beside me, Cal had stripped off his shirt. The fucker looked like a professional yogi, his body flowing gracefully as I attempted not to face-plant on the floor.

On my other side, Sully was contorted into an unnatural position, his face a mask of pure pain.

"You are all so locked in tonight," Jess said, her voice full of delight. "Let's take an extra set of breaths in downward dog." While we all stood with our hands flat on the ground and our asses in the air, she said, "Now sway your hips and regulate your breathing."

After a handful of breaths, she released us from the position and guided us to stand with our feet shoulder-width apart.

"Now I'd like to have some fun."

I sighed in relief. This sounded promising.

"We're going to do some arm balances."

Cal let out a little cheer that made me want to knock him over. Cocky bastard.

But arms? I could do arms. Not to brag, but my upper body was pretty strong.

"Widen your stance and sink into a deep yogi squat. Use your elbows to push your knees wider and tuck your pelvis."

Cal squatted deeply, his ass nearly grazing the floor.

Jesus, my hamstrings could not do that, so I settled for a traditional gym squat. Sully, likewise, bent his knees at a ninety-degree angle, glowering at me like he was not going lower.

"Now watch as I walk through the beginner progression for crow," Jess said.

She flowed through a sequence, then pushed forward onto her arms and tucked her knees behind her elbows, balancing on her bent arms. She pointed her toes, her spine curving gracefully.

Holy fuck. I couldn't stop staring at what her body could do.

Not only did she balance on her arms, all twisted up like a pretzel, but she stayed there, holding perfectly still, while we all stared. Her strength and control were mesmerizing, as well as the pure joy on her face, like sharing this insanity with a room full of people truly fulfilled her.

She rocked herself back, her feet gently hitting the floor, and pushed herself up to stand. When she was on her feet, she encouraged us to give it a try.

Several people around me eased themselves into the position, including Cal and Lo, managing to hold it for a few seconds.

"For more support, try a one-legged crow," Jess said, walking around the room, wearing a relaxed smile.

How was it possible for her to look so pretty and relaxed when it was hotter than the ninth circle of hell in here?

My muscles were screaming at me, but I wouldn't take the easy way out. I wouldn't give up. I was strong. I lifted weights and had been boxing since I was fifteen. I could do the crow.

Several attempts in, I realized that I could not, in fact, do the crow. I lacked the flexibility to tuck my knees up close enough, and suddenly, I discovered I had no balance.

I'd get it, though. I swore I would. Like everything else in my life, I'd muscle through.

After several more tries, I contorted into a position that somewhat resembled it. My arms shook violently, and I had to use every muscle in my body for balance, but I'd done it.

Take that, you dumb crow.

Just as I silently cheered myself on, I lost it. And instead of rocking back onto my feet as she'd shown us. I went down, face-first, into the floor. In an attempt to catch myself, I twisted, but that only caused my forehead to take the blow. I landed with a loud thump, and as I scrambled to regain my dignity, I was certain every set of eyes in the room was on me.

Keeping my attention on the floor, I picked up my water bottle, and when I tipped it back, I tried my best not to die of shame. This was so fucking hard.

"You okay, Counselor?" Jess loomed over me, her expression compassionate. Maybe it was a dehydration-induced hallucination, or maybe it was the blow to the head, but the candles created a soft halo around her blond ponytail, making her look like a bendy, sporty angel sent to earth to save me.

"Good." I grunted, shifting back into a seated position.

Lips quirking, she nodded. Then, without another word, she moved on, launching into an explanation of something called pigeon, which sounded just as painful as crow.

Hips were not supposed to do this. I was certain of it. Humans had not evolved to torture themselves this way. How the hell were the people around me not tearing ligaments? Was it the heat? I guzzled more water, and when I was finished, wiping at my mouth with the back of my wrist, I discovered Jess watching me with a concerned look on her face.

I looked over at Sully, who was wincing, his face red as he sank into pigeon pose.

"You okay?" I whispered. The tendons in his neck were tight, his eyes squeezed shut as he extended one leg behind him, the other bent in front of him, stretching his groin in an unnatural way.

He shook his head. "Tell my wife I love her," he whispered as he slowly tipped onto one side, like a felled tree.

I stifled a laugh as he flopped onto his back and stared.

But I was determined to push through. I peeled my soaked T-shirt off and wiped my face, then rejoined the sequence. I would not disgrace myself any further. I was on the wrong side of forty, but I wasn't dead, for Christ's sake.

Jess guided us through a few seated poses that were twisty but doable, then brought us back to child's pose, which was becoming my favorite.

"Well done," she said, her voice somehow soothing and energetic at the same time. "Now we'll move into shavasana. Also called corpse pose. This is how we end our practice. While you focus on relaxing, letting go of all the tension in your body, I'll come around with cool cloths infused with essential oils for your foreheads."

I lay back on my mat in what felt like an inch-thick puddle of sweat, my muscles burning.

Fuck, I'd certainly never underestimate yoga again.

Soothing music played while Jess guided us through cleansing breaths. And then it was just me and my thoughts. Eyes closed, breathing deeply, I worked to recover physically and emotionally from that experience.

As a cool cloth was pressed to my forehead, the calming scent of lavender infiltrated my nose. I opened my eyes and peered up at the angel come to comfort me.

She crouched beside me and adjusted the cloth. "You did great, Counselor."

I closed my eyes again. Primarily because the view down her sports bra was too tantalizing. I breathed deeply and tried to relax, since that was, after all, the whole point of this corpse on the floor thing.

But all I could focus on was how pretty Jess was. How magnetic. How the sound of her voice and the sight of her in that outfit had given me more energy than I'd had in years.

Lying there, sweaty and wrecked, I discovered that I'd been overcome by the peace that Cal was always going on about. Jess's presence grounded me. It pulled me out of the chaos in my head and made even this physical torture feel good.

A chime rang, and the room slowly brightened. I sat and surveyed my friends. Cal and Lo, who didn't really look worse for wear, were making moony eyes at one another. Sully was chugging water like he'd just returned from a week in the desert and shaking his head in disbelief.

After cleaning our mats and putting the other equipment away, I made my way over to the front, where a group of what I assumed were regulars were chatting with Jess.

"You survived." She bounced over to me, her pristine ponytail bobbing and her skin glowing with a light sheen of sweat. She looked incredible. I, on the other hand, looked like a swamp monster and probably smelled like a dumpster in August.

"Barely." I huffed. "Remind me never to underestimate yoga again."

"It will be easier next time." Her wide smile was half amusement and half challenge as she took a step closer.

With that small move, it was as if she'd crossed an invisible barrier. This close, the air between us crackled, the heat it caused was much more enjoyable than the heat of the yoga studio.

We both knew I'd be back, and it wasn't because I'd suddenly fallen in love with yoga.

"Great class." Cal elbowed me out of the way and hugged Jess.

"Your crow was fantastic," she said to him.

He bounced on his toes like a little boy. "That trick you showed me last time really helped."

Jealousy flared within me. I wanted to be her star student with the perfect crow pose. God, what was wrong with me?

Lo and Sully appeared, waving goodbye to Jess, and suddenly, I found myself rushed out the door.

"Gotta get home." Cal explained, giving Jess a friendly wave. "Bubbles has been looking pale again and I'm worried about him."

Lo's eyes widened. Shit, I'd had such a good feeling about Bubbles the Ninth.

As we walked home, my mind raced. That wasn't unusual, though I was typically thinking about legal briefs. But this time, I was consumed by thoughts of how painful it felt leaving her.

And then, as if summoned directly from my nightmares, Madame E appeared, blocking me on the front steps.

"Ah," she said, clapping her braceleted hands together. "The fool card appears."

"Um. Is that me?"

She nodded and patted my shoulder. "Every day. But I wanted to tell you. I had a dream about you."

I braced myself, last time she had a dream about me, it involved me pantsless with plungers. She claimed it was because I was spiritually and emotionally blocked.

Patting my face, she smiled. "A courtroom. And a feline judge."

Great, this couldn't be any fucking weirder.

"Two giggling children as the jury. And the verdict."

I looked at her expectantly.

"Undecided," she replied, shaking her head. What in the ever-loving mystic fuck was she talking about?

Desperate to end this conversation, I asked. "Was I at least wearing pants in this dream?"

She stared at me for a beat. "Not emotionally."

CHAPTER 19

Brian

My usual hyperfocus was hard to come by these days. Maybe it was the weather. It was June, after all, and the sun was out and the weather was perfectly warm. Or maybe Jersey was finally getting to me. Maybe the distraction was caused by all the parts of my life that were suddenly more interesting than work.

Like building Legos with the boys, or cooking dinner, or chatting with Jess when she stopped by.

As I sat at my desk with the window open, hoping to catch a breeze from the alley, I smiled. It was a bit embarrassing how much I looked forward to seeing her. Some days, our run-ins only lasted minutes, but that didn't stop me from finishing up early and hanging around upstairs with the kids, quizzing Greta on her state capitals and listening to Lake Paige with Kit so I could run into the woman who'd infiltrated my every thought.

My brain constantly replayed our almost-kiss. At this point, I'd relived it and analyzed it hundreds of times. If Dammit hadn't been such an asshole that day, spazzing out in my office the way he did, maybe I'd have even more to fantasize about.

But for now, this was enough. I couldn't stop envisioning the way her eyes had widened or the way she had bitten down on her plump bottom lip. We hadn't even touched, and it would go down as one of the most sensual experiences of my life.

Though after my pathetic attempt at yoga, I wasn't sure the almost-kiss moment was the one that stuck out most to her. When she thought of me, she probably replayed my face-plant in her studio.

Jess wouldn't be here for another hour, and I had at least two hours of discovery to deal with. If I re-caffeinated, there was a chance I could squeeze it all in before she arrived. As I was pushing back, determined to get another cup of coffee, a knock sounded on my door.

"Come in," I hedged, frowning. Cal, Sully, and Lo did not knock, and honestly, I rarely closed my door, since they'd all barge in anyway, but I'd hoped by shutting myself away like this, I could focus. Clearly, that hadn't helped.

Worried a client had found their way back here and that I'd completely lost my mind and had forgotten about a meeting, I splayed my hands on my desk, ready to stand.

The door opened slowly, and Kit appeared, followed by Greta, who gave me a friendly wave.

"I made you this," she said, handing me a large tumbler. "I noticed you come upstairs and make this every day."

I reached for the glass, touched. She'd noticed my afternoon protein shake?

"I added Greek yogurt and a banana, because Sloane said she didn't see you eat breakfast."

I took a sip. It was a bit lumpy but tasted like my usual. My heart warmed.

"Thank you, Greta," I said, watching her little face light up.

"Greta is an amazing chef," Kit said. "She makes amazing smoothies."

The two of them grinned at each other, exchanging some kind of sisterly look I didn't understand.

"I have to agree." I settled back in my chair and took another sip. "How was school today?"

"Awesome," Greta said, just as Kit shrugged. "Fine." Her attention roamed around my office, making me feel self-conscious. Although I kept it tidy, this place was objectively a dump, and I felt guilty that the best I could offer them was the old folding chair.

I hummed. "This time of year was always difficult for me. I just wanted it to be summer vacation already."

Kit gave a noncommittal shrug and sighed. "I don't know. Summer means moving, and..." She trailed off, looking at her hands.

My chest tightened with sympathy. "You don't want to move?" I asked gently.

She looked up at me. "It doesn't matter. Mom said you're a great lawyer, so you're gonna make it happen."

"She actually said you're the best lawyer ever," Greta corrected.

Kit glared at her.

That tightness suddenly became uncomfortable. I hated the idea of letting Jess down, but her daughters too?

I folded my hands on my desk. "I'm trying. Your mom is my client, and I always work my hardest to help my clients."

Kit zeroed in on me, her eyes narrowing. "That's actually why we're here."

I leaned forward, head tilted, confused.

She dropped into the chair across from me and squared her shoulders, pinning me with a glare. "You need to stay away from our mom."

I reeled back, caught off guard by her almost feral tone. I'd never known Kit to be anything but quiet and serious.

I looked over at Greta, who had her arms crossed. This interaction had gone south very quickly.

"I see the way you look at her." Kit arched a brow, as if daring me to deny it.

"Um. I—" I shook my head, grasping for words that would make sense.

"You seem nice," she said. "But I'm sure my dad seemed that way once too. And he's not a good dude. He was mean to her and treated her badly, and we're never gonna let that happen again."

"Never," Greta echoed.

Quickly, the fear that had hit me dissipated, and I was filled with pride. I smiled at the pint-sized piano prodigy and her little sister. They were good kids with protective hearts. And I understood. It took a lot of courage for them to come down here and talk to me. Yet they'd done it. They had stuck up for the person who meant the most to them. These kids were fighters, just like their mom.

Abandoned by their father and forced to grow up too fast, but they were on track to be just as incredible as Jess.

"Did you know I'm also an oldest child like you?" I asked Kit, steepling my fingers on top of my desk. "I've got a little sister, Dylan. She's four years younger than I am. I also lost a parent." I looked over at Greta. "My mom died when I was seven, and I always felt like I had to take care of my dad."

Their eyes widened.

"So I know what it feels like to want to protect the people you care about. I understand why it feels like it's your job. But it's not. Your job is to be kids. To have fun. Your mom is an incredible woman who is doing an incredible job raising you both."

Greta's lips twitched in the smallest of smiles. Kit remained unreadable.

"And she doesn't take any shit," I added

Kit gasped, her eyes widening.

I cringed. "Don't tell her I swore."

Both girls giggled.

"I care about her," I said, leaning forward. "She's my client. And as a lawyer, it's my sworn duty to help her. I would never hurt her."

While Greta seemed relieved by my answer, Kit did not. If she had been younger or a little less jaded, she might have accepted it. But sadly, that was not the case.

"Do you babysit all your clients' kids?" Kit folded her arms and stared at me.

My heart thudded. "Um. No."

"Do you cook dinner for your clients? Or go to their yoga classes? Or watch their kids' piano concerts?"

I shook my head. She had me there.

"So my mom's not just a client, then."

As I looked into her eyes, I traveled ahead in time to a moment when she'd be a composed, confident adult. It was incredibly easy to envision. "You are so much like your mom."

Her face fell.

Dammit. I'd forgotten how incredibly uncool that would be to a twelve-year-old.

"But I respect what you're saying," I said, recovering quickly. I hoped. "And I hear you."

"My mom doesn't need a boyfriend," she insisted. "She has us. She's happy."

Ah. I could see it now. The hurt. The cracks her dad's behavior had caused.

"I'm sorry," I said. "I would never hurt your mom or either of you."

"Good. So stop looking at our mom like that."

I sat back in my chair, hands on the armrests. "Like what?"

"Like she's pretty," Greta blurted out. "Like she's a pretty princess and you're in love with her."

A smile tried its best to overtake my face, but I tamped down on it. "She is pretty."

Kit's glare could have frozen lava. "Do *not* think my mom's pretty," she said through gritted teeth while Greta glared.

"Okay." I held my hands up in surrender. "Your mom and I have been friends a long time, but I promise I will not look at her like she is pretty."

"Good." Kit nodded once. "Because I love my mom, and I won't let anyone hurt her again."

Finally, I allowed myself to smile, but this one was small, soft. These kids were so damn sweet. They'd been through some shit, and I respected their strength.

"Thank you for speaking to me about this directly."

"Mom says we have to fight our people-pleasing urges and express our authentic selves," Greta said, sounding so much like her mom.

Damn. Every day, Jess impressed me more. And her girls did too.

"She's right. I promise you this: I'm going to work as hard as I can to make sure that you get whatever you need. But can we be friends?"

"We're already friends," Greta said cheerfully. Kit gave a slow nod, apparently satisfied with my response.

The minute the door closed, I put my head on my desk.

Jesus. How bad did I have it for Jess if I was getting called out by kids? Did Murphy and T. J. know? Had Tia clocked how gone I was for this woman?

And it was wrong. Unethical too.

Jess and her kids deserved their fresh start, and Kit and Greta were right. I couldn't just moon over their mom. I had a job to do.

With a sigh, I stood. I locked my door, ensuring I wouldn't be disturbed, and drank my lumpy protein shake, determined to start keeping my distance.

CHAPTER 20

Jess

"**I**'m so glad we're doing this." Lo stretched, her crop top riding up. She and Sloane had come to my flow class, and afterward, they'd come upstairs for charcuterie and wine.

They'd convinced me that I needed a girls' night, and while I felt guilty for leaving my kids at their place, both Kit and Greta had seemed excited about watching *Ghostbusters* with T. J. and Murphy.

"This tastes *so* good," Sloane said, sipping the rosé I'd picked up.

"I picked up all kinds of cheese too," I said. "I hope you girls don't mind. I'm over cooking."

"Bring on the cheese," she said, rubbing her hands together.

Lo picked up her bag and rummaged through it. "I brought Korean face masks."

"I may leave my husband for you, Lo," Sloane joked.

"We already live together." Lo shrugged, her expression wicked. "It'd be convenient."

I envied their easy friendship and how genuinely happy they were after all the changes they'd navigated over the past year. I'd only gotten bits and pieces, but so far, I'd learned that a year ago, Sloane and Sully had been separated and planning to divorce. Yet now their marriage was stronger than ever, and they'd just added baby Tia to the family.

What I did know about their backstories fascinated me. Though I hadn't yet figured out how three successful, wealthy men had ended up living together in what could kindly be called a fixer-upper in Jersey City.

"You can join us, Jess," Lo teased. "We can make room."

"Tempting." I laughed. "Especially with all the built-in help. I'm already taking advantage more than I should, though."

Sloane waved me off. "Not true. Kit and Greta have made my life so much easier. Kit scares T. J. into doing his homework and has got him reading chapter books. And Greta and Murphy are best Lego buds. Having them around saves me so much work. It frees me up to nurse and take photos of my gorgeous baby."

Lo raised a glass. "To Kit and Greta."

Chest expanding and cheeks heating, I lifted my wine in response. My girls were incredible. I'd never deny it.

"I know it seems weird," Sloane admitted. "But I honestly think the move to Jersey is what brought Sully and me back together. He moved in without us at first, and the distance was hard on him. When I did finally move in, I was forced to take a step back and look at our situation with a fresh perspective. Being forced together changed everything."

"Oh, yes," Lo added, topping off her wine. "We all grew in unexpected ways. And once we fell into a routine, taking turns, collaborating and working together both in the home and at the office, our friendships grew and strengthened."

"If you don't mind me asking, what forced you all to live together?"

The women looked at one another, as if debating who would explain it to me.

"Terry," Lo sighed.

"Cal and Sully's father," Sloane explained. "Brilliant lawyer and one of those people who just kicked life's ass every day."

Lo snorted into her wine.

"He was so proud of his sons, and he'd always counted Brian among them. But he was a bit of a wildcard."

"So he set up a trust with stipulations," Lo said. "When he passed away, it was discovered that in order for the guys to maintain ownership of the firm in New York, the three of them had to relocate here, to where the firm was founded. They're required to work and live together for one year." She rolled her eyes. "The trust also stipulated that they could only bring one paid member of support staff. Brian, of course, talked me into coming with them."

"I knew Terry for close to two decades," Sloane said, her voice soft and her eyes going a little misty. "His methods were unconventional, yes, and we still don't understand what the hell he was thinking, but he started his career in that building. And as much as we all hated it at first," she said, "especially this one"—she elbowed Lo—"getting out of the Manhattan rat race actually provided good perspective."

"The building we work out of now is a far cry from the Murphy and Machon office in the city," Lo mused. "My old office is twice the size of the postage-stamp space I work out of now. With top-of-the-line copiers. Here, we've got twenty-year-old shit boxes filled with maggots." She shuddered. "It's hard to believe it, but the place was actually so much grosser ten months ago."

"Says the woman who chose to move in." Sloane bumped her shoulder against Lo's. "I, on the other hand, was legally obligated to."

"Thank God for Terry," Lo quipped. "Before you and Tia, I was surrounded by testosterone. The entire building needs way more feminine energy."

I'd missed this. Girlfriends. Hanging out without feeling pressure to perform or impress anyone. Sloane and Lo accepted me and made me feel like part of their little family.

Kenneth's friends ignored me and their wives looked down on me. The other moms at the elite prep school the girls had attended were in constant cutthroat competition with one another. I'd never found my people. Yes, I had Lana, and she was my ride-or-die bestie, and I had my siblings, but for years, there'd been a void in my chest that suddenly felt full.

"Thank you," I said awkwardly. "For hanging out with me."

Lo tossed a piece of cheese into her mouth. "You're awesome. Thank *you* for hanging out with *us*."

Head dropped back, I laughed. "It's been a while since I had girl time. I'm usually working or momming, so I don't have much time to socialize."

"You're kind of stuck with us now." Sloane grinned. "Once our strange little family pulls you in, we keep you."

Warmth blossomed in my chest, but I tamped down the instinct to burst into happy tears.

She shook her head, her smile turning rueful. "I just can't believe it's really you."

My elation was quickly replaced by confusion. "What do you mean?"

"I met Brian when we were 1Ls. He, Sully, and I formed a study group for torts. We became good friends, and it just kind of went from there. So I've known him at his best and his worst. We studied for the bar together. He held my hair when I threw up after more than one karaoke night. And I've even talked him into singing karaoke with me from time to time. To this day, those are some of my biggest achievements." She laughed.

"When did you and Sully start dating?"

"Later that year. During midterms, I think. We danced around each other for a while, but when we finally hooked up, Brian wasn't the least bit surprised. Apparently, he knew it was inevitable from the very beginning."

"It was the accent, wasn't it?" Lo asked.

The two of them grinned at one another.

"Yes." Sloane giggled. "And because before him, I'd only ever dated boys. Sully was a man. He knew exactly how to care for me. He respected me. And the best part? He didn't care one bit who my mother was. I'd had more than one bad experience connecting with so-called friends or love interests, only to find out they were only interested in me because my mother is a judge. Sully never once brought her up. And honestly, I was obsessed." She sighed, her eyes going dreamy. "But," she finally said, straightening, "what I was getting at is that for the almost twenty years I've known Brian, he's always talked about this mythical unicorn woman from his past."

My breath caught. No. That wasn't possible. What we had was puppy love. Right?

"Jess," she said. "The girl he always thought about and compared others to."

Cheeks warming, I looked away. "It wasn't like that," I tried to explain. "We were kids."

Sloane cocked a brow, unconvinced. "Maybe for you it wasn't much. But you stuck with him."

Her words hit me hard. I'd loved Brian. Of course I had. But we'd been kids, and when life had gotten in the way, we'd said goodbye. I'd thought about him off and on over the years, the memories always fond, and yes, maybe I compared other men to him. But that was normal for one's first love, right?

"How did you meet him?" Lo asked, scooting closer.

My face was still burning. "Intro to psychology class. Freshman year," I murmured, assaulted by memories. He'd sat next to me, his auburn hair shaggy and falling in his face. "We chatted and became friends. He grew up with some girls in my dorm, so I'd run into him occasionally at parties. And then we just kept hanging out."

"Classic Brian." Sloane laughed into her wineglass. "He's not known for his seduction skills."

I felt a pang of jealousy as I considered just how many girls had had crushes on him back then. And since. It was silly to feel this way, yes, but impossible to control.

"Until one day, during my sophomore year, he asked me to take a walk with him. We spent four hours traversing the entire city of Boston and ended up eating pizza while sitting on the Longfellow Bridge."

"Aw," Lo said. "And you fell in love."

I shrugged. Basically, yes. It was that young, idealistic kind of love that songs were written about. Long walks and even longer nights spent talking about our lives and dreams for the future. Nights spent entwined with one another on a twin-size bed.

"He was one year ahead of me. The plan was that after he graduated, he'd get a job in Boston. I'd finish school, and then we'd apply to law school together."

Sloane straightened. "You wanted to go to law school?"

I nodded wistfully. "Yes. We had all these dreams about changing the world together. Honestly, I would have hated it." I exhaled, my shoulders lowering. "Eventually, I realized that social work was much more my speed."

"So what happened with you and Brian?"

"His sister had a baby. The father wanted nothing to do with her son. He was a senior when it happened. I was still a junior. He moved back to Brooklyn the day after graduation to help her." I couldn't help but smile. It was admirable, the way he'd stepped up for Dylan and her son. "He helped raise his sister after their mom died, and there was no way he'd let her do it alone."

Sloane nodded. "And Liam is an amazing kid."

That made me happy. Brian had loved his sister deeply, and he'd been head over heels for his nephew before he was even born.

"We hadn't figured everything out yet, but I assumed I'd finish school in Boston and we'd do long distance for a bit. But then my dad had his first heart attack."

My nervous system kicked into high gear, just like it had done when I received the call, and my heart rate spiked. The fear and the panic in my mom's voice had gutted me.

"My sister Jenn was in the marines and deployed, and my brothers were still kids. While Dad recovered, Mom ran the farm by herself. She burned out quickly, so after I finished school for the year, I went home for the summer to help. Pretty quickly, it became clear that I couldn't leave them. So I took classes at U Vermont to finish my degree."

"I'm so sorry," Lo said, gently squeezing my arm. "Did your dad recover?"

A wave of grief washed over me. No matter how many years had passed, it never got any easier. "Sort of," I explained. "He got back on his feet, but five years later, he had another heart attack, and that was it. He'd worked himself into the ground. He never got to meet his granddaughters."

I wiped a tear from my cheek and inhaled a cleansing breath.

"Brian and I were both drowning in our own family situations. We didn't have time to call, let alone visit. So we broke things off, both swearing it was temporary. But then we just... lost touch." Sadness hit me, mingling with the grief, and the tears I'd been fighting surged again. "So often, I wanted to call him. I missed him terribly. But by the time the work was done for the day, I was dead on my feet. And I always feared calling him late in the evening, worrying I'd wake the baby. So I didn't. And he didn't call either." I lifted a shoulder and forced a smile. "I figured he was better off."

"No," Sloane breathed, eyeing Lo.

Lo gave her a look I couldn't decipher. "When did you come to New York?"

"In my mid-twenties. About a year after my dad died. I got a job at a PR firm, and a couple of months later, I met Kenneth. By then, I assumed Brian had finished law school and had met a kick-ass female lawyer and was blissfully happy."

Sloane snorted. "Not at all."

They looked at one another again, exchanging some kind of nonverbal language I didn't understand that involved hand gestures and raised eyebrows.

"What?" I asked, hit with a surge of self-consciousness.

"Nothing," Sloane said with an easy smile.

Lo, on the other hand, wore a downright diabolical grin.

"You have no poker face, Lo," I said.

"He's single," she hissed, her green eyes dancing with mirth. "Very single. Super single. Been waiting around for you to walk through the door single." She rubbed her hands together like a supervillain.

"I'm not dating," I said weakly. My stomach flipped like a gymnast on the uneven bars. "I'm moving to Vermont. Brian is my lawyer."

Neither woman seemed fazed by my argument. Maybe because it lacked conviction.

It was getting more difficult to hide my feelings every day.

He had been wonderful when we were kids. Smart and kind and funny as hell. Now? Every one of those qualities had only compounded.

I looked forward to spending a handful of minutes with him each day when I picked my girls up. Made sure I fixed my makeup before walking over after work.

"Surely you feel the connection. We're all enveloped in secondhand pheromones any time the two of you are together," Sloane argued.

"I feel a lot of complicated things at the moment," I said gently. "Brian is amazing, sure, and he's helped me and my girls so much. No amount of legal fees would ever be enough to repay him. I am in debt to all of you."

Lo crossed her arms. "You're into him." It was a statement, not a question.

For the millionth time tonight, my face burned.

The last thing I needed was to make this situation more complicated, but I responded honestly.

"How could I not be? He verbally eviscerated my shitty ex-husband and then had him socially blacklisted because he'd wronged me. He shows up to support my kids, and he makes me feel like I'm special. Like I'm smart and capable and have my shit together."

"You are smart and capable," Sloane interjected.

Head dropped back, I groaned. "I know that, but when my marriage ended, I was destroyed. I had been for a long time, honestly. It's taken me this long to rebuild my life. And Brian sees that. He gets it. He makes me feel like I can do anything."

Lo clutched her chest. "Oh my God. This is it."

Sloane put her arm around her friend, pulling her into a hug. "It's the day we've dreamed of."

"Girls," I said firmly. "This doesn't change anything. He's my lawyer, and he's way too professional to make a move."

Sloane waggled her brows. "But you can make a move."

"No, I can't," I argued. "I'm about to relocate to another state, and furthermore, I would never risk our friendship. Having him back in my life has been such a blessing. And as a bonus, I got you two and the rest of your family. My kids are happy, and I've found the village I've always dreamed of having. I'm not going to mess that up by throwing myself at the guy I dated in college who probably isn't interested."

The two of them burst into laughter.

"Delulu," Lo declared.

"You're off your rocker if you think he isn't head over heels for you." Sloane patted my knee. "I promise, if I know Brian Machon, you'll soon find you can no longer resist him."

CHAPTER 21
Brian

Staying away felt almost impossible. Jess's girls were here tonight while she and Sloane and Lo had a girls' night. Asshole that I was, I stayed in my office, working through the Phillips trust reallocation, letting Sully and Cal handle babysitting duty.

But with each minute that passed, it got harder to remain in my office chair, focusing on work.

Through therapy, I'd learned to embrace my feelings.

But Dr. Johnson hadn't warned me that once I opened up, a dozen emotions I'd never understood would come rushing out along with those I knew I was suppressing.

Desire and longing plagued me, along with the constant fear that I was missing something essential.

Despite my determination to keep my relationship with Jess professional, my mind wandered. And Madame E certainly didn't help. She'd caught me late that night when Dammit and I were returning from our walk and had blocked me on the stairs.

"I must talk to you. The winds have spoken."

I looked down at the damn cat, who looked equally confused by this insanity.

"They said it's a great time for Lake."

I blinked, I was tired, overworked, and annoyed that my feline overlord had bullied me into a late-night walk. "Great. Should I throw myself in this lake?"

She frowned. "Lake is not water." Her bracelets jangled. "You need to open your third eye."

"It's almost midnight. I can barely keep these two open," I quipped and her lip curled.

"You need to see, Brian. See yourself. See her."

She thankfully moved, heading down the stairs toward the door. Where a seventy-something psychic was going at his hour was a mystery, but it was one I'd rather not solve.

Instead, I was left to obsess over her weird-ass predictions.

I'd never been much of a lake-goer, so I couldn't begin to guess which lake she was referring to. We weren't exactly surrounded by lakes in Jersey City. We had the Hudson River, but that was possibly the least romantic body of water in history.

So now I was spiraling about lakes, wondering if I should buy a boat, pick up life jackets, or research fishing. Fucking great.

It was almost midnight, and considering how quiet the apartment was, I assumed everyone had turned in. My stomach roiled, I wasn't sure if it was from stress or the protein shake Greta had made me that included what tasted like an aggressive amount of cinnamon.

I hung the cat's leash beside the door and headed to the kitchen for a glass of water. Halfway there, I found Sloane pacing the living room with the baby.

"Brian," she whispered. "We need to talk."

I strode toward her, concerned by her statement. "Everything okay?"

Nodding, she held the baby out to me. "Burp her for me. I gotta get Lo."

I cradled Tia against my shoulder, patting her firmly and congratulating her when she let out a belch that would make a Big 10 frat boy proud.

When Sloane reappeared, Lo was hot on her heels, dragging a sleepy-looking Cal by the hand.

"Brian," Lo squeaked, her tone high-pitched.

"Sully's coming," Sloane said, clasping her hands. "We have so much to discuss."

"Bloody hell. It's midnight. Do we really need to do this tonight?" Sully asked, running his hands through his hair.

"Yeah." Cal added. "I need to keep an eye on Bubbles. He's made a miraculous recovery since I gave him his fish vitamins. He's got a new lease on life." .

Oh Jesus. Lola flushed and I raised an eyebrow at her. Long live Bubbles the Tenth, I guess.

"Focus," Sloane chirped. "We need to talk about Brian."

Annoyance rushed through me. "I'm right here."

"And Jess," Lo added. "We loosened her up with wine and cheese, and let me tell you, that woman is into you."

"So into you." Sloane bounced up and down. "When she talked about you, she couldn't stop smiling, and her eyes got all dreamy."

I sucked in a breath. I'd kept my feelings under control by denying that there was any interest on the other side of this.

"Why are you telling me this?"

Cal threw an arm around Lo's shoulders. "Because you have to make a move, you plonker."

"She is my client," I gritted out, irritated that, after such a long, stressful day, I was now being subjected to a late-night inquisition.

"You've already filed her motion," Lo said.

"One of us can step in for the hearing if necessary," Sloane added.

Seriously? She was still on maternity leave, but she was offering to step in for the hearing? These people had lost the plot. This could not happen. For so many reasons, but most importantly because it was unethical.

"I know you're all happy and in love, but don't let that blind you to the facts. If I were to pursue a romantic relationship with a client, I could be disbarred."

Sully, who had his phone out and was scrolling, held one finger up. "Actually, according to the New Jersey State Bar Association code of conduct, if the romantic relationship preceded the representation, it's allowed."

Sloane beamed at him.

"Our relationship was twenty years ago. This is absurd."

As if sensing my frustration, Tia fussed in my arms, so I exhaled and willed my muscles to relax.

"Tomorrow I'll look for precedent on point," Lo added, ever the paralegal.

"Seriously," I said, keeping my tone even so I wouldn't upset the baby again. "We've spent the last year trying to save our firm. I'm not going to ruin all that by getting involved with a client."

Cal barked out a laugh, and Lo and Sloane joined in. Sully wasn't effusive the way they were, but even he cracked a smile.

"We've discussed this." Sully took the baby from me. "In fact, you and Cal were the ones who spelled it out for me when I was ready to let the firm go to save my marriage. Dad was trying to save us, dumbass. In his own weird misguided way. Not the firm. The wanker wanted to save us from ourselves."

"And the most ridiculous part is that it worked," Cal added. "Look at us. The Murphy boys are finally getting their shit together and making Dad proud."

Sully kissed Tia's head.

I pinched the bridge of my nose. They were all love drunk and had no idea what they were saying.

"And technically," Sloane said, "we're not saying you should jump right in and initiate a sexual relationship. We're suggesting you lay the groundwork. Show your interest."

"Because she is interested," Lo added.

The two of them high-fived.

Terror shot through me. Fuck, how had I ended up in their crosshairs like this? The Murphy brothers were typically the recipients of their shit.

"Her motion should be resolved soon," Lo said.

"And I can file a motion to appear as co-counsel," Sloane added. "Just in case."

Decades of professional conditioning butted up against the feelings that had been steadily growing stronger since Jess had walked back into my life. The situation was fucked up, and my brain was fried. All I wanted was to be alone. I wanted to climb into bed, read my Winston Churchill biography, and wallow in my obsession with my college girlfriend.

Cal, ever the negotiator, clapped my shoulder. "She's your first love. And she walked in the door after decades, desperate for your legal expertise and your broad, manly shoulders."

"Cal." I groaned.

"Lay the groundwork, mate." He shook me. "I got the girl because I strategized." With a grin, he threw Lo a wink. "Make a gesture."

"Yes," Sloane said. "Her ex sounds like a piece of shit, yet she's risen above it all. She's busting her ass to be a great mom. Show her you see her. Show her you want to be part of her and her kids' lives," she urged.

I respected Kit and Greta as much as I respected Jess, there was no denying that. They made the most of the hand they'd been dealt, and their presence in my life was breaking me out of my workaholic tendencies.

Hope, that sneaky bastard, bloomed in my chest. Was it possible? We should have a resolution soon. And depending on the outcome of the motion, either Cal or Sully could take on her case. Even Sloane when her maternity leave ended.

I paced to the kitchen and back, my mind racing.

What could I do to show my interest? My care?

I couldn't just go for it and kiss her. I was her attorney. I'd hate for her to misinterpret the act, to feel obligated to reciprocate to show her thanks.

She would have to make the first move.

But a gesture. Something to excite her and her kids. Something to prove that I'd gladly be part of their lives if they wanted me to.

"Lake," I said quietly. "They love Lake Paige. She's going on tour, right?"

Lo blinked at me like I was the stupidest man alive. "Um. Yeah. The Moonlight Tour."

"Okay," I breathed. "I'll get tickets. She must be coming to New York."

"You can't just *get tickets*." Lo spoke to me as if I were a child. "They've been sold out for months. The Lake fans crashed the ticket websites when they went on sale, and resale prices are astronomical."

"I'll figure it out." Cost was no object. If I had to drop a couple of grand, then so be it.

I whipped out my phone and typed *Lake Paige tour* into the search bar. Immediately, I found a list of dates, including one in New York in August. Shit, they'd be in Vermont by then.

"Dammit," I muttered, and the cat appeared, rubbing up against my legs, as if I'd actually called him.

The more I thought about it, the surer I was that taking them to see Lake Paige was the best way to handle this. Kit and Greta would lose their minds, and it would be incredible to experience this through their eyes.

I scrolled back up the list of dates and hissed. "Yes." With my phone held up in front of me, I said, "She'll be in Boston next weekend."

I had to try. They'd eventually move to Vermont, but I had to take a chance. I had to know whether it was possible that we could really be something. Because I felt it. Deep inside my bones. The universe had sent her back to me, and I didn't want to ever let her go again.

"I need to call Dylan."

CHAPTER 22

Brian

My pulse thudded in my ears. Was this too much? I didn't want to be the guy who threw money around like an asshole. From what I could tell, Jess's ex was that kind of man. Why the hell would she want anything to do with another dick who flaunted his money?

But Sloane and Lo had insisted that I make a gesture.

Despite my apprehension, I couldn't deny that this was perfect. Jess and the girls were huge fans, and seeing Lake Paige in Boston meant taking Jess back to the place where we'd fallen in love.

The thought of making her happy powered me through an almost sleepless night.

While I lay in bed, with the damn cat on my chest, my thoughts moved from one detail to another. I'd clarify with her that she was not obligated at all to spend any more time with me if it wasn't what she wanted. There would be no pressure. Nothing like that. No strings. She was still a client, after all.

The concert was next weekend and technically sold out, but if I knew my sister, she could make it happen for me.

"Hello, my lovely brother." My sister's voice was almost drowned out by the chaos swirling around her. It wasn't surprising. Dylan was the definition of a free spirit. My opposite in so many ways but also the person I cared about most. "You always call on Thursdays, but it's Monday. Are you okay?"

I winced. She knew me too well. I may be a little too attached to my routines. Yet another thing to bring up with Dr. Johnson next week.

"Dylan." I took a deep breath, gearing up to open the enormous can of worms this request would bring with it. "I need a favor."

"Name it."

"It's Jess."

The screech she let out all but pierced by eardrum. Eyes squeezed shut, I pulled the phone away from my face.

"I knew it," she gloated. "I told you that garnet crystal I sent would do the trick. Finally. You've been so lonely and grumpy for so long."

"Hey," I grumbled. I had hardly been guarding a bridge for all these years.

"Hold on." A rustling sound. Then, "Cortney!"

I pulled the device away again.

"Brian needs us."

"Everything okay?" Cortney asked, his deep voice a little farther away, like Dylan had put the call on speaker.

My brother-in-law was careful and a planner. The exact sort of man I would have chosen for my free spirit sister. He also managed Boston's MLB team—a team I'd been raised to hate my entire life, but we couldn't win them all.

"Start from the beginning and tell us everything," Dylan insisted. "It's hard for me to read your aura over the phone, but I'm getting some deep green vibes."

I walked them through the last few weeks, doing my best to remain neutral and impassive so as not to excite Dylan too much. If I let her get too far ahead of herself, she'd probably show up here tomorrow with her sage and smudge the whole place to clear out my love chakras.

"So you're in love with her," she declared.

"No," I said sharply. "I don't know. I can't do anything but be her friend while I represent her. But I want to show I care. I want her to know I'm interested."

"The ball is in your court," Cortney finished.

"Yes." I sighed. "I don't want to be creepy or go too over-the-top, but I've worked hard; I can afford to do something special. So..." I blew out a breath. "She and her daughters are huge fans of Lake Paige."

"Aw, shit. Hold on," Cortney said.

"What are you doing?"

"Calling Beckett on the intercom. He's gonna want in on this."

Dylan had lived with her three best friends and their kids before meeting and marrying Cortney. Now that she and her friends had all found their partners, they were neighbors. Each had their own brown-stone on the same street in Boston, equipped with a state-of-the-art intercom system so they could contact one another easily and keep track of their kids. Beckett technically lived next door, but despite the walls, there were not a lot of boundaries.

"I do not need Beckett Langfield to help me impress a woman," I said through gritted teeth.

Cortney barked a laugh. "Normally I'd agree with you, but this time, you're wrong."

Within minutes, Beckett Langfield, billionaire owner of the Boston Revs and Cortney's boss-slash-best friend, greeted me.

"I'm here to fix your problems," he declared. "Let's switch this thing to video."

"We don't need video," Cortney said. "What are you doing?"

"Butt out, Man Bun."

"Guys," I said over their scuffle, "I'm the one who called you about tickets."

"Tickets? Dylan said this was an urgent love crisis."

Before I could explain, my phone rang with a FaceTime request. With a sigh, I answered, coming face to face with Dylan, Cortney, and Beckett.

Beckett, who was dressed in a full suit, cocked a brow. "So what's the situation and how are we fixing it?"

"The universe has granted Brian another chance with his first love," Dylan trilled, one hand dragging the rose quartz pendant at her neck along its chain—a habit of hers for as long as I could remember. "And he wants to make a grand gesture to show his interest."

I took a deep breath. "She and her daughters are huge Lake Paige fans. And she's playing Lang Field next weekend."

"Yes," Beckett said. "We're all going. The girls are losing their minds."

"I can buy resale tickets," I went on. "Money isn't the issue here. I just want to make it extra special. Think you can help me out?"

"Absolutely. You're welcome in the owner's box with us. I'll make it happen. Get here early and join us for the preshow backstage meet-and-greet too."

"Seriously? They can meet her?" I asked, my heart in my throat.

"Yes, Brian. It is my stadium, and Lake is my sister-in-law's best friend. What's the rest of your plan?" He raised his dark eyebrows expectantly.

That was as far as I'd gotten. Obviously I'd coordinate transportation and get a hotel room. But seats in the owner's box and backstage passes? Already, it was more than I could ask for.

"The Miller Group just acquired the Greenbriar Hotel," Dylan said. "Let's reserve the penthouse."

She looked at her husband expectantly.

"Would you want that?" Cortney asked me.

"Ooh, yes." Dylan clapped before I could respond, her golden eyes—the same color as mine—danced. "We'll have a big sleepover with all the kids. And do hair and makeup and outfits for the concert. That way you and Jess can get some alone time."

Beckett offered his fist, and she bumped it.

Based on the ease with which the two of them were making plans, this was not the first time they had played matchmaker.

"Okay, then, that's settled." Cortney said. "Backstage passes and hotel."

"That's not a plan," Beckett said. "What else? Do you need the plane?"

"No, we can take Amtrak."

"Amtrak?" He slammed his coffee mug on the table, causing liquid to splash over the lip.

Cortney reacted immediately, wiping the coffee off the pristine surface.

"Now you're just ducking with me," Beckett ranted. "Take the helicopter at the very least. It's faster, and the kids will love it. Your girl too. It'll really make her feel special. And it's easier than getting a runway at Logan these days, anyway."

"That must be a you issue," Cortney teased him.

"Duck you. The entire team had to circle for forty minutes last week."

"Because I wasn't with you. Air traffic control never gives me shit."

"I can't," I hedged, interrupting their banter. "It's too much." In the span of five minutes, my plan had evolved from acquiring hard-to-get concert tickets to an over-the-top circus.

"It worked for Cal." Okay, he did have a point there. "You think your first love just walks through your office door every day?" Beckett grunted. "Get it together."

"Lay off him." Cortney interrupted. "He's got a plan. Don't bulldoze him."

Beckett threw his hands up. "I'm not bulldozing. He just doesn't know what he needs."

Cortney groaned. "And you do?"

A slow smile spread across Beckett's face as he turned to Dylan. "I got you your wife, didn't I?"

Dylan giggled as Cortney let out a sigh.

"She's still my client." I scratched at my beard. "Nothing can happen."

"Gotta play the long game," Beckett said. "You can't leave anything to chance. Make a plan and execute."

"Easy for you to say." I huffed. "You forced your crush to marry you."

Smiling, he held his mug up in a toast-like gesture. "Yes. Best decision I ever made. You wanna win big, you gotta swing big."

"I'm with Becks," Dylan said. "Fate has intervened, and you cannot ignore the will of the universe. I suggest you sage the apartment and light some jasmine candles immediately."

"Don't duck it up," Beckett warned.

I let out a sardonic laugh. "I guess I'll see you all next weekend."

CHAPTER 23

Jess

When I was sure Brian wasn't looking, I pinched myself.

This could not be happening. The girls had been screaming and crying nonstop since he'd delivered the news.

He'd scored us tickets to see Lake Paige in concert.

When he'd casually mentioned that we'd get to meet her? Kit had burst into tears, and Greta had run laps around the apartment, yelling at the top of her lungs.

"Is this a dream?" Kit asked, looking out at the helicopter that was waiting for us.

"I'm not sure," I replied honestly.

Greta hadn't let go of my hand since we'd arrived, holding it so tight she was cutting off blood flow. Brian was across the room, ensuring all our bags were accounted for. He'd insisted on carrying them all himself, but he probably regretted the offer once the driver had pulled them all from the car. Greta had been beside herself when she realized she didn't have months to recreate one of Lake's iconic music video looks, so we may have overpacked a bit. But hopefully we'd have enough glitter, pink, and fringe to have a good time.

The girls let out a fresh round of happy squeals and twirls. "Lake

Paige," Kit trilled. "Her new album is everything. It's like she's more musically complex after she took time off to have a baby."

Greta peered back at Brian. "You have a helicopter?"

He shook his head, looking slightly uncomfortable. "No. A friend lent it to me."

She released me and darted across the room. Arms flung out, she launched herself at him and hugged him tight. "You're the best."

Kit joined in, though she was a little more successful at playing it cool.

Brian, who still had a bag slung over each shoulder, wobbled a little on his feet.

"Girls, I think we need to get inside and listen to the pilot." I dropped my focus to the floor in front of me, hoping Brian couldn't see the color staining my cheeks. Their excitement and their affection for Brian tugged at my heartstrings.

He'd been so sweetly sheepish when he'd delivered the news. The girls had screamed and jumped around wildly, waking Tia from her nap.

Now, as he carried our bags out onto the helipad, I truly had no idea how I would ever thank him.

Okay, maybe that wasn't completely true. My dirty mind had a few ideas...

And said mind had been on overdrive these past few weeks. Because while Brian, ever the gentleman, always professional, could control his lustful urges, I could not.

I was a woman starved. Every time I saw him at the end of the work-day, with the sleeves of his dress shirt rolled up, I swooned a little.

When I stepped into the apartment and found him building Legos with Greta or helping Kit multiply fractions, my attraction grew.

Because not only was Brian objectively handsome, he was also objectively *good*. I'd known it back in college and I knew it now. He was serious, and sure, he could be a grump, but he took care of his clients, his colleagues, and the little family that had formed in the old building in Jersey.

He'd even grown to love that monster cat, no matter how annoying he swore it was.

The girls were animated, squealing often as we flew to Boston. Every few minutes, Brian would look back from his seat in front with the pilot and smile at me.

The girls were busy watching the scenery and taking helicopter selfies with my phone, so I sat back and tried to focus on enjoying the views. The whole way, my stomach jumped with anticipation. My friendship with Brian was changing and evolving every day, and for as good as it felt, it was also confusing and overwhelming.

It certainly didn't help that my kids were so attached to him and our new friends. Nights spent with them in that strange building had become precious to me. The whole crowd had enthusiastically embraced Wednesday dance parties, and we'd taken to stopping by even on my day off, when the girls didn't need to be watched, just to visit. I'd worked so hard to insulate and support my little family that I hadn't even considered how much fun it would be to welcome others into the fold.

As we landed on the roof of the Greenbriar Hotel in Boston, the harbor stretching out in front of us, Kit pointed wildly out the window. "We can see Lang Field from here."

Sure enough, the outside of the stadium was adorned with Lake's signature pink bows, marking her arrival. Seaport Boulevard had been temporarily renamed by the mayor of Boston to Lake Paige Boulevard in honor of her.

Once we'd disembarked and were inside, away from the wind the chopper's blades created, Brian grimaced down at his phone.

"I was hoping to get out of this part, but my sister is here, and she's threatening to call the Boston Police Department to detain me if I don't bring you guys to meet her right now."

"Dylan?" I frowned in confusion.

Brian had always talked about how laid-back she was. Yet she was making threats?

"Yeah." He scratched the back of his neck. "It may actually be her friend Delia, but I can't tell. They're here with their daughters, doing hair and makeup for the concert."

"Hair and makeup?" Kit's eyes bulged. "Mom only let me pack sparkle eyeshadow."

That was how we found ourselves headed up to the hotel penthouse.

It occupied the entire top floor of the hotel and was easily bigger than both my apartment and Brian's apartment combined.

There were kids everywhere, and I hadn't made it through the door before I was being hugged by a beaming redhead.

She pulled back, and as she cupped my cheeks, she said, "Jess," like my name was a sacred prayer.

Too stunned to respond, I stood frozen to the spot, letting her study me.

"Just as I suspected. Totally purple. And totally perfect for my brother." With a pat to my cheek, she stepped back and greeted my kids. "Hello, girls. I'm so excited to meet you. Kit, Brian sent me a video of your piano performance. You are so talented. And Greta, my husband really wants to meet you so he can convince you to be a Revs fan."

The girls were truly charmed by her sweet, friendly face and were eagerly peering around at the bright space. Light streamed through the massive windows as Boston's skyline spread out in front of us.

Dylan gestured widely. "Come on in. The gang's all here."

Everywhere I looked, children were running and playing, and Lake Paige music was blaring through the speakers.

As Dylan led us deeper into the room, two young boys darted in front of us with rushed *sorrys* as they blew by. We met Liv and Delia, whose tween daughters immediately guided my girls to the hairstylist who'd been hired for the occasion.

"Mom," Greta yelled, holding up a champagne flute full of sparkling cider that a server had brought out on a tray. "Can I get hair tinsel?"

"Sure." I gave her a thumbs-up as another server approached me with champagne.

Dylan, I learned, owned a chain of daycare centers. Liv ran the

Boston Revs, and Delia was a prosecutor and philanthropist. Between them, they had something like ten kids. They clearly led busy lives, but the love and affection they shared was palpable instantly.

Dylan plied me with champagne and charcuterie, asking question after question about me and the kids. Every so often, she'd look at her brother pointedly, as if trying to tell me something.

Brian was across the room with a handful of men, talking about what I could only assume was baseball and empire building, given the folks involved.

In theory, these were the kind of people I avoided at all costs. While I was married to Kenneth, I'd never fit in with the crowd of folks who owned corporations and sat on boards and owned helicopters. They had always made me feel insignificant and small. Like they could sniff out that I was a farm girl from Vermont and not one of them.

But this group could not be more different. These women welcomed me with genuine smiles, and their children had been kind to mine from the first moment. And there was no putting on of airs around here. It was so unlike what I was used to. No showmanship, no one-upping. Just honest friendships and fun.

When a wave of emotion welled up inside me, coming dangerously close to spilling over, I excused myself to the bathroom. After a couple of cleansing breaths, I recovered, and when I came back out, I detoured to the floor-to-ceiling windows. I was there, soaking in the view, when I felt his presence.

"Having fun?"

I turned toward him, my eyes filling with tears. So much for collecting myself. "This is too much."

He put his arm around my shoulders and pulled me into his side. For several seconds, we stood like that, silently watching a plane land at Logan Airport across the harbor.

"Nothing is too much," he said softly. "You'll never be too much."

The silence returned, a calm descending over us even with the chaos going on in the penthouse.

Despite how overwhelmed I was, I couldn't deny just how perfect this felt.

I was definitely in love with this man. With his kindness and thoughtfulness and his heart. I'd been denying it and avoiding it for too long.

The timing could not be worse. Nothing could happen. But I could at least enjoy this perfect moment.

CHAPTER 24
Brian

I'd never felt anything like this.

The smiles and selfies and constant quoting of Lake Paige lyrics. I hadn't realized this artist had created an entire subculture of friendship and empowerment around her music, but it was on full display tonight.

It had taken minutes for the daughters of Dylan's best friends to bring Kit and Greta into the fold. Now they were all glittered up and screaming nonstop. It was energizing and exhausting at the same time.

I loved it.

Jess looked so beautiful it was difficult to keep my eyes off her. She glowed with happiness, and the slinky dress didn't hurt.

Dylan, of course, had racks of clothes delivered to the hotel penthouse for all the women and girls to choose from.

Room service had brought up snacks, and the girls had engineered a fashion show that eventually transitioned into a dance party. I'd never seen Kit so animated and excited. She was in her element, chatting with the older girls and consulting on shoe choices.

In typical Jess fashion, she'd chosen a bright pink dress with sparkly straps. The makeup artist had made her lips look even more delicious and kissable than usual, making it impossible for me to stop staring at her mouth.

I wanted it. To kiss her, to hold her. To show her how much I cared about her. But I couldn't cross that line. Not yet.

Thankfully, we'd been so busy that I hadn't had much time to even contemplate it. I'd been put on photography duty, and I took my role seriously, memorializing every moment for the girls.

At the stadium, we were whisked through a VIP entrance and up elevators manned by men with earpieces. It was all very official and unlike any experience I'd ever had at a ballpark.

Beckett led us through a maze of hallways, then ushered us into a well-furnished room to wait.

While the kids choreographed yet another elaborate dance routine, I stood by Jess, watching her face as she took it all in. She was so beautiful. But what caught my attention now that I'd had time to get used to the extra fullness of her lips was the sheer joy on her face.

Every detail mattered to her. Every moment was special. Not just today, either. She was like this all the time. Dancing and singing and cooking and smiling through all of life's mundane moments as well as the exciting ones.

It made me want to share all of them with her. And the curiosity was killing me. I wanted to know what she looked like first thing in the morning. I wanted to watch her face light up when I surprised her with flowers. I was desperate to discover if she would flush, like she used to, when I made her come.

Focus, Brian.

For now, this had to remain friendly and nothing more.

It was going to be a long weekend if I couldn't keep my fantasies in check.

Before my mind got away from me again, the door opened, and two burly security guards entered, followed by Lake Paige herself. She looked like a smaller, younger version of the billboard currently in front of this stadium. Long brown hair, signature red lips, and an infectious smile.

The screaming and excitement took over, and I shifted back into photographer mode.

She chatted with each of the kids, giving hugs and high fives, complimenting their outfits and asking about their favorite songs.

When a warm hand landed on my arm, I looked away from my phone's screen. At my side, Jess wore a wobbly smile, her eyes misty. "This is amazing," she mouthed.

As Lake approached Greta, I bumped Jess with my elbow. "Get in there."

She threw her hands up. "Oh no. No old ladies in the pictures."

"You look gorgeous." I pinned her with a serious look. "Now get in there and take photos with your daughters."

Finally, she shuffled toward Lake. And when Lake threw her arms open for a hug, Jess stumbled, starstruck. As they embraced, she peered down at her girls and wiped a tear from her eye. The four of them posed, making peace signs and silly faces. Lake took time to make each of them feel special before moving on to the next fan. Eventually, though, she was whisked away to the stage. The moment the door shut behind her, the room erupted again.

"I'm deceased," Kit declared, a hand over her heart, her tween angst on display. "Bury me, Mom. This is the best day of my life."

Jess playfully rolled her eyes. "Can we at least wait until after the concert before making funeral plans?"

"Fine." Head thrown back, she sighed. Then she turned to me. "Thanks, Brian." She pushed a strand of glitter hair behind her ear and tackled me in a huge hug.

Greta piled on, and then Jess wrapped her arms around both of them, her hands barely making it to my back.

I was unprepared for the affection, and it was a bit of a shock just how good it felt to be appreciated like this. Making Jess and her kids happy made me happy too.

We were herded out of the conference room minutes later, and as we followed the group to the owner's box, I was struck by how much fun I was having. I wasn't usually one for crowds and noise, but the energy was undeniable, and it felt special to share this with Jess.

When the opening act came on, she danced and sang, jumping in with the kids' dance routines.

When Lake took the stage, energy crackled in the air. It seemed impossible that one could feel complete safety in a crowd of sixty thousand people, yet here I was, without a care in the world. I was surrounded by glitter and friendship and hugs. And our entire group, even grumps like Beckett and me, had a great time.

Each time Jess brushed up against me, my blood heated and I had to remind myself that I was playing the long game. Laying the foundation for a connection I didn't yet understand but needed more than I needed my next breath.

So much was unknown, but in my bones, I was certain that this woman was worth all of it. I'd just have to be patient and hope that one day, she could be mine.

The security posted at the entrance to the owner's box had passed out light-up bracelets, which were now flashing in time with the beat.

Blinding lights flashed as Lake strutted across the stage, and as backup dancers appeared, a round of fireworks exploded overhead.

The crowd sang along to every word, never tiring, never missing a lyric.

With my heart in my throat, I snuck looks at Kit and Greta, who were shaking and jumping wildly. I'd only ever felt this kind of affection a few times in my life. Liam, of course, had stolen my heart the day he was born. And I was partial to Sully's and Cal's kids. It blew me away how quickly these two girls had chipped away at my heart and found homes there.

As the music slowed and Lake launched into her famous love song "Hold Me," cell phone lights turned on one by one. My bracelet flashed blue, pulling my attention down to where my hand rested at my side.

Like this, Jess's fingers were a few inches from mine. As I stared, the need to touch her, to hold on tight, overwhelmed me.

It took more willpower than I'd like to admit to fight the urge. With a sigh, I turned back to the stage, trying to ignore the persistent tug in my chest.

I was still battling with myself when Jess, as if reading my mind, clutched my hand and smiled up at me.

Time stopped as we looked at one another, the music, lights, and crowd fading into the background.

It was dark, but there was no hiding the emotion in her eyes. It was palpable, a deepening connection that neither of us could fully embrace yet.

Heart racing, I turned back to the stage, focusing on the feel of her palm in mine. This was more than I could have hoped for. When tomorrow came, I'd have to take a step back, erect those boundaries again. But for tonight, I'd hold on and enjoy every moment.

This was meant to be. It was right. Thank fuck my friends had pushed me to do this.

Nothing could happen. That was still true. But if this moment was anything to go by, at least Jess got it now.

She understood she was special to me. That I'd do anything for her and her kids.

The only downside? I'd have to admit to Lo and Sloane that they were right. That a gesture could speak volumes, even while I was still prohibited from telling her how much she meant with words.

God, they'd be insufferable.

But this sensation, the strange combination of excitement and comfort as we held hands, made it all worth it.

During intermission, while I was at the bar area inside the box, fetching waters for the kids, a hand landed on my shoulder with enough force to make me fumble the bottles I was holding. I managed to hold on to them all as I turned and found Beckett Langfield watching me.

"Thank you," I said, emotions still rushing through me. This man was a billionaire, one of the firm's most valuable clients, and a sort-of friend. He owed me nothing, yet he'd helped me get here, to the top of the world.

He eyed Jess and the girls, who hadn't left their spots, and raised his whiskey glass to me. "Happy to be of service. Don't duck it up."

With that, he strolled over to his wife and two of their daughters.

Once I'd handed out waters, I focused on breathing, working to center myself.

"Brian." Kit rushed toward me and threw her arms around my waist. When she looked up, her eyes were wet and her small face was stained with tears and rainbow glitter. "This is the best day of my life," she sobbed. "Thank you."

Before I could react, Greta and Jess were joining her. All three of them squeezed me as they bounced up and down. "You're the best, Brian," Greta said, her voice muffled.

I held them as tightly as I could, savoring the moment.

Across the room, Beckett caught my eye and raised his glass.

Shit, he was right. I could not duck this up.

CHAPTER 25
Jess

"I've missed Boston." I twirled in a circle, my face tipped toward the sky. It wasn't as busy as New York, and there wasn't the same urgency, but the city had always had a place in my heart. The history and the architecture were enough to make anyone stop and take in the sights. Being here made me feel like the main character in the story instead of one of the teeming masses the way New York did.

The air was crisper too. Though it was June, the cool breeze was enough to keep me on my toes.

"Think the girls are okay?" Brian asked. "We can head back."

I scoffed. "They were more than happy to see us go."

When we'd left, the whole crew was busy making friendship bracelets and s'mores while talking endlessly about last night's concert.

Dylan had arranged for a massive camp-out movie night in the penthouse, tents and sleeping bags and all, and the hotel staff had gone all out, providing snacks and lanterns. She'd mentioned her husband Cortney's family owned the hotel chain, so it made sense that they'd let her do whatever she wanted. If the last day hadn't been so strangely surreal, I'd have questioned it. Right now, I was floating along in a fairy tale, so it didn't seem so far-fetched.

The girls insisted that they'd prefer to stay at the camp-out overnight —again—so I'd have my very luxurious hotel suite to myself. I should be thrilled to have a night off after having gone without one for so long, yet I had no idea what to do with myself.

So I asked Brian to take a walk with me.

We'd been invited to dinner with some of Dylan's friends and their husbands, but I'd declined, preferring a quiet evening after the chaos of the previous day. The girls and I had spent this morning walking the Freedom Trail and the afternoon at the Museum of Science, and though my feet hurt, I needed the quiet and the fresh air to process the events of the last thirty-six hours.

The concert might have been the greatest experience of my life, aside from the days the girls were born. The pure happiness radiating from Kit and Greta had filled my heart with joy. Yes, I was still riding a high, but secretly, it had more to do with holding Brian's hand than meeting Lake Paige. The act had been so innocent, yet it felt significant. The intensity in his eyes when he looked at me had made my heart race, and the gravity of what he'd done for me and my kids had hit me like a bus.

I was falling in love with this man.

Not the boy I'd fallen for a lifetime ago.

The man standing next to me right now.

Weeks ago, I'd made my peace with the attraction. Attraction was normal. But this urgency, this ache in my chest, was so much more than lust.

He wore jeans and a T-shirt as we traversed the city. It was a look I hadn't seen on him in twenty years. The casual attire made him look younger, which sent my thoughts skipping back in time to the days we'd often walked these streets together. Young, carefree, and in love.

The differences were like night and day. Life now was complicated and difficult, and every day contained challenges my young mind could never have conceived of back then.

We'd had a lot of fun roaming these streets, dreaming and chatting and holding hands. But we were different people now. Grown and weary and tired. That version of Jess was so far away from me, I could barely feel her, even back in Boston.

And Brian? The grown-up version of him made my knees weak.

"This is so beautiful," I remarked as we strolled along the Rose Kennedy Greenway. "I remember when this was an ugly highway."

His response was easy, mundane, his expression introspective.

For a long while, we were silent, but with each step, emotions bubbled up inside me. When I was bursting, unable to hold back, I stopped abruptly and wrung my hands.

He stopped too, turning back and frowning at me in concern.

"Thank you," I blurted out. "For everything. This whole trip has been a dream come true."

"You're welcome," he said, dipping his chin. "But the look on the girls' faces last night was all the thanks I need."

I shook my head. "Someday, I'll find a way to repay you. But for now. Just let me say this."

With my heart thudding heavily, I clutched his hand and forced myself to hold eye contact.

"Thank you. For your friendship and your kindness to my kids. Thank you for being someone I can depend on. It's been a long time since I had someone in my corner, on my team. I forgot how good it feels not to have to face every battle alone."

He sucked in a breath.

"Sorry," I said, dropping his hands. "I wasn't trying to make things weird."

He ran a hand through his hair. "You didn't. And I am on your team. As are Cal, Lo, Sully, Sloane, Tia, and the boys. Even the damn cat. Our whole dysfunctional family."

"You have no idea how lucky you are," I replied, tears pricking at the backs of my eyes. "The work you do is so important, and you get to do it with people you love and who love you back."

He blew out a long breath. "I should be thanking you," he said, his brow creased. "It wasn't until you showed up that I realized how much I've been holding back. My priorities have been muddled."

Without waiting for a response, he tugged me toward the crosswalk, where the signal had just changed.

Being here with him was surreal. The city had changed so much, but while we walked the streets together, it felt as though we'd fallen back in time. We talked endlessly, laughing and reminiscing, the present and past mingling together.

"We had fun," he said softly as we navigated the cobblestone sidewalks of Boston's North End, heading toward Genaro's.

"We did." I smiled, overcome by the ghost of a once familiar light, magical sensation that came with being young and in love and free from all the burdens of adulthood.

"I hope the pizza is still amazing after all these years."

"Enzo, Delia's fiancé, swore that it is. He's a Boston guy. Knows his stuff."

He held the door open for me, then guided me past the small seating area with checkered tablecloths and candles in wine bottles, straight to the takeout window.

The smell hit me hard, followed by a wave of nostalgia. I loved pizza, but no New York pizza shop smelled like this.

A tiny woman with gray curls tied back in a bandana popped her head up over the counter. "Whatcha want?" she asked, her Boston accent thick.

Brian looked at me, and I nodded. After all these years, my order hadn't changed.

"A slice of mushroom and a slice of pepperoni," he replied.

Paper plates in hand, we stepped outside again. The slices were as big as they'd been twenty years ago, hanging off the plate at each point. The crust was so thin I had to use both hands to keep it from falling as we walked across the street to North Square Park.

"It's nicer than it used to be," Brian said as we found a bench. Between bites, he surveyed the sculpture garden and impeccable landscaping.

Since my hands were both occupied, I nodded toward the small gray clapboard house. "That's the Paul Revere House. I'm glad this little spot is getting some love. We learned on our Freedom Trail tour that this was a public gathering place back as far as the sixteen hundreds. There used to be a meeting house here too. It's where several important parts of the Revolution were planned."

He smiled at me. Around us, tourists chatted and took photos, and the cool night air smelled of delicious food and possibility.

"You have room for cannoli?" he asked. We were wedged on a small stone bench, our knees touching as he munched on the crust of his pizza. Nothing had changed. He could still inhale a slice, no matter how large, and have room for more.

I straightened, nodding. "Mike's or Modern?" I asked.

He stood, taking my paper plate from my hands. "Obviously Modern. I know a lot has changed since we were last here together, but you can't actually think I'd abandon all my cannoli principles."

"Wasn't sure if you'd switched allegiances," I quipped.

He reeled back, a hand on his chest. "Never."

His beard almost hid the speck of pizza sauce on the corner of his lip. If I hadn't been studying him so intently, I probably would have missed it. But now that I'd seen it, I couldn't stop myself from wiping it away with the pad of my thumb.

We touched frequently, but never intimately, unless one counted the hand-holding at the concert. I blamed my lack of judgment on the nostalgia clouding my brain.

The minute my thumb touched the corner of his lip, I knew it was a mistake. So, breath held, I drew my hand back quickly.

But he caught me by the wrist, his golden eyes molten as they locked with mine. Holding me firmly, he angled in close, though not too close. In his proximity, all I could think about was his lips and how desperately I needed to kiss him.

My lack of self-control was ridiculous. I was a forty-one-year-old single mother, not a lovesick college student.

But none of that mattered.

So I closed the gap.

The moment our lips met, fireworks exploded behind my eyes. And rather than sweet nostalgia, I was hit with a wave of pure heat.

He pulled me closer and cupped my chin, his soft lips intent.

As if my body had a mind of its own, I found myself pushing toward him, almost landing on his lap.

The kiss wasn't indecent. We were in public, after all. But it was intentional. His lips were firm and focused, teasing my mouth open as I melted into him. It was new and old and invigorating.

But then it stopped.

"I'm sorry." He heaved a breath as he pulled away and stood. Silently, and without meeting my eye, he gathered our paper plates and deposited them in a nearby trash can.

My heart fell into my shoes. Had I done something wrong? Did I have horrific pepperoni breath? I touched my tingling lips, trying to make my brain process what was happening.

I stood, brushing the crumbs from my lap, avoiding looking at him. God, leave it to me to completely misread the situation.

But I hadn't attacked his face, had I? No, he'd kissed me back.

"Jess," he said softly, the regret in his tone making me wince. "Look at me."

I took a fortifying breath. Then, slowly, I lifted my face and forced myself to zero in on him.

"I'm sorry about that." He swallowed thickly, his throat working. "I got carried away. I shouldn't have done that."

Oh God, this was mortifying. I scuffed the loose cobblestone with the toe of my sandal, wishing the ghost of Paul Revere would ride through here on his horse and save me from my utter humiliation.

He sighed. "Wanna keep walking?"

I nodded, desperate to get away from the confusing moment we'd just shared. I'd thought it was a magical kiss, a transcendent experience. But clearly, I was alone in that.

One would think that after the failed marriage, I'd stop romanticizing every little thing. God, I was an idiot.

We headed down Hanover Street and back toward the waterfront, hugging the piers as we zigzagged along Boston Harbor, silent the whole way.

With each block, my embarrassment grew until I was certain it would consume me.

But he had leaned in. He had kissed me back. I replayed the moment over and over, certain that I hadn't made that up. About the time we made it to Fan Pier, the embarrassment turned to anger.

We'd sat side by side, eating pizza in our spot, flirting. He'd been the one to grasp my arm. He'd been the one to lean in like the hero in a goddamn movie.

"What the hell?" I finally snapped, stopping at the railing and focusing on a massive container ship out in the distance.

He came to stand beside me, silent.

I waited for a family with a stroller to walk by before I turned and poked him in the chest. "You kissed me back," I hissed quietly. "You leaned." With a groan, I threw my hands up. "You were into the kiss, and it was a good fucking kiss. How dare you act like it was a mistake?"

My body temperature rose with each accusation. We'd been dancing around this for weeks. He'd whisked me and my kids off to Boston for a once-in-a-lifetime adventure. How could I not read into all of that?

"Jess." He grasped my hand, his palm warm. "Jess, please listen."

He was even more handsome in the moonlight reflecting off the harbor, shadows making the sharp angle of his jaw even more prominent.

"It was a great kiss," he said, giving my hand a squeeze. "And yes, I leaned. I wanted it desperately. I want you desperately."

My heart thudded heavily. What?

I swallowed, collecting my thoughts. "You want me?"

He cupped my cheek and took a step forward so we were standing almost chest to chest.

"So fucking much," he growled. The sound was full of determination, but an instant later, his face fell, and he hung his head. "But I can't. You're my client. I've tried to manage these feelings, but I only have so much self-control. And then you kissed me, and it was like every dream I've ever had coming true."

My stomach fluttered. He felt it too. He wanted me just as much as I wanted him.

But… "Who cares if I'm your client?"

He rested his hands on my waist, bringing me closer. "The New Jersey Bar Association cares. A lot. It's not ethical."

Screw the New Jersey Bar Association. I didn't want this night to end. I didn't want this trip to end. The last thirty-six hours had been truly magical, and I had this man to thank for it.

"What if…" I trailed my fingers up his chest and ran my nails through the scruff of his jaw. "What if we just let go and see what happens? We're not in New Jersey. This entire trip has been magical. What if, just for tonight, we're not lawyer and client, but two people who can't keep their hands off each other?"

He gave me a sad smile. "We can't."

"Brian." I popped up on my tiptoes and kissed him softly. "I am just a mortal woman."

As I pulled back, I studied his face, noting the desire in his eyes, the way his lips parted. I kissed him again, a bit longer this time.

"You can't expect me to resist you," I whispered. "Especially here. My kids are having the time of their lives with your sister, and I have a massive hotel suite all to myself."

He looped an arm around me, pulling me flush against him, and captured my mouth in a searing kiss.

"Fuck," he growled into my mouth. "Jess."

"I am an exhausted single mom," I confessed. "I have no idea what the future holds. But no matter how hard I try, I cannot fight my attraction to you." Hands on his chest, I peered up at him through my lashes. "And if you truly meant it when you said you wanted me, then let's do this. Let's go back to the hotel and give ourselves a night to take what we want."

"One night?"

"Yes. One night where I'm not putting my kids first and you're not putting your career first. Where we live only in the moment."

His breath hitched. "What if I want more than a moment?"

Unease curled around the desire coursing through me. There it was. The slippery slope. The promise of a perfect man who would ride up on a white horse and solve all my problems. That was a fantasy, not real life. I'd learned that the hard way.

Our lives were going in different directions. We could never be more than a brief moment. But I wanted our moment. And dammit, I'd earned it.

"It's all I can give." I stroked his beard. "Take it or leave it, Machon. You want to come up to my hotel suite, get naked, and ravage me?"

He kissed me again, sloppy and desperate, and pulled back, out of breath and eyes wild.

"Fuck yes, I'll ravage you."

CHAPTER 26
Brian

It was just as I'd suspected. Once we'd opened the floodgates, there was no going back. Jess and I had to stop several times on the walk back to the hotel to kiss.

Her mouth.

Fuck. It was soft and firm, and kissing her felt better than anything I'd experienced in two decades. She was familiar yet totally new, stoking the fires of my lust.

As we got into the elevator, an elderly gentleman joined us, tipping his hat at Jess. She stood, hands clasped, the face of innocence, while we rode up silently.

All the way up, I stole glances, wishing we were alone so I could get my hands on her body.

Instead, I closed my eyes, thanking every deity I could recall for the woman standing next to me. Being this close to her, I was more alive than ever, invigorated and so fucking happy.

Our time in the park, simply eating pizza side by side, would go down as one of the most romantic dates of my life.

Finally the elevator reached our floor, and when we stepped into the hall, she arched a brow and held her key card up. "Race you?"

She took off running down the hall, and after a heartbeat, I followed, catching up to her quickly. Without slowing, I threw her over my shoulder. Only when she pointed at the door to her suite did I stop.

Giggling, she handed me the card. Once inside, I strode straight through the massive living area to the bedroom.

I deposited her on the king-size bed and kicked off my shoes before climbing on top of her, caging her between my arms and stealing another kiss.

This one was ravenous. I was fucking starved.

She gripped my hair and tugged, sending bolts of electricity up my spine as our tongues danced and I finally got to explore her body.

She was lush and soft in all the right places. Fuck, she felt so good.

My fantasies didn't do justice to the goddess spread out below me.

As I kissed her neck, she grasped my belt and pulled roughly.

"Slow down." I buried my face in her neck, relishing her intoxicating scent.

"No," she snarled. "You've been all sexy and kind and helpful for weeks. I'm not holding back."

Though I didn't know it was possible, my cock got harder. Goddamn this woman.

As we wrestled one another's clothes off, I knew I should stop and take a moment to drink in the sight of her. But I was too busy exploring her skin with my mouth and hands. Every inch of her was perfect, and each little gasp and sigh pushed me to keep going.

Slowly, I pulled the straps of her bra down, and when I found her pink nipples already rock hard, I growled, angling in and taking one in my mouth.

Back arching, she wrapped her fingers around my length through the fabric of my boxer briefs and squeezed, and I fucking saw stars.

Willing my body not to get ahead of itself, I breathed deeply once, then again. Then I kissed down the length of her, imprinting the feel of her skin on my subconscious.

It was imperative that I remember every moment, because nothing would ever feel this good.

By the time I reached her blue panties, I was dizzy with lust and barely holding on. I hooked my fingers into her waistband and inched them down, and I was rewarded when I discovered she was soaked.

"Is this all for me?" I gently stroked her clit, certain that I'd died and gone to heaven.

"Yes," she moaned as I sank one finger inside her. Studying her face, I removed the digit and licked it clean with my tongue.

Her pupils blew out, almost eclipsing her dark irises. "Dirty," she sighed.

I slid my finger inside her again. But this time when I removed it, I held it up to her lips.

Without hesitation, she laved it with her tongue, maintaining eye contact with me the entire time.

"You're in charge," I said, barely holding it together. "This only goes as far as you say it does."

"I'm all in." She pushed up onto her elbows, making those luscious breasts jiggle.

"Tell me what you want," I urged. There was nothing I wouldn't give this woman.

"I want you to fuck me," she said. "Fast and dirty. You make me feel sexier and more desired than I have in my entire life. I need you inside me."

"But." I lowered my face and licked her clit. The move gave me the opportunity to taste her. It also allowed me time to get myself under control.

I needed to rein my desire in. Otherwise I'd embarrass myself with my dream girl.

"There's plenty of time for that later," she moaned, tugging on my hair. " You said whatever I wanted. And I know what I want."

With a sigh, I looked up at her. Before I could disappoint her by telling her I hadn't come prepared, she smirked wickedly.

"I packed condoms."

I pushed myself up on my elbows, searching her face for any reservation but finding none.

"I'm an optimist." With a smile, she rolled over and snagged a makeup bag from the nightstand. She deftly unzipped it and pulled out a roll of about a dozen condoms, then tossed them onto the bed.

My heart seized in my chest. Holy shit. In this moment, I knew beyond a shadow of a doubt that I was in love with this woman.

She tore one from the end and pushed at my chest, silently encouraging me to stand. When I was looming over her, she looked up at me with those big brown eyes and pushed my boxer briefs down.

My cock bobbed, and as she gently stroked it, tingles shot up my spine.

Deftly, she rolled the condom on. Then she pushed herself back onto the bed, unabashedly spreading her legs wide.

The sight of her alone almost made me pass out. Blond hair everywhere, hard nipples begging for my tongue, and a look of pure want on her face.

A heartbeat later, I was on top of her, lining myself up at her entrance. But I hesitated there, needing confirmation once more. This moment would change everything.

"Please," she whispered.

The last thread of my self-control snapped. I pushed inside her, teeth gritted because it felt so damn incredible. She whimpered, head thrown back, begging for more.

"Wider," I said, pushing her thighs open. "Spread for me."

She obeyed, and I thrust home. My vision tunneled, and I swore I could have gone off right there, but I refused to be that asshole. So I sucked in a sharp breath, tensed every fucking muscle, and found a rhythm that made her pant and moan.

She clawed at my back, meeting me stroke for stroke as I lost myself to the feel of her underneath me.

I thrust hard and fast, knowing I should be going slower. But this woman unraveled me. She pushed me and surprised me and made me feel like a superhuman.

"Brian." She gasped, her nails digging into my skin. "I'm so close."

Fighting for control, I snaked one hand up, gently collaring her neck. "Good girl," I growled as she cried out. "Eyes on me when you come."

I kept my fingers on her pulse as I felt her begin to convulse around me, gasping and shaking. It was fucking bliss, watching those eyes darken with lust as she came on my cock. I willed myself to keep going, but it was too much for me, and I followed her into the abyss, my orgasm ripping through me as she moaned my name.

CHAPTER 27
Brian

Bliss. Pure fucking bliss. My arm was numb from being curled around Jess all night, but I'd gladly lose a limb if it meant I could sleep next to her.

She was curled up against me so tightly it made my heart clench.

Mine.

The words had been a drumbeat in my brain on repeat since the night of the concert. Mine, mine, mine.

The sensation was one of both exhilaration and calm. Like we'd struck some kind of cosmic balance.

I hadn't felt this way in a very long time.

Not since college.

All those years ago, I'd assumed that it was just what it felt like to be in love. But I'd never been able to replicate it. I'd never found someone I craved and respected and adored like this.

Love.

As I looked out at the Boston skyline through the gauzy drapes, I knew it.

I was in love with Jess.

Mind, body, and soul. Fuck, this was a problem.

She shifted next to me, and I found myself smiling like an idiot. This was the kind of moment I wanted to hold on to and never let go of. Revel in and enjoy, because as desperately as I wanted it forever, it wouldn't last.

"Brian." Her voice was husky.

I swelled with pride, knowing I'd made her scream last night.

Other parts of me swelled, too, as she sat up, causing the sheet to slip and reveal her naked breasts.

I pulled her on top of me, kissing down her collarbone, and with a husky chuckle, she wriggled against me. Last night had been an appetizer. This morning, I was only hungrier.

Hands cupping her breasts, I worshipped one nipple, then the other.

Her hand was already wrapped firmly around my cock, her firm hold making my eyes roll into the back of my head.

"Brian." This time her voice wasn't breathy. It didn't drip with need. It was insistent, serious.

So I pulled back, searching her face.

She gave me a sad smile. "We need to talk."

And just like that. My hope—and my cock—deflated.

She pushed herself off the bed and stepped into the bathroom. She came out a moment later wrapped in a fluffy white robe.

Fuck, she was adorable.

Now that she was covered up, she perched on the side of the bed.

"God, Brian." She raked her fingers through her wild hair, gathering it into a lopsided ponytail. "The things you do to me."

A smirk overtook me without my permission, though I quickly tamped down on it, because her expression was suddenly one of distress.

"You were hot in college. But God, now? All manly and serious? You make it hard to think straight. You've got this whole Michael Fassbender thing going for you. Successful professional on the surface, but deep down, you're still a blue-collar kid from Brooklyn who was a champion boxer. Like you'll negotiate contracts in your fancy suit and then turn around and kick a guy's ass for disrespecting your woman."

I laughed. I'd always enjoyed her rants, but this time, as she talked about how much she was attracted to me, I wanted to encourage her to elaborate.

Turned out I didn't have to do any encouraging. "And you're all muscular and bearded," she went on, lamenting me, "and good with your tongue."

I bit the sides of my mouth to keep from smiling.

She, on the other hand, got progressively redder. Yet she didn't stop. It was the single biggest ego boost of my life.

She let her hair down and pulled it back again. This time, the ponytail was relatively straight. "You're the best combo of loyal golden retriever and stern brunch daddy."

"What?" I frowned. What the hell was a brunch daddy?

She waved a hand. "Forget it. Bottom line is, you are incredible."

That was it. There was no fighting my smile any longer.

"But."

All the air escaped me. Aw, fuck. There was always a but.

"As much as I hate it, we can't do this again."

I let the weight of her words sit between us for a moment. She was right. There was no denying that. She was still my client. And she'd been very clear about her intentions last night.

As much as I wanted to plead my case and convince her of how great we could be together, I couldn't do that to her. I wouldn't undermine her choice or try to convince her she was wrong.

I was torn in two, and the two sides were at war. I was her lawyer, and I wanted to win her case so she could move to Vermont. Yet I was her friend, or maybe more, who wanted to explore the connection we clearly had.

But this woman had been counting down the days until she could leave Jersey since before she walked into my office and we reconnected. It wasn't fair to ask her to stick around for me.

She scooted over and laid her head on my chest.

"You will never know how much this has meant to me. How much you mean to me. But I know myself. If we keep this up, I'll fall in love with you." She tipped her head up and eyed me, worrying her lip. "Hell, I'm already halfway in love with you."

Her sweet honesty made my stomach drop.

"If we went any further only to part ways when my request is granted, it would break me." She sighed. "I worked so hard to rebuild myself after my divorce, to forge a stronger version of the woman I used to be. I can't lose that, and I won't let my kids suffer either."

I kissed her forehead, eyes closed, wishing things could be different but knowing she was right.

"And you're a risk, Brian. A kind, smart, sexy risk. But still a risk. And I've got to stay focused. Deal with the legal stuff and start over in Vermont."

"I understand," I whispered into her hair. "And not because I don't want more with you. I want it more than you could ever imagine. But I respect that you're rebuilding your life for your children. I would never get in the way of that."

Her head was tilted down again, her shoulders shaking, and suddenly, my chest was damp. Fuck. She was crying.

I wrapped both arms around her and held her close, helpless, wishing I could fix everything for her.

I cleared the emotion from my throat. "You've made a wonderful life for your girls."

"Hardly," she scoffed.

"Bullshit," I said. "Do I need to spell it out for you?"

"Actually." She sat up, inspecting my face like she was looking for a lie. "Yeah."

"Okay." Sighing, I took her hands. "First of all, you love so fully. You love with your entire being. Your words, your facial expressions, your touch. Even on dark days, those kids feel your love in every nook and cranny of their lives."

Her eyes misted over again. "Wow."

"The way you speak to them and about them is so effervescent. It fills everyone around you with joy. You've created a magical life for those girls. You work hard to make every day feel special with all your traditions."

"Thank you." The tears were flowing now, but I wasn't finished.

Maybe I couldn't keep her, but she wasn't leaving this hotel room without understanding what a remarkable human she was.

"The way you make room for their individual personalities and all their activities and passions is admirable. You taught yourself piano just so you could understand what Kit was talking about."

"YouTube taught me." She let out a watery laugh. "And just the basics."

"Take the damn credit, Jess." I squeezed her hand. "Those kids hit the mom jackpot. Everyone who knows you has. You brighten the day of everyone you meet. I'm proud to be your lawyer and your friend. And if that's all I get, I'm still the luckiest guy in the world."

She took a shaky breath and let it out slowly. "Thank you." As she wiped at her eyes, she stood, putting distance between us.

I wanted to grab her and never let go. But I wouldn't do that to her. I wouldn't confuse her or ask her to give up a single thing for me.

"What time are we heading back to Jersey? I need to shower."

I leaned across the bed and snagged my phone so I could check the time. "We have a couple of hours. I'm going to hit the gym and get some coffee."

With a nod, she shuffled toward the bathroom. At the open door, she turned, her lips tugged down. "My younger self is screaming at me right now for not taking a shot with the best guy I've ever known. But I'm a forty-one-year-old mom, barely hanging on by a thread. I can't take the risk."

My chest constricted so forcefully it took effort not to double over. "I understand."

Nodding, she disappeared. But before she shut the door, she said, "I don't think I'll ever set foot in this city without having hot-sex flashbacks."

When the door was closed and the water was running, I threw myself back on the bed and covered my face.

We wanted each other, but our situation was impossible. History was repeating itself. And now I was old enough to understand what I'd lose by letting her walk away.

But at least we'd always have Boston.

CHAPTER 28

Jess

I was sweating through my blazer, and if I wasn't careful, I'd make my cuticles bleed. Picking at my nails was a terrible habit, one that Kenneth had chided me about for years, but I couldn't help it.

We might not even get a decision today.

It was just a hearing. The judge would ask questions, and Brian would make arguments. Then we'd wait. According to Lo, we were in good shape. Kenneth had withdrawn his opposition, and we'd filed the best interest evaluation ahead of schedule. Judge Gordon occasionally ruled from the bench, but that didn't mean he couldn't choose to issue a written decision instead.

Regardless of what happened today, the process was moving along, and this was the first big milestone.

Living with this uncertainty got harder every day. At this point, I needed an answer. My heart couldn't live in two separate places, and now that school was out, the need to make plans for our future felt more urgent. The girls were doing well at the day camp I'd enrolled them in, and they still enjoyed spending most afternoons with T. J. and Murphy.

They'd gotten comfortable with Brian's found family quickly, and that fact made me decidedly uncomfortable.

Since our night together, he'd been a perfect gentleman. Kind and understanding and totally professional.

But I was haunted by memories of our time in Boston.

I'd been the one to insist this couldn't go further. I'd sworn that I couldn't let myself fall for him.

But I was a damn liar. I'd already fallen.

Yet the man was as cool as a cucumber, seemingly unaffected by what had transpired, behaving just as he had before he'd told me he wanted me and then rocked my world.

And I couldn't avoid him. Especially with the hearing coming up. And because the universe hated me, Kit and Greta had decided he was their all-time favorite person. Since the concert, they talked about him nonstop. They had made glittery thank-you cards and baked brownies from a mix. When they'd presented him with them, he had savored each bite as if it was from a Parisian patisserie.

My stomach ached as I considered the choices ahead. Each time I worked out the logistics of my move to Vermont, I felt a tug toward him. To that strange building and the people I now wished I hadn't fallen for almost as deeply as I'd fallen for Brian.

The ragtag family that had embraced me and my kids and given us a soft place to land during a difficult time.

The thought of leaving them made my nose sting and tears threaten.

Brian looked as cool as ever, his dark blue suit making his eyes pop and his freshly trimmed stubble making me want to lick his neck.

He typed on his laptop while we waited for my case to be called. Every few minutes, he'd glance over at me. His intention was probably to reassure me, but it only made my gut twist more.

All the walls I'd built up, all that hard-earned cynicism, had been demolished by this sharp lawyer with muscled forearms and soulful eyes.

We waited while case after case was called. Divorce had been my first introduction to the legal system. It wasn't until then that I understood what a snoozefest it could be. TV made it seem fascinating, yet in my experience, it was mostly drudgery, forms, and waiting. Endless waiting.

After another recess, Judge Gordon returned, and the clerk stood and read off the docket sheet. "NJ-5001-4B. Mosely."

Brian snapped his laptop shut and led me toward the bar. He opened the door and stepped aside so I could walk through the swinging door first.

Once we were seated, the judge riffled through a stack of papers, then peered up at us over his glasses. "I see the father withdrew his opposition to the motion."

Brian stood, smoothing down his tie. "Yes, your honor. He has declined visitation per the custody order, and my client has full legal and physical custody of the minor children. In addition, the father moved out of state last year. If you refer to exhibit four-A and seven, you will find both the custody orders and the confirmation of the out-of-state move."

Nodding, he flipped through the big book of exhibits Lo had prepared.

With every second that passed, my muscles locked up tighter as Brian and the Judge talked through the law.

"I see no reason to deny the petition." He straightened. "We will enter a judgment and issue a written opinion for the record."

I froze, my breath stalling, as I processed his words.

"Clerk, please enter on the record. The motion to relocate is granted. The petitioner will have one hundred and eighty days to file residency paperwork with the court."

The gavel sounded, startling me. Heart pounding in my ears, I blinked once, twice, a third time. Was this actually happening? Were we finally free to leave New Jersey?

Beside me, Brian gathered his things. Then he cupped my elbow and guided me to my feet. It wasn't until we'd exited the courtroom and were in the cavernous hallway that my mind came back online.

"We did it." I leaped at him, catching him, and myself, off guard.

He hugged me quickly, then set me on my feet and ensured I was steady before releasing me completely.

"Er. Sorry." Ducking, I smoothed my skirt.

"I liked it," he replied, immediately loosening his tie. "And congrats. You are a free woman."

A thrill shot through me. "Because of you," I breathed, beaming at him. "Thank you."

"It's my job." He nodded toward the exit, then skirted around me.

I shuffled to keep up, annoyed with his humble routine. He'd answered all those complex questions with confidence and ease. Had prepared things the judge didn't even know he wanted.

Sloane was right. He was the best.

Yet this victory felt hollow at best.

"How did you do it?" I asked as we headed toward his car. "Get Kenneth to withdraw his opposition?"

"I had his number. The guy is a coward and a shithead. That made it easy," Brian replied, not really answering my question, as he tossed his briefcase, jacket, and tie into the back seat. Straightening, he methodically rolled up one sleeve, then the other.

I couldn't help but gawk, drinking in every tiny movement. God, it was sexy, the way he was removing his legal armor. As I watched, the traitorous slut that was my brain came up with all kinds of fun ways to celebrate this court victory.

When he caught me looking, I averted my gaze, my face flaming.

"I think it's because you took away his toys," I said, hoping he wouldn't call me out. "His baseball tickets and that charity thing."

"Oh, I took away all his charity things," Brian said cryptically as he slipped into the driver's seat.

As he cranked the AC, I buckled my seat belt. "What do you mean?"

"After my call to Dylan about the charity event the night of Kit's performance, she talked to her mother-in-law. Evelyn Miller doesn't fuck around. She put the word out, and now Kenneth can't get an invite to save his life. Every socialite in New York knows he's a deadbeat. They don't want his money. He couldn't get invited to the opening of an Olive Garden in Times Square now."

When he looked at me, his grin was pure sex.

I resisted the urge to fan myself. Barely. I never could have guessed that messing with my ex-husband would be such an aphrodisiac.

As we drove through the city, I found myself looking out the window and daydreaming. But not about Vermont. Though the move should have been paramount in my mind, I couldn't stop thinking about Brian.

I should have been going through my mental checklists, preparing for the next phase of my life, yet all I wanted to do was ask him to be my boyfriend. Which was the most ridiculous, juvenile thing ever.

He was a rich, hot lawyer in his early forties. Men like that didn't have girlfriends. They took lovers, sophisticated European women who collected fine art.

Not hot-mess single moms like me. Yes, we'd had fun together in Boston. A lot of sexy, orgasmic fun. But that was done and over with.

My phone vibrated in my purse, forcing me to rein in my runaway thoughts. I breathed a sigh of relief, though it was quickly followed by a bolt of panic. Worrying that it was summer camp calling about an emergency, I dug it out quickly.

When the name of Kit's piano teacher appeared, I slumped back in my seat and slid my thumb over the screen to accept the call.

"Hello, Jessica," Jenine said. "Is this a good time?"

"Yes." I inhaled deeply and let the breath out through my nose, trying to compose myself.

Brian probably thought I was a complete train wreck.

I cleared my throat and forced a professional tone. "How can I help you?"

Jenine rarely called. She mostly sent long emails filled with details about Kit's performance and practice work that I could barely understand.

"I've secured Katherine an audition at PPAS."

I frowned. "Excuse me?" The Professional Performing Arts School was one of the best schools in the country. Thousands of students auditioned for only a few dozen spots every year.

She was silent for a moment, then, "She is going into sixth grade, correct?"

"Yes." I shifted in my seat. "But the application deadline was months ago. And we decided not to pursue it." PPAS had been Kit's dream for years. I'd agonized over the decision not to apply, but ultimately, after long talks, she and I had decided it was better to stay focused on moving to Vermont.

I was relieved, when we chose not to pursue it. For as talented as my daughter was, I wasn't sure a pressure cooker school filled with highly competitive musicians was the best thing for her at this age.

"Katherine asked. After the showcase last month," she explained. "I have a friend on the admissions committee, and apparently, this year's crop of applicants was... lacking."

I squeezed my eyes shut, frustrated that Kit had gone behind my back. "Jenine," I said, keeping my tone even. "I appreciate you pulling strings. But—"

"She's talented, Jessica. Talented and passionate. An elite school could open many doors."

I let out a sigh. It didn't seem possible for my life to get more complicated than it already was, yet here we were.

"Thank you, Jenine," I said firmly. "Send me the details and I'll consider it."

Once I'd disconnected the call, I threw my head back against the headrest. What other curveballs were coming today?

"You okay?"

"Yes," I said softly, my eyes closed. "Kit got an audition at a prestigious music school."

"That's fantastic."

"It is." My heart softened a fraction. I let my head loll to one side, taking in his profile. "She deserves all the best things. But I'm trying to get my kids out of the city and into a less intense life."

He nodded, his attention never leaving the road.

I considered not even mentioning it to Kit, but immediately, I threw that idea out. Guilt gnawed at my stomach at just the idea. I had to tell her. Auditioning would be a great experience for her, even if she didn't get admitted.

But what if she got in? Would she want to stay?

"So you guys are heading to Vermont to visit in a few days?" Brian asked, distracting me from my mom guilt.

"Thursday morning," I replied, forcing myself to sit up again. "I'm taking PTO. The plan is to get acclimated, then come back here the following weekend."

He peered at me, though he kept his face forward. "Do you have a moving date in mind?"

"Not yet," I said vaguely. "I've got a lot to wrap up here, and I haven't let myself think too much about it, just in case."

"Let me know how I can help."

As I nodded my acknowledgment, a pit opened up in my stomach. There was so much to celebrate. Instead, I just felt dread.

We drove the rest of the way to the office in silence.

While my brain should have been cartwheeling with plans and to-do lists, my thoughts had drifted elsewhere.

To Brian's genuine happiness for us. His commitment to helping me.

As we walked across the parking lot of his building, I wasn't consumed by thoughts of farm life and vast mountains, but the sinking sensation that I was close to losing something even more precious.

CHAPTER 29

Jess

Maplewood, Vermont, was the kind of idyllic, postcard town that people flocked to for a taste of authentic New England.

It was the place I'd spent the first half of my life trying to escape and the last several years trying to come back to.

"Can we get ice cream at Scoops?" Greta asked from the back of the car.

I smiled as I kept my focus on the road. "Of course."

"Can we hike to Cora's Rock and go behind the falls?" Kit added.

"We sure can." With every mile, my shoulders lowered, and now that we'd hit town limits, the tension had all but vanished. Already, I was itching to take my mat out into the maple grove. As a kid, I'd spent a great deal of time among the trees, sometimes jumping and maneuvering around the tubing, to get a little peace and quiet.

Three siblings, a working farm, and two parents who loved loudly made me crave stillness from time to time.

I was flooded with memories as I drove through town, passing the general store where I'd worked in high school, then Clem's Diner, where I'd drowned my sorrows in poutine after Joe Willis didn't ask me to prom.

Every building was pristine, making it feel like the complete opposite of Jersey City.

It was America's most charming small town, after all. A designation that was taken *very* seriously. Stoneridge, thirty miles north, had been angling to steal the title from us since before I was born. The rivalry had always been heated, and here and there, it turned ugly. Any person who'd grown up here had been raised to have an automatic dislike of any resident of Stoneridge. Like Maplewood, the town consisted mostly of farmland, mountains, and covered bridges. But we'd always had an edge, and every citizen worked hard to keep it that way.

Rural life had changed so much since I was a kid. The granite mining industry had died down, and most timber came from overseas, meaning there simply weren't many good-paying jobs to keep young people in state. If not for the tourists, I feared, this town would fall apart.

Some neighboring areas had been hit hard by opioids and the loss of manufacturing jobs, but Maplewood had survived. Berkshire Maple could be thanked for that. Though in part, the town was still thriving because the people here reinvested in it. The festivals, the covered bridges, and the waterfall brought people in for all four seasons, keeping shops and businesses open year-round.

After almost six hours in the car, the girls were desperate to escape. The moment the tires crunched over the long gravel drive, they cheered, and I'd barely shifted into park before they threw the doors open and ran straight through the field toward the river.

The temperature today was mild, though the air was sticky with that stifling humidity that descended every July.

As I popped the trunk and grabbed our bags, I considered which trail I'd walk to clear my head and stretch my legs. The distant clucking of the chickens in the far barn and the fresh air wafting around me further settled my nerves.

The farmhouse where we'd grown up had been transformed. Josh had added a shiny metal roof and new siding, and he'd expanded the porch to face the pastures and forest. When I stepped inside, I was certain I'd find even more improvements. Lately, I'd begun worrying about the number of projects my brother had taken on. But I supposed it wasn't unexpected. Josh had always had a restless mind that could only be quieted by working with his hands.

As I hauled our things up the path, admiring the black-eyed Susans and coreopsis blooming on either side, I yearned to text Brian.

To check on him. Show him the view and the wide blue skies.

Though just crossing the state line had relieved a good deal of stress I was under, we weren't here for vacation. Yes, I intended to rest and spend time with my family, but this was a working trip. I had many details to take care of in the week we'd be here. I had to register the girls for school, apply for jobs, and negotiate rent with Josh, who continued to insist that he wouldn't charge me at all.

Knowing him, he'd made significant changes to the cottage on the property. That alone had probably cost thousands, so there was no way I wouldn't contribute. He'd warned me the renovations weren't finished yet, so the girls and I would be staying at the farmhouse this week.

The thought of how I'd repay him instantly soured my mood.

Now that uprooting our lives had become a reality, the idyllic dream I'd held tight to had morphed into thoughts of all the tasks I'd have to complete.

I couldn't deny the pull of this place, the happy memories, and the slower pace. Vermont would be good for the girls and for me. Yet for the last several days, I'd begun to consider all we'd be leaving behind in Jersey.

Lana and Max, Kit's piano teacher, Greta's sports friends, Sloane and Lo. And, most importantly, Brian.

In a few short months, he'd become an irreplaceable part of my life. A friend and a confidant. And during that weekend in Boston, a lot more.

Josh appeared in the doorway of the barn, his baseball cap low, his beard untamed, and his giant dog, Bruce, at his side.

"Jessie," he called as he jogged toward me. Before I could argue that I didn't need help, he'd taken all the bags from my hands. "I'm so glad you're here."

Josh was the quiet one, but the brightness in his dark eyes gave him away. He was delighted to see me.

I threw my arms around him and, with my face buried in his chest, said, "I've missed you, little brother."

"Come on, I'll get you settled. I take it the girls are running wild and barefoot already?"

With a grin, I nodded. Then I pushed thoughts of Brian away. We were here now. Exactly where we were supposed to be.

While the girls played with their cousins that evening, Jenn and Mel made dinner. Mel had gone to culinary school and had once been an editor at a big-time food magazine in New York. She'd worked herself into burnout, then gone on a hiking trip in the Green Mountains to clear her head. She'd accomplished her goal, and she'd also met my sister.

She never went back.

While Jenn had always worn her hair pulled back and lived in Patagonia gear, her wife rocked a trendy buzz cut and designer clothes. Now, several years, a thriving coffee shop, and two sons later, Mel still hadn't lost her New York edge.

After the girls were in bed, as my siblings and I sat on the porch, watching the fireflies dance in the distance and catching up, my sister abruptly cut off the story she and Josh had been telling about the latest casualties in the town cheese war and shifted in her seat.

"How are you?" she asked, her brows pulled low in concern. "Really."

"I'm okay." I gave her a small smile.

She looked at Josh, and he eyed her in return. Jenn was the definition of overprotective oldest daughter, and Josh, while younger, was deeply protective and had been my rock during the divorce proceedings.

He'd paid the retainer needed to hire my first lawyer before the courts had ordered Kenneth to cover my legal fees. And he'd coached me through every step of the process. That had been back when Mom was alive and before we understood how bad things had gotten up here.

"I'm good," I said, my words more firm this time. It was the truth. Things had been so bad for so long, and I'd worked damn hard to turn it all around.

"He's leaving you alone, right?" Josh asked, his tone dark.

I nodded. Kenneth's harassing phone calls and texts had stopped a long time ago. And life had improved drastically for the girls and for me. Though the guilt of our broken family, the guilt of walking away and not pushing through, sometimes edged its way back into my mind.

Doubts about myself crept back in, whispering that I hadn't been good enough.

At first, the mental abuse was almost undetectable. It started small, with little criticisms and backhanded compliments. But then he'd get mad.

I would accompany him to a client dinner or an event, and after, in the car, he'd pick apart everything I'd said. He would get mad if I laughed too loud or talked too much. So I learned to be silent.

But even that wasn't good enough. From there, he more blatantly criticized my clothes, my hair, and my body.

It took time, but eventually I realized I'd never win. He had decided that he was superior, that he'd settled for me. And then the cracks began to show.

But I was a devoted wife. I took care of the girls, volunteered, and constantly networked, be it at the country club or at school fundraisers.

All with the hope that one day, he'd look at me and see my value.

That he'd see the beautiful family unit we'd built. That he'd want to fight to preserve it. So I stayed small and silent.

The family unit was beautiful and sacred. And I wanted that.

I would have done anything to keep it intact.

And I did. For years, I made myself smaller. I stopped voicing concerns and opinions, and I let him walk all over me.

Jenn squeezed my hand, silently supporting me. Only then did I realize I'd been lost in my thoughts.

I sniffled a bit, not wanting to put a damper on our reunion by rehashing the past. After the loss of our parents, we'd spent so many nights on this porch crying, grieving. It was time to make happier memories.

I reclined in my chair and focused on the sunset. I couldn't count the number of hours we'd sat out here. All six of us. Watching the sunset like this, counting the fireflies or just avoiding coming in to do homework while our parents rocked in their chairs, relaxing after a hard day's work.

"Farm looks great. And the house?" I asked, changing the subject. "It's astonishing. Did you secretly study interior design while we weren't paying attention?"

Josh hung his head, his lips curving into a bashful smile. "Not quite. You know I like projects."

I scoffed. "Repairing a fence is a project. Fixing a creaky stair is a project. You demo'd the aggressively eighties kitchen, bumped the wall out, reconfigured the layout, and outfitted it professionally. Martha Stewart would cut a bitch to have your kitchen."

Humor flashed in his eyes. "Is that a compliment?"

I threw a piece of popcorn at him. "Of course it's a compliment."

He lifted one shoulder and let it fall. "The farm runs itself."

Jenn snorted. "Farms do not run themselves. They're financial sinkholes that drain people of their labor and spirit." She sat forward in her chair. "You are a genius."

"I didn't do much. Just developed a few models, made some investments, and capitalized on market fluctuation."

"Blah, blah, financial genius bullshit." Eyeing me, she gestured to him with a thumb. "Do you believe this?"

"I do not," I replied. "You're amazing, and if your big sisters aren't gonna tell you, who will?"

Before he could downplay his accomplishments again, the sound of an engine coming up the drive caught our attention.

"Jas?" I said, getting to my feet. "He's back?"

Josh nodded. "'Course. You know how much he loves the girls." He shifted forward and lowered his voice. "He's been working extra shifts lately, so he's constantly exhausted. Something is definitely up with him."

Jas was young when we lost Dad, so he'd been raised by a grieving mother and his older sisters. I'd even go so far as to say that parenting tasks had mostly been crowdsourced. Several friends had helped out when they could.

And because of that—or maybe not; maybe it was just his nature—the boy was wild. Not dangerous wild, but fun wild.

Loved a party, found himself in all sorts of weird situations. Meeting celebrities, backpacking through countries I didn't even know existed, that sort of thing.

And he was a notorious ladies' man. The kid was the definition of charming. He didn't take himself too seriously, and he possessed a one-two punch of dimples and a six-pack.

His car, a Mustang, was his pride and joy, so though one would expect him to tear down the driveway like a bat out of hell, he rolled slowly, careful not to kick up stones.

"Jessie," he called as he climbed out.

I darted down the stairs and leaped into his arms, a piece of my heart locking into place. Jasper Lawrence was a goofy little kid in the body of a six-foot-three, heavily tattooed firefighter.

He spun me around until I shrieked, then put me on my feet and held my elbows to make sure I was steady.

"What is this?" I tugged at one side of his mustache. "What did you do to your handsome face?"

He ran his hands through his hair. "God, you sound like Mom. It's just something I'm trying."

"You look like a seventies porn star."

Smirking, he rubbed his jaw. "Can't grow a beard because of my respirator."

"You can't grow a beard at all," Josh joked, gesturing to his own full beard. "Not man enough."

Ignoring him, Jas gave me another hug. "I'm so happy you're here, Jessie. Where are my nieces?"

"Sleeping in the princess suite Josh made for them."

"Bummer. I rushed home hoping to catch them awake." He took a seat next to me. "The Sticky Notes are playing at the Drip Line tonight."

"Didn't you date the lead singer?" Jenn asked.

He dropped his head back and rocked, huffing. "No, that girl sang with Mapleback, and she moved to New York." Brow arched, he gave her a pointed look. "And you know I don't date. But since you asked, the new bartender is super cute." He leaned forward, eyeing Josh. "Wanna head over there with me? I'll buy you a beer and teach you to talk to women."

Josh shook his head, his expression serious. "Some of us have to get up and work in the morning. And I know how to talk to women. I just don't want to."

Jas stuck his tongue out, falling back into his role as the annoying little brother.

Jenn stood, her oldest sister instincts kicking in as well, and went inside to make him a plate of leftovers.

For the next hour, Jas fired off question after question, asking about our drive, the girls, my jobs, and the relocation request.

When the air got crisp, Josh slid a small blanket off the back of his chair and held it out to me.

The softness of the yarn in my hands brought back a powerful memory. One of my mom, rocking in this very chair, crocheting. Even after a long day of work and raising four kids, she still couldn't keep her hands still. Josh had clearly inherited that from her.

Every child born in this town had a blanket custom made by Maryann Lawrence, and she'd donated thousands of hats to the maternity ward at the county hospital over her lifetime.

As I sat here with my siblings, the ache of losing her filled me. There was so much I wanted to tell her. And, selfishly, I craved the way she would have looked at me with pride after I'd freed myself from a bad marriage. She'd never said a bad word about Kenneth, but she had never been particularly warm toward him either.

"Did Mom hate Kenneth?" I asked, interrupting the silence.

The three of them froze.

Jasper, with a roasted potato halfway to his mouth, went wide-eyed. "Um."

Josh gave Jenn a pointed look, and she sighed, her shoulders slumping.

"Yes," Jenn said. "She despised the man. She swore he was a covert narcissist, insisting that no one had realized it yet."

I pressed my lips together, considering, trying to recall a memory of any kind of comment like that she'd ever made to me. But I came up empty.

Jenn gave me a sympathetic smile. "But she loved you and wanted you to be happy."

"She'd always rant about how you could do better," Josh added. "How you needed a man who really saw you, who made you feel safe enough to be yourself. Who appreciated your quirks."

"Yes." Jenn added, "like that sweet guy you dated in college."

My heart lurched, and I stopped rocking. The move was apparently violent enough to draw everyone's attention, because suddenly, all eyes were on me.

"What?" Jenn asked.

Josh raised his eyebrows at me, ok I guess I had to tell her.

I fiddled with the blanket on my lap while I worked to school my features. I wasn't ashamed of hooking up with Brian, but it wasn't the sort of thing I wanted to admit at the moment. Especially given my track record with men.

"It's just funny that you mentioned Brian. My college boyfriend," I clarified. I squeezed my eyes shut for a moment.

"Why?"

"Funny story." I peeked one eye open, then the other. "He's actually my lawyer now."

"Brian? Tall redhead with the goofy smile?" Jenn asked.

"His hair is auburn," I corrected. "But yes. He's a hotshot attorney now. One of his partners has been coming into my studio for the last several months. He and his girlfriend convinced me that Brian could help me secure the court order to relocate to Vermont."

"And he did it," Josh said, rocking back.

I nodded, a smile breaking through. "He did. He's one of the best."

"Small world." Jasper shoveled another potato into his mouth, eyeing me with suspicion.

With a sigh, thankful the conversation was over, I scanned the horizon.

"What aren't you telling us?" Jenn asked, bursting the peaceful bubble I'd slipped into.

My stomach twisted, but I kept my expression neutral. "Nothing."

"Nope. Don't buy it." She grasped her armrests. "When you said his name, you broke into a dopey smile."

"He's become a friend." I shrugged. "His partners and their wives have too. The girls spend time with their kids too. And last month, Brian took us to see Lake Paige in Boston."

Jenn's eyes widened. "He got you Lake Paige tickets?"

I nodded, leaving it at that. If I mentioned the helicopter or the preshow meet-and-greet or the hotel penthouse makeovers, she'd lose her mind.

"That isn't the kind of shit a man who is just a lawyer does," she said.

"Or just a friend." Josh crossed his arms, protective brother mode clearly activated.

Jasper eyed me warily, still chewing.

I rolled my eyes, swatting at a bug. "It's not like that. I needed legal help, and he gave it. Throughout the process, we all became friends. We went to the concert, and sometimes he takes my yoga classes. That's it."

They eyed me and one another warily, but they dropped it when Jasper jumped in with a story about how Bitsy Brambles's goats got loose. He'd had to chase one through town before finally catching it in the alley behind the diner. His job as a firefighter and paramedic meant he always had wild stories to tell, and Jasper had the charisma to make even a run-of-the-mill small-town emergency sound fascinating.

By the end, he had us all howling, and soon after, the day had caught up with me, and I could barely keep my eyes open.

Mel and Jenn loaded up their sleeping kids and went home, and after I insisted that I'd do the last of the cleanup, Josh headed up to bed.

Mel had done the majority of the work, but Jasper and I finished loading the dishwasher, and as I wiped down the counters, I mentally went through my to-do list for the next day.

"Jessie."

I turned to my baby brother, smiling softly at the way his hair flopped into his face like it did when he was a little boy, then chuckling at his ridiculous mustache.

"I know you're in love with him," he said quietly. "That Brian guy. I don't remember him. I was probably too busy running through the barnyard and fields to even talk to him, but Mom mentioned him a few times. Said he was the one that got away."

I shook my head. "I'm not."

"Everyone thinks I'm the dumb, oblivious one."

That got my attention. He was a barrel of fun, yes, but I'd never once thought he was dumb. Before I could tell him that, though, he held up a hand.

"But I know what I saw when you talked about him. It's okay. I won't tell Josh and Jenn." His lips twitched. "You know how those two get."

I stared at him in the dim light, unable to come up with a denial.

He squeezed me tight and kissed the top of my head, then padded to the stairs.

"I'm happy for you, sis," he said over his shoulder. "You deserve good things."

His words rang in my ears as I got ready for bed. Because he was right.

I was happy to be back in Vermont.

But something was missing.

Or rather, someone.

CHAPTER 30

Brian

"You're scaring me," Sully said, gripping the edge of my desk. "You gotta get it together. You do need to sleep once in a while."

As I loosened my tie, I glared at him. "I'm fine."

He shook his head and snagged the walkie off my desk.

"Code red. Brian's throwing a nutter. Need backup."

Before I could throw a stapler at him, Cal and Lo appeared, both panting like they'd run down the stairs.

"What are we dealing with?" Lo asked. "Is it like when Judge Walsh deleted the motion? Or when Fuzzy peed on the Gainsborough exhibits thirty minutes before trial?"

"Worse." Sully roughed a hand down his face. "He's gone mental because his girl is gone and he's finally realizing he's in love with her."

"Bugger," Cal hissed. "We knew this day was coming but..." He checked his watch. "I thought we had at least a couple more weeks."

The three of them looked both deeply satisfied and confused as they crowded into my small office, blocking the door so I couldn't escape this bullshit.

I eyed the window, cursing the bars that played a role in holding me captive.

Of course I missed Jess and the girls. They'd become daily fixtures in my life. Without them, I had nothing but work and the damn cat lying on top of the file cabinet, flicking his tail. The life I'd lived happily for decades was suddenly a joyless prison. My mood had been shit, and my knuckles were bruised and bloody from all the boxing I'd been doing in an attempt to cope.

For my whole career, all it had taken was securing a win for a client to fill me with a deep sense of satisfaction. This job was my life, and I took pride in helping people.

But since the day Judge Gordon issued the order, giving Jess legal permission to relocate to Vermont, my life had felt empty.

That first day, the overwhelming emotions had been relief and pride, of course. Because I'd won for her.

But within hours, reality had set in.

She was leaving. I'd helped her leave.

I'd worked my ass off to pull off a legal miracle, and in doing so, I'd paved the road the people who meant so much to me needed so they could walk away.

My brain could not reconcile the goal I'd attained with the storm of emotions churning in my chest. Winning felt like losing.

But she'd been so damn happy.

Her beautiful face had lit up, and she'd hugged me fiercely just outside the courtroom.

"I don't want to talk about this." I sat up and focused on my computer, blindly moving the mouse and clicking. Maybe I'd been a bit bearish since they'd gone to Vermont a few days ago—and how could I not be, now that the reality of living without them was settling in?—but come on, I had work to do. We *all* had work to do.

Lo put her hands on her hips. "Tough. It needs to happen."

"Have you at least called her?" Sully asked.

"No, of course not," I replied without taking my eyes off the screen.

"Why not?"

Because I had no right to. We weren't dating. We weren't anything. We had been lawyer and client. Now that the representation agreement had been fulfilled, we were nothing to each other.

"There is no reason to bother her. Her legal matters are wrapped up."

Lo threw her hands up in frustration. "What about Boston?"

The sharpness of her tone caused me to stare at her. How the hell did she know about Boston?

"He's in denial." Sloane appeared, baby monitor in hand. "He's in love with her and can't figure out how to accept it and move forward."

"So emotional constipation?" Cal asked.

Sloane chuckled. "You could say that."

"Can you all please stop talking about me like I'm not here?" I asked, my rage barely contained.

"No." Cal tossed a mini basketball into the air and caught it. "You can't just stomp around this building all day and night, growling at everyone. You've got to tell her how you feel."

Sully nodded. "Sloane said she'd smother you with a maple-scented pillow in your sleep if you didn't stop snapping at us."

Sloane smiled at him, hearts in her eyes.

"You've got to do something," Sully said. "Make the gesture. Take the leap. Learn from me, mate. It's worth it."

He put his arm around his wife and kissed the top of her head.

That's when it hit me.

I only had one shot at this. The two of them had almost gotten divorced, for fuck's sake. They'd been dangerously close to losing one another because they'd both been stubborn. And here I was, sitting in my office, having a nervous breakdown.

"I need to go to Vermont," I said.

My friends gave me looks that ranged from curious to smug.

Now that I'd put the words out there, it was as if a lightbulb had turned on. I needed to go to Vermont and see Jess.

Despite the complex situation I was in, this was simple.

"When?"

"Now," I replied, logging off and powering down my computer. "I'm going now."

"It's eleven p.m."

"So?" I plucked my briefcase off the floor and confirmed that my laptop and charger were inside it. "I've got a tank of gas and some feelings to work through."

"Do you need company?" Cal asked. "We can come along for the ride."

I shook my head. "Nah. The solitude will do me good."

"I'll pack snacks for you," Sloane said, slipping into mom mode, "And brew some coffee."

"I'll clear your calendar for the rest of the week," Lo chimed in.

"You should propose," Cal quipped.

Sloane and Lo shot him matching dirty looks.

"May want to be a bit more subtle." Sully glowered at his brother, then focused on me, brow arched. "When are you coming back?"

"I don't know." And I wasn't sure I cared. If Jess was in Vermont. I wanted to be in Vermont. End of story. In this moment, nothing else mattered.

I climbed the steps two at a time and packed a bag, my mind totally clear. With my toothbrush and toiletries packed, I said goodbye to the cat. Then I headed for the car.

For the first time in as long as I could remember, as I strode across the parking lot, my thoughts weren't racing. My objective was clear.

I had to go get my girl.

It wasn't until I'd crossed the GW Bridge that I realized I didn't know where I was going. Luckily, when I called Lo, I discovered that she was ten steps ahead of me. She texted the address of Jess's family farm, and once I clicked *Go* on the GPS, a wave of relief hit me. I'd head there and then figure the rest out. It was the middle of the night, so traffic was nonexistent, and as I reached the town of Maplewood, Vermont, the sun was beginning to rise.

This place was charming as hell. Everywhere I looked, I found picture-perfect rolling hills and farmland, flanked by green mountains and a vast, cloudless sky.

Since it was only five, I stopped in town for coffee and to stretch my legs. I'd visited the farm once during the summer between my junior and senior years of college but didn't remember much about the town itself.

In the early morning light, when the only sounds were the wind rustling in nearby trees and birdsong, it was like walking onto a movie set. The downtown area looked like the definition of New England, with cobblestone sidewalks, Revolutionary War monuments, colorful shops, and impeccable landscaping.

I parked along the street in front of a hipster-looking coffee shop called Bean There, Sipped That and headed in, desperate for a hit of caffeine.

When I checked my reflection in the rearview mirror, I almost didn't recognize myself. My hair was a disaster, probably because I'd run my hands through it repeatedly to keep myself awake. I hadn't trimmed my beard in a week, and today, it had officially begun veering into mountain hermit territory. Then there were the dark circles under my eyes that looked more like bruises. Shit, I was a mess.

The shop was mostly empty, though there were a few older folks sipping from large cobalt blue mugs in one corner. Their eyes followed me intently as I approached the counter.

On one wall was a massive mural of the mountains I'd admired on the way in, with hand-painted road signs displaying the distance to various world landmarks.

The other was dominated by a chalkboard menu with every type of drink one could imagine and an impressive selection of pastries and breakfast sandwiches, each with special notes about the origin and sustainability of its ingredients.

The lanky teen behind the counter looked me up and down, his lip curled with what might have been disgust, though his question held a hint of concern. "You okay, dude?"

"Um, yes," I replied awkwardly. "Can I get a large black coffee, please? And one of those croissants."

He pulled a large mug that matched the ones the patrons were using from under the counter.

"Can I get that to go, please?" I asked, pointing at it.

"Did you bring a reusable mug?" he asked, his pierced brow arched, his teenage attitude on display. It was impressive for such an early morning, really.

"No."

"So you're okay with killing a tree so you can have a cup of coffee?"

His words barely registered. I was too lost to sleep deprivation and caffeine withdrawal. In hindsight, I'd really let myself go to hell since Jess left last week.

"Sure," I replied, eye twitching.

With a scowl, he produced a cardboard cup from under the counter.

"Hey, kid," I asked as he poured. "What day is it?"

He peered at me over his shoulder. "Monday."

"Munchkin Monday," I murmured. "Do you have Munchkins?"

"Does this look like a Dunkin' Donuts to you?" he snapped back.

I rolled my eyes. Teenagers.

Frowning, I scanned the bakery case, which was the size of a school bus and filled with dozens of amazing-looking treats.

"Can I get a few donuts, then?"

He set the coffee beside the register and grabbed an empty box. Then he looked at me expectantly.

I did a few calculations in my head, though my thoughts were jumbled. Jess was at the farm with the girls and her brothers and her sister and her kids. I should get a lot. Plus, they looked delicious, and I couldn't remember the last time I'd had a donut, so I wouldn't mind having more than one. Or leftovers.

"That one." I pointed to the top shelf. "The lemon curd—no, make it two. And three of the maple bacon. Nah, I'll eat those while driving. Just give me all the maple bacon. And the Mexican chocolate ones too."

The kid dropped the donut in his hand into the box and leaned back. "Hey, Mom," he hollered. "There's an unhoused guy in a suit out here who wants to buy all the maple bacons."

A moment later, the kitchen door swung open and a plump woman with a blond ponytail and a full sleeve came striding out.

"Elijah. What are you talking ab—oh, shit."

She froze in the doorway, her eyes going wide. "You're here."

I studied her, trying to place her, but my exhausted brain and blurry eyes made it impossible.

She dropped the last few donuts into the box and shoved them at me. "Take 'em. Elijah." She turned to the teen. "Give him the lavender-infused vanilla. Those are her favorite."

As he dropped a couple of those into a bag, I pulled out my wallet.

The woman shoved the bag into my face and waved me off.

"But I have to pay."

"Later." She pointed to the door. "Just go. Huge red sign. Can't miss the farm."

CHAPTER 31

Jess

I was standing on the porch when the car came up the drive. Jenn had texted, giving me a heads-up, while the girls and I were feeding the chickens. I left them to finish up while I jogged back to the house.

My heart fluttered as I caught a glimpse of his car coming up the drive. I'd missed him. More than I'd expected. More than I thought I could miss someone.

Especially a man I wasn't even dating.

But over the last several weeks, Brian had become a fixture in my life, and although my days here were busy, I'd thought about him constantly.

When he stepped out of his car, his suit wrinkled and a look of exhaustion on his face, my heart ached. Even like this, he was handsome.

His expression morphed into something more bashful as he caught sight of me.

"Get over here," I said, opening my arms.

He obeyed without hesitation, and when he got close, I threw my arms around his neck.

"I missed you," he said into my hair.

His warmth enveloped me, bringing with it a peace I didn't realize I needed. "Did you drive all night?"

He backed away and nodded, running his hand through his hair, which was sticking up on one side of his head. "How did you know I was coming?"

"You caused a stir in town. Not many racing green Audis up here."

"It's not even six."

"Farm town." I smirked. "Also, my sister texted me. She owns the coffee shop."

"Ah. I knew she looked familiar."

I looked down at my phone screen and read the message she sent. "She said 'a lovesick dude in a five-thousand-dollar suit just came in asking for Munchkins. I assume he belongs to you?'"

He smiled. "Do I? Belong to you?"

The sincerity, the uncertainty, in his voice made my stomach drop.

"Let's get you inside." I grasped his arm. "You look exhausted. You didn't have to drive all night, you know. You could have called."

"I wanted to see your pretty face." He caressed my cheek with the back of his fingers. "And I wanted to touch you."

My knees wobbled. This was so strange and awkward but maybe the most romantic moment of my life.

Blushing, I looked away, only to spot Josh and Jasper with their arms resting on a nearby fence, spying on us.

"We have an audience," I declared, nodding toward them.

Brian waved at them, though he never took his eyes off me.

"I brought Munchkin Monday donuts," he rasped. His voice was thick, his words slow. "They are not Munchkins. The kid at the store was very offended when I asked. Which makes sense." He frowned. "They are not holes. But they have holes? Wait, I'm confused. Anyway, I bought a few dozen."

He stumbled toward the car and opened the passenger seat. "Delicious," I said, following him. "But let's get you inside. Do you want to take a nap or a shower?"

"I don't want to impose." He clutched the donut box to his chest. "There's an inn nearby. Lo made a reservation."

"You're staying here," I said firmly.

"You can send me home." His eyelids were heavy and his feet

dragged in the gravel as I guided him to the porch. "I know I'm interrupting. But I was going crazy without you."

God, could this be any more adorable?

"I want you here. With us," I said.

A slow smile spread across his face.

"But," I hedged, "you need to sleep for a little bit."

The smile turned a little wicked. "Will you nap with me?"

The warmth that had settled into me when we first touched burned hotter. "Only if you promise to behave."

"I don't think I have a choice. Your brothers look pissed." He peered over my shoulder at them. They'd now left their post at the fence and were wandering this way.

"Don't mind them. The town text chain has been blowing up. They're just curious."

I led him into the house, and when my brothers followed, I made introductions. By the curiosity in Jasper's eyes and the look of concern Josh wore, it was obvious they had questions, but I left them to stew in them, and eat donuts, while I took Brian up to my old bedroom.

Josh had upgraded the space significantly since I'd lived here. Rather than a twin, a queen-size bed sat centered on one side of the room. The sky-blue quilt brightened the space, complementing the board-and-batten walls perfectly. Above, a wooden ceiling fan circled lazily, and the floors that had once creaked terribly were mostly silent.

He'd even found photos I'd taken in high school, when I was certain I wanted to be a professional photographer, and had framed them and used them to create a gallery wall. It was technically home, though with all the changes, I felt like a guest.

"I want to hear all about Vermont." Brian dropped heavily onto the bed, head tipped back, his bloodshot eyes on me.

"Later," I said, giving him a gentle shove. "Take a nap first. I'll show you all the sights as soon as you've rested."

I gestured for his phone and plugged it in on the nightstand. Before I could back away, he snaked a long arm out, looping it around my waist, and pulled me onto the bed. When I was flush against him, he sighed.

"Five minutes," he whispered into my ear as the comfort of his body relaxed me and his scent flooded my senses. "I've been dreaming about this."

He was asleep, breathing softly into my neck, minutes later.

I was still in shock that he was here. But as he held me, I closed my eyes and allowed myself to savor the relief of having him close.

I'd missed him more than I could have imagined. And every day, no matter how hard I tried, I found little enjoyment. Because I knew without a doubt that every activity would be so much better if he were here with me.

We had a lot to talk about, especially after his spontaneous all-night road trip. But for now, I let myself relax.

CHAPTER 32
Brian

While I was being given the official town tour, I discovered just how right Jess had been when she said I caused a stir. People here were quite curious about me. As I was being shown around, I was led up and down every street in the downtown area and forced to consume goods from every store, including two cheese shops. We'd spent the afternoon hiking a long trail to the town's famous waterfall, and then the girls had led us to a tiny secret cavern behind the falls. I was too big to fit, but I took photos of them posing.

Greta and Kit—especially serious Kit—seemed so much younger here. They were more carefree, running barefoot while collecting eggs and giving me a tour of the sugar shack where they boiled syrup every spring.

We laughed, spent most of the day outside, and ate ungodly amounts of delicious food. I could see why Jess loved it here. The entire town shone with joy and charm.

Back at the farmhouse, no one mentioned the little snuggle nap Jess and I had taken. Though when I woke up, I was subjected to questions from both her brothers.

Josh, who'd been a teenager when I visited twenty years ago, was now a broad, serious investment banker turned maple farmer. Jasper, the baby of the family, had been a little boy when I met him. Now, he was a tall, lanky fireman covered with tattoos, and he sported the kind of confidence that came with being under thirty and having visible abs.

While neither of them had explicitly asked about my intentions, I got the sense that we were two beers away from a full-blown interrogation.

I'd spent the day preparing for the eventuality. So when two little spitfires cornered me after dinner, I was thrown off-kilter.

When Kit and Greta asked me to help them get a few board games from the upstairs closet, I gladly followed them. Yet as I peered into the open closet, Kit shut the bedroom door behind her and crossed her arms over her chest.

"We need to talk to you," she said.

Greta stood next to her, making sure to block my exit. "Have a seat." She gestured to an old wooden rocking chair next to a large picture window.

I eased into the seat, careful to make sure it was sturdy before giving it all my weight. My heart hammered, because the serious expressions the girls wore were unfamiliar and a tad worrisome.

Five minutes ago, they had been competing with their cousins to see who could fit the most brownies in their mouths, cackling and full of glee. Greta, in fact, still had some chocolate smeared above her lip. Yet here we were, and by the way they scrutinized me, it was clear they meant business.

"Our mom is awesome," Kit said.

"The best," Greta echoed.

"And our dad sucks."

"Kit." Greta's little brown eyes widened in shock.

"You know it's true." She huffed. "He doesn't think of anyone but himself."

Greta's lips turned down, but she nodded in agreement.

I was tempted to get up and hug her. Kenneth was a motherfucker. Right here, as I sat waiting for their lecture, I vowed to find more ways to fuck up his life when I got back to Jersey.

"We made a deal that we would never let anyone hurt her."

I surveyed the girls, who both looked so much like Jess. "I would never hurt your mom."

Greta's body relaxed like she was satisfied with my response, but Kit only narrowed her eyes.

"I told you to stay away from her. But now she's all giggly and happy and talks about you all the time." She sighed. "She hasn't been herself since we came up here, but then you show up, and suddenly she's smiling again."

My heart swelled with pride and hope. My rash decision to come here had been out of the ordinary for me, but the moment I stepped out of my car and Jess smiled at me, I'd known it was right. I wanted to be here. Jess, Kit, and Greta were my people.

"We also agreed that we would not let her date anyone unless they were extremely super awesome and got our approval."

"How does one earn your approval?" I asked in my most professional tone. "Is there a written application? Lo can prepare some paperwork."

Kit smirked. "Just an interview."

"An interview? Will I have time to prepare?"

"Sure. But we're gonna be tough."

"Bring it, kiddos, because I really like your mom."

The girls looked at one another, and Greta giggled. Kit, to her credit, did not, but I swore her lips twitched.

"That's a good start," Greta said, giving me a thumbs-up.

Kit nodded. "But this isn't over."

I couldn't help but grin. "Your mom is lucky to have you."

After I was released from the first of what looked like it would be a series of interrogations, I headed downstairs and found that everyone had migrated outside. Josh had built a massive outdoor fire, and Jenn's boys were already roasting marshmallows. Kit and Greta darted over, grinning and squealing, as if they hadn't just been giving me the third degree upstairs.

As I strolled closer, dogs and shockingly domesticated goats ran around me.

"Didn't you visit once, years ago?" Jenn asked as she poured a finger of maple whiskey into a glass.

I nodded. "Between my junior and senior years of college. Your parents were very kind to me."

"My mom liked you," she said, holding the glass out to me. "And she was a good judge of character."

"I'm sorry for your loss," I replied, my tone subdued, knowing how raw the wound still was for Jess.

The four of them reminisced a bit, talking about their parents and the hijinks they used to get up to on the farm, then catching up on town gossip. I listened quietly, content to let the warmth of the fire and the good company wash over me.

After Jess got her kids to bed, Jasper stood and stretched. "I'm out. Don't wait up."

"Where are you going?" Josh asked with a frown.

Jasper shot him a wink. "Bachelorette party at Timberline." With a wave, he jogged to his Mustang.

"Don't do anything stupid," Josh yelled after him.

Jasper barked out a laugh without turning back. "I always do."

"It's like he's still sixteen," Jenn said.

Josh stood and added wood to the fire. "Someday he'll calm down."

Jess perched on the arm of my Adirondack chair, her movements languid, like the whiskey was loosening her up.

While Josh poked at the fire and Jenn had her face buried in her phone—probably texting her wife, who'd taken the kids home—Jess leaned against my shoulder. "I still can't believe it," she murmured. "That you came all the way here."

"It's not far."

She frowned down at me. "But what about work?"

"The guys got me covered, and Lo moved all my meetings. Trust me, they practically kicked me out the door. I've been such a bastard since you left."

"Really?"

"Yes." I roughed a hand down my face. "I was a bear without you."

She broke into a slow smile. She looked so beautiful illuminated by the firelight. I wanted to pull her into my lap and kiss her senseless. But the presence of her siblings and the various farm animals kept me in check.

"Do you want to take a walk?" she asked softly.

My chest tightened. It was as if she'd read my mind. "Sure."

She took my whiskey glass and set it down on the small table beside my chair. Then she grasped my hand, encouraging me to stand. With a quick farewell to her siblings, she guided me away.

But she didn't lead me back toward the farmhouse.

"Where are we going?"

"My secret spot," she said with a devilish grin.

We were quiet as we strolled hand in hand down the dirt road that led to barns, paddocks, and what looked to me—a man who knew nothing about farms—like storage sheds.

"This place is magical," I eventually said.

"Yes," she sighed. "This is the best time of the year. The animals all have babies, and everything is in bloom. Early fall is incredible too. Those couple of weeks when the leaves change, before they've fallen, offer some of the most beautiful views I've ever seen. But then Halloween hits, and from there, it's nonstop snow and darkness until May."

We fell into silence again, and shortly after the house was completely out of sight, Jess stopped and turned to me.

"Why did you come here?" She nibbled her bottom lip, her dark eyes depthless in the moonlight. "Does it mean what I think it means?"

"It means whatever you want it to mean. I'm selfish. I needed to see you. But say the word and I'll be back on the road. I will never pressure or push you." My hands suddenly felt slick. I only hoped she didn't notice. "I just want to be around you."

"I'm moving." Her tone was sad, defeated.

"I know." I kicked at the ground, head lowered. "Lo has already sent me the paperwork I'd need to apply to the Vermont bar."

She tilted her head back and let out a laugh. "Of course she did."

"I just want to be with you." I tucked a strand of hair behind her ear. "The rest is logistics."

"But logistics matter," she insisted.

I brought her hand to my chest and pressed it to my heart. "Not as much as you and the girls do."

Blinking rapidly, she stood on her tiptoes. For a moment, she studied my face. Then, in one quick move, she pulled me down into a searing kiss.

Our mouths tangled in desperation as I grasped her hips and she clawed at my chest. This wasn't a sweet kiss. It was pure lust, driven by the deprivation we'd sentenced ourselves to for the last few weeks. We were explosive together, and as I ground against her, keeping her locked to my body, it was more apparent than ever.

When we were out of breath, she pulled away and tugged me toward the tree line. "Follow me."

I jogged along, sticking close as she darted behind a small barn at the edge of the wood.

"Where are you taking me?"

"The only place we can truly have privacy in this damn town," she replied over her shoulder.

As we approached another small, darkened building, she pulled a tiny flashlight out of the back pocket of her jean shorts and opened the door.

"This is my secret spot," she said, leading me inside.

It was mostly empty and had been swept clean, though there were a few boxes and some equipment stacked in the back.

"My mom briefly went through a pottery phase," she explained. "She used to come out here and make misshapen coffee mugs just to get away from us."

She shone the flashlight around the space.

"It's too small for livestock and not quite big enough to fit the large tractor. But it's sturdy and well-maintained."

The ceiling was lined with decorative trusses, and several large windows on one wall were all that separated us from the maple forest.

"It's kind of beautiful," I said.

"My grandfather built it. I'm in love with the architecture. I always dreamed of converting it into a little house. Like a barndominium-type of thing."

Lips pressed together, I nodded. "I could see that."

"Come on, we're going up to the hayloft." She waggled her brows.

I bit back a grimace at the thought of literally rolling in the hay. I was a city boy, and never in my life had it been more apparent than now.

"There's no hay," she said, clearly reading my mind. "That would be scratchy and terrible. Come on."

I followed her up the narrow staircase to the open loft, and at the top, I peered down at the barn below, noting the beach chairs and a couple of lanterns, then turned back to scan this space. "Are those sleeping bags?"

She smiled at me. "Yup. I thought maybe I'd bring you up here. Seduce you, farm-girl style."

CHAPTER 33

Jess

Brian wasted no time. His lips and hands were all over me the minute the words left my mouth.

And he wouldn't hear a complaint from me. I'd barely been able to keep my panties on all day.

He'd come all this way to see me. He'd missed me.

And he'd told me that, with words, repeatedly.

My heart could barely contain my happiness.

He guided me to the floor, the sleeping bags our only padding, and undid the buttons on my jean shorts. "If you don't let me eat this sweet pussy, I think I'll die," he said. "I've thought of nothing but the taste of you for weeks."

Heat flooded my core. Damn.

I was a generous gal, so I was more than willing to give this man anything he asked for.

Once he'd tossed my shorts and panties aside, he clutched my hips and pulled me closer, throwing my legs over his shoulders and spreading me wide.

In seconds, I was babbling incoherently. Every flick of his tongue sent me spiraling further into the abyss.

I'd missed this. Intimacy, trust, and experimentation. Being with Brian felt both safe and exhilarating.

The comfort of being with him spurred me to chase what I wanted without abandon. So I grasped his hair, pulling him closer, and rolled my hips.

"*Yes,*" he growled, sinking one finger inside me. "Ride my face."

I had no choice but to comply. The combination of his hands and mouth was life-altering. Damn, he knew what he was doing. Over and over, he teased me, bringing me to the edge, then backing down again.

From the sounds he made, I swore he enjoyed it as much as I did, edging me closer and closer.

"You are a sadist," I cried out, my voice echoing off the rafters.

As he withdrew his fingers and licked them clean, my body felt like a bomb about to detonate.

"Delicious," he growled. "If you want to come," he said, lowering his face and ghosting his lips over my clit, "all you have to do is ask."

"Please," I squeaked. "Please, you are so fucking good at this."

He smiled up at me from between my legs and dove back in, licking and sucking until I was hit by a massive wave of bliss.

I cried out, my legs shaking as he pinned me to the sleeping bag.

"Keep going," he growled, not stopping the sensations that were making me scream.

"I-I can't—"

He trailed one finger down my crease, gently teasing at my back door. "Yes, you can." He insisted. He massaged the area while flicking my clit with his tongue.

Before I could argue, he pushed his finger inside me, filling me completely, and another orgasm washed over me, leaving me unable to speak.

I wasn't in a barn on the family farm. I was floating through space, because pleasure like this did not exist on earth. I clenched around his fingers as wave after wave hit me.

"You are such a good girl," he said, pressing a kiss to my stomach as I ran my fingers through his hair.

"Brian," I said softly. "I can barely speak."

The grin that spread across his face was one of the sexiest things I'd ever seen.

"No need. On all fours, farm girl," he commanded.

I happily obliged, scrambling onto my knees and throwing him a saucy look over my shoulder.

"My God," he said, caressing my hips. "What did I do to deserve you?"

He stood and shucked his pants, then pulled a condom out of one pocket.

"Look at you," I said. "Being the prepared one this time."

His eyes glimmered in the low light. "I'm an optimist."

He was sheathed and pushing inside me in the blink of an eye, his hands on my hips.

"That's it." He groaned. "Perfect. Relax, Jess. You've got this."

I threw my head back, my nerve endings lighting up. He was both rough and gentle and hitting every single spot that drove me crazy. A cry escaped me, the aftershocks from the mega orgasm hitting. But damn if I wasn't ready for more.

He ran his fingers gently down my spine while thrusting forcefully, making me feel safe and defiled all at once. I didn't normally enjoy this position, but the feel of him dominating me made me feel safe and cherished. Like I was giving myself and my pleasure over to him, and he knew exactly how to take care of me.

Spreading me wider, he thrust deeper, making me cry out, causing my pussy to pulse around him. "You just got tighter," he growled. "That's it. Come again for me." His fingers found my clit, and I almost blacked out, my arms shaking as he picked up the pace.

Just as I thought this man could not wring any more pleasure out of my forty-one-year-old body, I detonated, sheer bliss firing through every nerve ending as I moaned his name.

Cursing, he chased his own orgasm, following me quickly over the edge.

We lay on the sleeping bags, sweaty and spent, staring up at the moonlight sneaking through the roof trusses. "I fucking love Vermont," he said, burying his face in my hair.

"I think farm life agrees with you," I replied.

He kissed his way down my neck. "It could be that. Or I'm just in love with a hot farm girl."

CHAPTER 34

Jess

"Do I need to come out and ask, or are you gonna give up the goods?" Sloane asked.

"*Yes*. It's just us," Lo purred. "We know something happened, and we're so happy for you."

She and Sloane had come to my restorative class tonight and had stayed after to help me stack the blocks and wipe down the mats.

Lana, who was extinguishing candles, smirked. She'd covered my classes while I was in Vermont and had bonded with Lo and Sloane. I'd given her some details during my drive back to Jersey, free to talk openly since the girls had convinced me to let them stay another week with Josh. I already missed them, but it was nice to have a break.

Especially because things with Brian had heated up so quickly. He'd headed home the day before I did, and from the moment he parked his car in the lot, he'd texted me almost hourly. And when I got home? I found him waiting out in front of the studio, pacing the sidewalk. We'd spent the night together and woken up with our limbs intertwined.

I pretended to be deeply involved in hanging straps from the hooks on the walls, hoping, in vain, that they'd drop it.

"You two aren't fooling anyone," Sloane said, crossing her arms and narrowing her eyes. "I've known Brian since law school. I can read him like a book."

"He's been so smiley." Lo clapped, giddy. "Cal hit him in the head with his basketball the other day during a meeting, and he just smiled."

I turned to face them, finding them standing only a few feet from me.

"Did you two plan this?" I asked, looking from a grinning Lo to a more serious Sloane. "The good cop, bad cop routine?"

Lo smirked. "I'm flattered you think I'm the good cop." She put her hands on her hips. "And no. We're just that good. So give it up. We know Brian, and we know something happened. He left here a rabid dog and came home a cuddly puppy."

Lana put her arm around my shoulder. "And I know you. I swear you're walking a little funny. Not to mention the constant singing to yourself." She leaned in closer to Lo and Sloane. "Our girl is in love."

"Lana," I hissed.

Sloane waved dismissively. "You're among friends."

"Do you need wine for this?" Lo asked.

I shook my head. "I'm just working out my feelings right now. I'm not ready to talk about it."

"You've clearly been working something else too," Lana said with a wink.

My face flamed, and I prayed the floor would open up and swallow me so I wouldn't have to put up with the teasing.

Lo fist-pumped. "I knew it."

"Come on. Let's order dinner and get the details out of her," Lana said, rubbing her hands together.

Once the four of us were settled in my apartment with Thai food, the pressure to spill my secrets became too high.

"I think I'm in love with him," I admitted into my Pad Kra Pao.

"'Course you are."

"It happened to both of us," Sloane said, thumbing at Lo, then herself.

"Me too," Lana said. "When I met Max, I wasn't interested. The next thing I knew, I was pregnant with his child and changing my name."

"But what do I even do?" In Vermont, I found myself living in the moment, and it had all seemed too easy. But back in Jersey, as I began packing up my apartment, it was clear we had no future.

"I'm moving to Vermont," I reminded them as I dropped my chopsticks into the cardboard container.

Sloane hummed. "That's not necessarily a deal-breaker. But tell us more. What's the plan? What's in Vermont that you can't get in Jersey?"

I sipped my water while I worked through how to explain the situation. It was complicated. Vermont wasn't just a place; it was an idea.

A goal.

A town where the girls and I could be happy and healthy. Where I could put distance between myself and my failed marriage.

But lately, I couldn't help but wonder if that was the right thing to do.

I'd begun to consider that maybe it would be better to own my story than to run from it.

"Family," I finally said, keeping the rest of those thoughts to myself. "My parents are gone, but my sister and brothers are there. It's a lot cheaper to live up there, and it's slower-paced."

The girls all nodded, splitting their attention between their food and me.

"I had a great childhood. I want that for my kids. Running through the woods, farm chores, spending so much time outside."

"What about Kit? Can she continue her piano studies there?" Sloane asked. "Sully has been raving about her since he and T. J. went to the concert."

My stomach sank. "Sort of," I hedged.

Vermont did not offer anything close to the opportunities she had here, but...

"Her teacher is going to continue to work with her virtually," I explained. "And my brother is restoring an old piano so she can play at home."

What I didn't mention was that there would be no showcases with the best and brightest and no specialized program at school. I could probably negotiate with the local junior high to get her some practice time, but we wouldn't be footsteps away from world-class musicians and teachers.

I closed my eyes.

My nose burned, and tears pricked at the backs of my eyes. "Sorry." I dabbed at my face with my napkin. "It's hard. Moving would be so good for all of us. It would give us a support network and allow the girls an idyllic childhood. But in moments like these, I start to doubt myself."

Lana grasped my knee and squeezed.

I sniffled and shook my head, straightening. "My daughters were born in the city, and part of me will always love New York."

Sloane nodded slowly. "I can relate. For a while there, I was unhappy. I'd lost my identity, and Sully and I even lost our way. During that time, I convinced myself I needed big changes. A totally fresh start."

My heart ached for her and her husband. I didn't know the entire story, but I'd heard enough to understand that they had come very close to divorce.

"I was convinced I needed space from Sully in order to grow and find the person I was destined to be. But in the end, I found my fresh start with him. He supported me and encouraged me. He cheered me on as I rediscovered who I was and helped me figure out what I really wanted."

"That's beautiful." I patted her hand. She was truly blessed to have ended up where she was now. What must it feel like to be loved so deeply?

"Just take your time and think things through," she cautioned. "In my case, what I discovered when I really took the time to reflect was that my marriage wasn't holding me back. I was holding myself back."

I nodded politely, cleaning up to avoid making eye contact.

Her words stung. But I'd needed to hear them. I'd spent the last few years completely focused on Vermont, believing that moving there would be the answer to all of my problems.

But I was beginning to think that I'd missed the forest for the maple trees.

And that maybe the girls and I didn't need Vermont to have a fresh start and follow our dreams.

CHAPTER 35
Brian

"Do you like it?" I asked, stuffing my sweaty hands into my pockets. I hadn't set foot in here in months, and given that I'd lived in this house for seven years before I was forced to relocate to Jersey, that was strange.

But somehow, even through the rat infestation and the maggots and the giant cat that practically suffocated me each night, I'd come to think of Jersey as home. A strange home, but still home.

"This is your house?" Jess turned in a slow circle, her lips parted in what I'd like to think was awe.

Tired of renting, I'd purchased the brownstone in Carroll Gardens. I'd fallen in love with this leafy block and the one-hundred-year-old building that, at the time, needed a lot of TLC.

"I feel like I'm in a romantic comedy," she said. "This neighborhood is like a movie set. And this house. How is this even possible? It looks so skinny from the outside, but inside, it's so spacious. And there is so much light."

"I can't take credit." I peered out the window at the street. "Terry set me up with an architect friend who helped me figure out how to make the most of the space."

"Is that a backyard?" She scurried deeper into the living room. "In the city?"

The garden was the width of the house and extended to the block behind us. It was flanked by brick walls, and I'd had a small patio installed, where a grill I used on occasion sat. There was even some decent shrubbery. It wasn't much, but it was my own little slice of paradise.

"Wow." She walked around, muttering to herself. "This is not what I expected."

"Because I hired an architect and a designer," I explained. "They did the work, not me."

"You know what I mean." She turned to face me, her hands clasped in front of her. "I would have taken you for a new-construction skyscraper, modern-minimalist type of guy."

I stalked over to her and tipped her chin up to kiss her. "Nope. I like what I like."

She smiled at me, her dark eyes warm, before she took off to explore the rest of the house.

Next month, we'd complete the year we'd been required to spend in Jersey. Next month, I'd be moving back here. It was hard to wrap my head around. What felt like a prison sentence had turned into maybe the biggest blessing of my life. Of all our lives.

"How many bedrooms?" she asked, running her hands along the quartz countertops.

"Four." I followed her as her curiosity took her up the spiral stairs at the back of the kitchen.

She walked into the primary bedroom and stopped dead in her tracks. "I am deceased," she said, clutching her heart. "Look at this place."

I crossed my arms, trying to rein in the joy that was bubbling up inside me.

This place had been a disaster when I bought it and had taken years and a ton of money to renovate. But it was my place. My shelter from the storm. And I wanted her to love it as much as I did.

She squealed when she took in the original fireplace, and she wore a thoughtful expression when she noticed the solar shades. The chandelier in the powder room earned a giggle. I'd buy another brownstone and fix it up all over again just to see her this excited.

"Wanna move in?" I kept my tone casual, wanting to gauge her response.

She pinned me with her mom glare. "Be serious, Brian."

I walked her backward until she was pressed against the wall and caged her in with my arms. Then I dipped down to kiss her softly. "I am serious. Come live here. I've got the space. I'll make some calls and have a piano delivered tomorrow."

She blinked rapidly, her jaw unhinged.

"Or"—I kissed her again, a little longer this time—"I'll sell it and move to a farm in Vermont. Whatever my girl wants. I'm flexible."

With an unintelligible sound, she ducked out from under my arm to keep exploring.

"Don't avoid me," I said, following her into the living room.

"You don't mean it," she said, running her hands over the deep couch. "Your firm is here. Your life is here."

"A year ago, I would have agreed with you wholeheartedly. But now I know better. Geography doesn't matter. We can make anything work if we set our minds to it."

She launched a throw pillow at my head. "Can you please stop being so perfect?"

I gave her an exaggerated wink and eased myself onto the couch. "I'm only perfect for you."

She plopped down next to me, letting out a groan. "Oh my God. It's like a cloud. And so deep my feet don't even touch the floor."

I pulled her over so she was on my lap. "You know," I said, ghosting my lips over the shell of her ear, "I have this fantasy that includes you riding my cock on this couch. Wanna make it come true?"

She moaned against my mouth as she straddled me, her hands buried in my hair. "I really do," she said, already breathless. "But I feel like we need to talk about all of this first."

I grasped her hips and pulled back with a sigh. I wanted to strip her naked and make her come five times, but she was right. Yes, I was delirious for this woman, but we were adults with responsibilities. If we wanted to be together, we had to work out the logistics.

"Anything you need."

She climbed off me and scooted over to the far side of the couch.

Instantly, I missed the warmth of her body. But this was good. The space would help me think straight.

"I want this," she said softly. "For so long, I didn't let myself want things. I denied my own needs and put everyone else first. But I want you. I want us."

My heart swelled.

"But..."

I deflated.

"I need to go at my own pace."

"Done."

She held up a hand. "We need to figure this out together. But please know this: I have to be a priority. You are dedicated to your work, and I respect that. But I won't ever be a corporate widow again. I won't ever beg for scraps of attention."

I scooted over and hauled her into my lap again. "Never fucking ever," I growled. "I'm not perfect, and I work a lot, but do not think for one second that you and the girls will not be my top priority."

She leaned forward, resting her forehead against mine, and closed her eyes. For a moment, we stayed like that, just breathing.

Eventually, I cleared my throat and pulled back. "Please trust me when I say that I'm nothing like him. I'm all in, happy to go at whatever speed you set. I want to do what's best for you and the girls."

"Thank you." Her body relaxed in my arms. "They adore you, but I don't expect you to be a surrogate father to them. They have a father. He sucks, but you don't have to replace him. They're fine with our family the way it is."

My heart broke. Those kids deserved a hell of a lot more than Kenneth.

"You're right," I said. "They don't need Kenneth because they have you. And they've got the support of our little Jersey City family and your family in Vermont. They're lucky kids. I'd just be grateful to be part of their lives."

"Thank you." Sniffling, she threw her arms around me and buried her face in my neck.

"I would never dream of replacing Kenneth. He occupies his own circle of hell. But instead of being a replacement dad, can I just be their Brian?"

Head tilted, she frowned. "What do you mean?"

"I want to be the guy who builds Legos, who helps with math home-work and loves Lake Paige dance parties. Think that's possible?"

A single tear rolled down her cheek, followed by another and another. "Yes. I think they need a Brian."

I kissed her gently as my heart swelled. "Then I will work tirelessly to be the Brian of their dreams."

CHAPTER 36
Brian

Having Jess in my bed—my actual bed—was a dream come true. A king with a cognac leather headboard and Egyptian cotton sheets. In my bedroom in my house. The house I'd bought so many years ago for reasons I couldn't articulate at the time.

Those reasons were crystal clear now. I bought it because I was waiting for her.

And she was finally here. We had two days together before she had to pick up her kids, two days before I needed to be in the office. And I intended to make the most of every single second.

"This bed is unfairly comfortable," she complained, lying back, her hair fanning out over the pillow.

"Don't get too comfy." I crawled up the length of her body to kiss the sliver of stomach exposed by her tank top. "I have plans."

She looked down at me with a grin. "As long as those plans involve orgasms and this bed, and possibly some snacks, I'm game."

"Excellent." I hooked my fingers in the waistband of her leggings and slowly pulled them down a few inches and kissed her exposed stomach.

She gasped under me, and I relished the freedom I'd been given to touch her exactly the way I wanted to. To take my time and savor her the way she deserved. To prove to her that I was all in. I'd never been good with words, but my cock could usually be counted on to step up when needed.

"Stop," she said sharply.

Immediately, I froze, my heart thumping heavily.

"Sit up," she commanded. "You always get to play. Now it's my turn."

I obeyed, getting comfortable as she shimmied out of her leggings in front of me, revealing her bare pussy. She tugged off her sports bra next and tossed it on the ground, leaving her completely naked. And all mine.

"Stand up." She scooted to the end of the bed and reached for my shorts.

I stood, heart pounding, and let her ease my shorts down. As she freed me from my clothing, my cock sprang to attention, already achingly hard for her.

She looked up at me with a dirty smile and licked the tip, sending shockwaves through me.

"Do you like this?" she asked, wrapping her fist around it and lowering her mouth slowly.

All I could do was moan.

She licked it again. "Use your words, Brian."

"Yes. I fucking love it," I growled as she lowered her mouth, taking me to the back of her throat. "You are so sexy. I've fantasized about this so many times."

She paused and looked up, licking her lips. "Really?"

The sight of her made my legs shake. "Yes. Every morning I jerk off in the shower thinking about your mouth, your tits, your pussy. Every part of you makes me fucking wild."

Seemingly satisfied with my answer, she ceased with the questions and took me in her mouth again, working her hands and tongue and lips over me in a rhythm guaranteed to kill me.

I cupped her breast, squeezing hard as I hit the back of her throat. I didn't want to hurt her, but I wasn't in control right now. She was, and if the way she wiggled against the bed in response was any indication, she liked the rough touch.

"You want to come, don't you?" I pulled her hair back from her face and fisted it while she worked my cock.

Her responding moan dripped with need, making the heat in my abdomen flare hotter. Fuck. I pulled out of her mouth, so desperate to fuck her I could barely function.

She spread her legs wide, fingering her drenched pussy, showing me just how desperately she needed me.

I fisted my aching cock, squeezing to maintain the thread of control I was clinging to. This woman made me crazy in the best way.

"Please," she said.

"Hold on. I need a condom."

"Don't." The word was short and sharp. "Please, Brian."

I held my breath, studying her wide eyes and flushed cheeks. "Are you sure?"

She nodded. "I'm healthy and have an IUD. I just want to feel you bare. I trust you."

With those words, I almost came on the spot.

"I had a physical a few months ago, and before Boston, I hadn't been with anyone for years."

She spread her legs wider, pushing one finger inside herself and moaning. "Years? look at you. How is that possible?"

I guided her onto the bed and kissed her deeply. "Because I was waiting for you, Jess."

"You don't have to wait anymore. I'm here."

I lined myself up, aching to be inside her. "Yes." I thrust inside her. "You are here. And now you're mine."

She clenched around me, gasping and crying out.

"Say it," I urged, holding her hands above her head while I lost myself in the feel of her.

"I'm yours," she cried out as I bit down on one of her nipples.

I fucked her harder, spurred on by her cries and moans. I wanted her to come so hard on my cock that it would block out the memory of every other man she'd ever been with.

I'd been her first, and I would be damned if I wouldn't also be her last.

CHAPTER 37

Jess

The third floor of Brian's brownstone consisted of three good-sized bedrooms and a full bath, as well as a small spiral staircase that led to the attic.

When I hit the landing, I gasped.

Through the medallion window, the view of the city in the moonlight was incredible.

The scenery looked nothing like that of the farm, but I loved it, nevertheless.

This space was small, but it called to me. It silently urged me to find a yoga mat and spread it out in the middle of the room. I imagined sunrise yoga up here before the city woke up. I envisioned padding downstairs to make coffee and kiss Brian, who would undoubtedly be talking about trusts and motion filings in his sleep.

I settled into an old armchair, curled my knees up, and looked out at the skyline, desperate to untangle my jumbled thoughts.

I had once been the girl who followed her gut. Who believed in intuition and never doubted herself.

Then I'd met Kenneth, and I'd let him tear down that part of me.

It wasn't the shitty marriage or the divorce. It was being with a person day in and day out who didn't respect me. Who regarded me as incapable.

Who'd made a fool of me. In the beginning, I'd believed he was fair and honest. That he would do right by me and the kids.

Even after we separated, even after I'd realized the kind of cruelty he was capable of, I couldn't have envisioned him turning any of that on his children. I imagined living close to one another so we could both be involved in the girls' lives as much as possible. I truly thought we'd sit next to each other at Kit's piano recitals and Greta's soccer games.

Never in my wildest dreams would I have thought he'd become a deadbeat dad who had no interest in his daughters. Who used them as pawns to get women and sympathy and nothing else.

It still made me shake with rage. How could he?

Every time these thoughts consumed me, they always circled back to guilt. Did I not encourage him to bond with them enough in infancy? Should I have pushed him harder to take more time off and be more active as a dad when they were little?

So many *shoulds*.

Each one made me sick.

It made me nauseas, knowing they hadn't gotten the life they deserved.

My childhood hadn't been perfect, but my siblings and I had been raised by people who loved us and loved each other. We'd worked hard, spent time together, and sat at the table every night laughing.

Once in a while, Dad would take us out after dinner, and we'd lie in the bed of the farm truck, looking up at the stars and coming up with fantastic stories.

Mom ran a tight ship, putting us to work peeling apples for pies and sweeping floors before welcoming neighbors over. At the time, we hated it, but now, those were some of my fondest memories.

We may have frozen when we tapped the trees and ran the lines, but the cold made the hot chocolate waiting for us at home that much better.

Every day, I'd woken up certain of my parents' love for me. It was a warm blanket around my heart, insulating me from the cruelties of the world.

And here I was, years after my divorce, still letting my ex-husband mess with me. There were days I could not get his constant criticism out of my head.

So after the divorce, I sat down and mapped out my life. I finished my master's and transitioned the girls to a new home and new schools. Then every one of us went to therapy. When I could think straight again, I planned for the day we could move to Vermont.

I'd been so fixated on that plan that I hadn't stopped to listen to my gut. To look around at the life we'd built in Jersey and see just how much it meant to us.

My children came first. Always. And I loved Brian. He swore he'd go anywhere and do anything to be with us. But was that actually possible? I couldn't let him walk away from the law firm he'd fought so hard to save.

As the sun warmed my face, I thought about what Sloane had said. That she and Sully had carved out a fresh start for themselves together. That she hadn't had to run away from her marriage to find herself after all.

Though thought after thought raced through my mind, I managed to doze off, sleeping fitfully in the old chair. I stirred, though, when warm arms wrapped around me and picked me up.

His woodsy scent enveloped me before I even opened my eyes.

"I was worried you'd gone home to Jersey," he said into my hair.

I shook my head. "I like it up here."

He made a low humming sound. "I knew you would." Gently, he set me on my feet. "Why'd you disappear?"

"Couldn't sleep," I admitted.

"Come back to bed." He cupped my cheek and ducked closer, and the kindness in his eyes nearly broke me.

Before I could get myself under control, I was crying. "I feel like I can't get it right. No matter how hard I try or how hard I work, I'm fucking something up."

"Jess," he soothed, caressing my cheek with his thumb. "You can't believe that. You are an incredible mother."

"I push them to be individuals, to follow their dreams and be authentic. But now Kit can't audition for PPAS and Greta can't try out for the club soccer team."

"There will be other opportunities in Vermont," he reminded me.

My heart thudded. "I know, but not these opportunities. And my job. I love my job. The hours are good and I get to help people. It took me years to finish my degree and finally get on staff. And I love Lana's studio and my regular students."

He pulled me into his chest and stroked my hair. "Okay."

"I want all the things at once. I'm a selfish bitch who can't make up her mind. I want you and all my friends here. But I also want music school for Kit. And I want the farm and my siblings."

I hiccupped, burying my face in his shirt. I couldn't stop the tears.

"This is embarrassing," I said when I caught my breath. "I'm having an adult tantrum."

Brian laughed. "It's the cutest tantrum I've ever seen." He tilted my face up so I was forced to look at him. "It's okay to be overwhelmed. It's okay to be confused. I'm here for you. I'll listen, I'll snuggle, and I'll help you figure it out. But it's four a.m. Let's get some sleep. I promise we'll work it out in the morning."

"Stop it." I swatted at his chest. "You're being too nice."

He gently wiped the tears from my cheeks. "No. I love you, and I'm in this for the long haul. We've got work to do, problems to solve, and plans to make, but I'm not afraid of any of it, as long as I've got you by my side."

"Stop being so perfect and sexy, and stop saying all the right things," I whined, throwing my head back. "Because now I'm wide awake, and all I want is to lick every inch of your naked body and forget all my problems."

Eyes flashing, he herded me toward the staircase. "Excellent plan."

CHAPTER 38

Jess

As I walked down the street, an unfamiliar pep in my step, I marveled at how colorful and fun it was. For so long, I'd viewed Jersey City as a sad prison, a place where I'd gone because I had no place else to go. But I was realizing more and more that I had vastly undersold this place.

I approached the deli, my steps slowing. I could use a cinnamon raisin bagel. When I came back out, I was loaded down with a dozen to take back to Brian's office, knowing the kids would devour them as an afternoon snack. And given's Brian's habit of working through lunch so he could finish early and spend time with me and the girls, he was probably starving.

Kit and Greta had spent the day with Sloane, who had found homemade slime recipes online for the kids. I wasn't sure how she balanced the patient mom part of her with the badass lawyer part. She seemed to have figured it out. How to be a whole person while raising kids. Not to mention her clearly hot and heavy relationship with Sully. She was technically younger than me, but she seemed to have solved the puzzle that had eluded me for so long.

I was already a hot mess with multiple jobs, two kids, and a lot of confusion surrounding my potential upcoming move. Then I'd thrown Brian into the mix.

Despite the mess my life had become, I couldn't help but smile. We were having fun. Brian and I talked or texted constantly, sharing funny stories and revealing more and more about ourselves. And every day I fell more in love with this man.

The office was busy. Cal had on his orange suit, and Lo was frantically sorting through a massive pile of documents while Amy looked on, thoroughly confused.

"The exhibits have to be in order, Amy," Lo said through gritted teeth. "They each have a lettered tab. G does not come before D in the alphabet."

"Bagels?" I interjected with a smile.

Lo gave me a smile. "Got any gluten-free? I'm crabby and could use a treat."

"Yep. Got one specifically for you. Cal," I said, narrowing my eyes on him, "the poppy seed is for Brian." I set the bag on the conference table and headed toward his office.

He was standing with his headset on, pacing while speaking and holding what looked like a lumpy smoothie. I waved at him and he gave me a wink, which sent a spark through me. God, he was so handsome.

He turned, headed the other direction, and took a big sip. He winced, but he choked the smoothie down.

"Yes," he said. "The discovery deadline is the nineteenth, and Judge Maxwell is not going to give you another extension."

He took another big gulp, and with what I swore was a shudder, he set the cup on the desk.

"Okay. Interrogatories by Friday could wor—" He winced. "Sorry, Mark. I—" His face paled. "I'll call you back."

He looked up at me, his eyes wide, then dashed out of the room.

He ran down the hall and disappeared into the bathroom before I could get my wits about me. What was happening? Was he ill?

Slowly, I crept down the hall. The closer I got to the bathroom, the louder his retching got.

"Brian?" I asked gently. "Can I help you?"

Sully popped his head out of his office and gave me a concerned look, then hollered, "Are you sick?"

"Yes," Brian groaned, his voice muffled through the closed door.

"Can I get you anything, water?" I rested a hand on the flimsy piece of wood between us. "A towel?"

"A priest?" Sully quipped, now standing next to me.

I glared at him and he shrugged.

In response, Brian retched some more. Eventually, he went quiet and flushed the toilet.

When he didn't emerge, I worried that he'd passed out, so I slowly eased the door open.

Brian, sweaty and pale, stared up at me from the mustard yellow linoleum floor.

I helped him up and led him to the couch in the reception area, then scurried to the mini fridge and pulled out a bottle of water.

"Do you think you caught a bug?" I asked as I uncapped it and handed it to him.

He sipped tentatively. "It was the smoothie. Usually I chug them, but this one was off. Tasted like pickles, but I hadn't eaten, and then all of a sudden..."

He ran his hands through his sweaty hair. Smoothie? Pickles? What the hell was he talking about?

I stalked back to his office and picked up the almost empty tumbler. It looked like a chocolate protein shake, but the liquid was lumpy and separated. Maybe he'd used expired milk by accident. I loosened the lid and was immediately hit with the distinct smell of brine.

Marching back toward him, cup in hand, I demanded, "Who made this?"

"Greta," he said, head tipped back and eyes closed. "She makes them for me some days. When I haven't had lunch."

I squeezed my eyes shut and silently cursed. Had my nine-year-old put pickles in his smoothie?

"Sometimes they're great. Sometimes she gets creative. But you know, she's a kid. And—"

I held up a hand, the pieces clicking into place.

"Drink a little more water. Take small sips. I need to talk to my kids."

I stomped up the stairs, fuming. Greta liked to cook with me. She knew damn well pickles wouldn't be appropriate for a chocolate protein shake. Was this a childish prank gone wrong? After all the kindness Brian had shown us?

I found the girls sitting at the massive table, playing with glittery slime and giggling while Murphy demonstrated his newfound ability to floss.

"*No*," T. J. corrected. "Like this. Arms and hips opposite."

It would have been a heartwarming scene had I not been filled with rage.

"Greta, Kit, can I speak to you for a moment?"

Both girls looked up at me with wide smiles, though when they saw the tumbler in my hands, Kit's eyes widened and Greta immediately looked away.

Once I'd marched them downstairs to Brian's office, I gave them my best mom glare.

"Did you make a smoothie for Brian?"

Greta nodded. "He never eats lunch, but he sometimes comes upstairs to make a protein shake in the afternoons. So I thought I'd help and make it for him."

She blinked rapidly, one of her tells.

"Why does this smell like pickles?"

She said nothing, just stared at me.

"I need an answer. Because while a chocolate shake can be enhanced by many ingredients, pickles are not one of them. And I know you know that."

I stared at her in silence, waiting it out. Kit and I had endured some epic standoffs over the years, but I knew Greta would crumble.

After about three minutes of disappointed mom glare and silence, she did.

"It wasn't just pickles. I added nutritional yeast. For Unami. I just wanted to see."

My stomach sank. "But why?"

"To see if he would drink it. He's drank all the other ones."

"Other ones?" Dear God, had my third grader been slowly poisoning my boyfriend?

Ugh. Boyfriend? That sounded weird in my head.

Partner? Guy I was dating? Shit, this was weird at forty. Another thing to put on my endless to do list, appropriate vocabulary for whatever Brian and I were doing.

"I've made a bunch for him. Some are regular. And sometimes I add fruit, like a banana." She looked at the floor, her feet shuffling. "But..."

"But what?" I barked.

"But then I got curious. He likes you so much, and he's so super-duper nice to Kit and me. I just wanted to test him."

I took a deep breath, swallowing back the urge to yell.

"Test him how?"

"At first I added a little hot sauce. I wanted to see if he liked you enough to drink it. And he did. He even pretended it was great. So then Kit said—"

"Wait." I held up a hand and spun toward my eldest daughter. "You were involved in this?"

She shrugged. "I never made anything. My hands are clean."

Damn, she was crafty.

"But you knew about it."

"Yeah. And it's hilarious. Greta needed suggestions, so I helped." Her flippant attitude made me want to shake her. "She's right. The guy is obsessed with you. For a while, we didn't like it, but we get it now. Brian's cool."

"I made them," Greta admitted. "It was Kit's idea to make normal ones too, so he wouldn't get suspicious."

I pinched the bridge of my nose, trying to wrap my mind around her confession. When Brian and I had agreed to give this a try, I'd sat down with the girls and asked for their input.

Guilt spiraled inside me. This was too fast. I was hurting them, and now they'd be even more traumatized.

"It's not because we don't like him," Kit said, sensing my distress.

"We love Brian," Greta added.

"I'm sorry," I said. "I shouldn't have brought someone into your lives so soon." My lips wobbled, dammit. "If my dating bothers you—"

"We don't mind," Kit said.

Greta peered up at me. "Especially Brian."

"So you're okay with us dating?"

"Yes," they said in unison.

"Then why did you put pickles in his protein shake?"

Greta shrugged. "I dunno. We'd put pickles on the list a while ago, and I saw a jar in the fridge."

I stood silently for a moment, trying to come to terms with this madness.Were they diabolical future serial killers? Or kids being curious and somewhat dumb?

"At first, we were mad because he liked you so much. But then when we saw how much you like him back, we wanted to make sure he was committed."

"By poisoning him."

"Mom, that's a bit hyperbolic," Kit said.

Impressive vocabulary aside, the urge to shake her returned.

"Brian is nearly passed out on the couch. He just spent ten minutes in the bathroom throwing up," I said.

Both girls' eyes widened, and Greta's even teared up. They were ashamed. Good.

"You made him sick. He was being kind to you by drinking your concoctions, and now he's ill."

Greta's face had gone wan. "I didn't want to make him sick. I just thought it was funny."

Dammit. I was raising sociopaths.

God, I was fucking this all up.

Someday I'd be on a Netflix true crime documentary, musing about how it had all gone wrong.

I should have known. They were made up of 50 percent of Kenneth's DNA, which meant there was plenty of asshole in their genetic code.

"You are both grounded," I declared. "You will apologize to Brian and do extra chores to atone for what you did. In the meantime, no screens, no playdates, and no dessert for two weeks."

After a prolonged apology, in which the girls agreed to clean Fuzzy's litter box and organize the office supply closet, Brian perked up.

When the girls ran upstairs to find crackers to settle his stomach, he pulled me close and wrapped his strong arms around me. With a kiss to the top of my head, he chuckled. "Your kids hazed me."

"It's not funny." I sighed, my heart heavy. "I need to call their therapist tomorrow. Nip this in the bud before it becomes the starting point of a life of crime."

Brian laughed harder. "I'm not worried. They're good kids, and they're protective of you."

I slumped against him. "But you got sick."

He squeezed me harder. "Worth it. They were testing me. And I passed the test." He pulled back, his golden eyes dancing.

"Testing you?"

"Yeah, I'm part of the family now."

"We do not haze people into our family," I declared. "This is a major parenting fail."

"Nah." He kissed my neck gently. "My gorgeous girlfriend has taught me to see the positive in every situation. If I have to chug a little pickle-and-oat-milk protein shake in order to keep you, then it's more than worth it."

CHAPTER 39

Brian

"Are you sure you can deliver it this weekend?" I asked into the phone.

Lo passed by, her brows high on her forehead, and I gave her a thumbs-up.

Kit had an audition at the Professional Performing Arts School this afternoon, and we'd planned a little celebration for after. T. J. and Murphy had made signs using glitter, and Lo had picked up balloons, ice cream, and cake. Greta had been putting a playlist together for the dance party, and I was going to top it off by showing her the piano I'd purchased for my brownstone.

"Yes, sir. We're the best piano movers in Brooklyn. Been doing this for generations."

"And you'll tune it once it's in position?"

"Yes. The tuner is on standby."

"Thank you for the last-minute help." With a harsh breath out, I ran a hand through my hair.

I was so nervous for her. Kit had not stopped practicing in the last two weeks. She'd pushed herself so hard, her dedication impressive. It was a long shot, but just the chance to audition was a big deal.

And while I was nervous, Jess was a full-on disaster. She'd shown up at the office the other day wearing mismatched shoes because she'd been up half the night worrying and could barely think straight.

"Thanks again for the Metros tickets." He laughed. Ernie and I had worked out an understanding that had helped me jump to the top of his waitlist.

While Jess and I had only talked casually about moving into the brownstone together, it was important to me that the girls felt comfortable there. So I was turning the formal living room into a music room for Kit and the basement into a game and playroom for Greta. The foosball table and giant beanbag chairs had been far easier to source than a Steinway baby grand piano.

A home I'd been so ambivalent about a few months ago had now become an incredible opportunity. Sure, I'd miss the camaraderie we'd created while living in the Jersey apartment, but things had changed. We'd changed.

Cal and Sully had been my best friends before, but now we were brothers. We'd survived Terry's death, saved the firm, and fixed our lives all in the span of twelve months. The circumstances that had originally felt like a prison sentence had freed us. They'd allowed us to grow and change in incredible ways.

And I could not wait for what was next.

I rolled my shoulders and checked the clock. I'd have to leave by noon to get to the city in time. The audition was closed, but I planned to meet them for the school tour and then wait in the hall with Jess while Kit played for the admissions committee.

We'd head to the Jersey apartment after and surprise Kit with our little family celebration. I'd also get to surprise the girls with the changes I'd made to the brownstone. While it had been a challenge to find alone time with Jess over the past couple of weeks, the two of us had been having a lot of fun. The more time I spent with her, the more I wanted. After years of playing it safe and avoiding risks at all costs, I was ready to jump off a cliff for her and her kids.

I was packing up when the phone rang.

"Landon?"

"It's the old man," he said. His voice was strained, as if he'd been crying. "We don't have much time."

My heart sank into my stomach. We'd known Cliff didn't have a lot of time left, but he'd looked so good last month when I dropped by with papers to sign.

I held on to my desk to steady myself. This was one of the hardest parts of my job, but it was the most important. Making sure my clients, people who had become friends, felt supported so they could leave this world unburdened.

Grief swelled inside me. It didn't matter that he had lived a long life. Each time I lost someone, emotions that had clung to me my whole life came rushing to the surface. The helplessness and sadness flooded in, and once again, the hole in my life where my mother had been yawned open.

Despite the pain, this was why I'd gone into family law. So I could help people get their lives in order. So I could give them a modicum of control over the uncontrollable—death.

"What can I do?" Mentally, I created a to-do list, considering which forms I'd need and which paperwork to file with the state to ensure the plans we'd spent years carefully crafting were carried out to his precise instructions.

"He wants to see you," Landon said. "We're at the Alpine house. How fast can you get here?"

I rarely got a chance to say goodbye to clients, so this was a blessing. And Cliff was so much more than a client. He had been my friend and a mentor for fifteen years.

"I'm on my way," I said, checking my watch. I'd figure out how to get to the audition later.

Once I disconnected the call, I fired off a quick text to Jess that something had come up and I'd meet her at the school. Then I grabbed my keys and headed for the car, praying I'd make it in time.

As I rolled toward the gates of the Phillips estate, they creaked open slowly. Landon met me at the entrance and ushered me inside, where the sunroom, which faced the large garden, had been converted into a makeshift hospital room.

The hospice nurse greeted me with a kind expression and led me to Cliff's bedside. He looked tiny and frail tucked beneath the sterile sheets and blanket, but he had a big smile on his face.

"Brian, so glad you could stop by." His tone was breezy, his words a little slurred.

Tears threatened as I took him in. And when I opened my mouth to speak, nothing came out. So I resorted to squeezing his hand instead.

"Sit with me for a bit." He pointed to a wooden chair next to his bed, and when I was settled, he gestured to the garden. "Isn't it glorious?"

It really was. A wild riot of color blanketed the grounds, and the sun shone down, its light bringing extra magic to the setting.

"Betty and I loved this room. We'd sit in here and stare out at the flowers, talking about our days. She loved those flowers. Chose and planted every single one."

The pride in his voice made my chest ache.

"I want to go home to her," he said softly.

I blinked back tears. I was here to support him, so I was determined not to make even an instant of this about me.

"It's no fun here without her."

I swallowed once, then again, searching for an appropriate response. When my mind came up blank, I focused on breathing and took in the colors and the shapes and the sun-dappled grass beyond the windows.

"She forced me to turn it off. To stop and pay attention. And thank God she did. If I hadn't, I'd have missed all this and so much more."

"Cliff," I croaked.

He raised one wrinkled hand. "Let me speak, son. I've got a lot to say and not much time."

"Everything is in order," I said.

"I know that. I've known that for years. The last thing I'm thinking about right now is my money or my businesses. I've only got a little time left on this earth, and I've got wisdom to impart. So I want you to sit and listen."

I smiled. Even on his deathbed, Cliff was a force of nature.

"You're a good kid. Smart and hardworking." He rested his head against the elevated mattress. "I know you'll help Landon when he takes over and that you'll keep him in line. For a long time, I thought my legacy was my business and my baseball team, but I know better now."

He coughed violently, and the nurse rushed in. She stood at his side, ready with a nasal cannula, but he waved her away.

"That's the easy stuff," he rasped. "We can draft papers and make plans for that. Relationships are much harder. But from where I sit, they're all that matter."

I sucked in a breath, letting his words wash over me, immediately envisioning Jess and her girls.

"We only get one beautiful and wondrous life, Brian. Promise me right now you won't waste yours."

My vision blurred and my nose stung as I listened. Had I wasted my time? I'd always done what I thought was best, giving everything I could to my family and my clients and the firm. But I hadn't been happy. I'd been treading water until the day Jess walked into my office.

"I won't." I closed my eyes and repeated the words to myself silently. *I won't.*

"Did you tell the girl you love her?" he asked.

A smile overtook my face, despite the somberness of the moment. "I did."

"Thank God—" His last word was cut off as he launched into another coughing fit. "I knew you had it in you. Now hold on tight and never let her go. If you do that, then you'll be just fine."

I thought about Jess and Vermont. That I'd go anywhere and do anything to be with her.

"I plan on it," I said, my brain racing ahead several steps. Would she want to get married again?

I wanted to grow old with Jess. I wanted to sit beside her and look at the flowers in our yard.

"Give me a hug and then get going," Cliff said gruffly.

I stood and bent over him, wrapping my arms around his frail form.

"I'm gonna go get my girl now," he said, patting my cheek. "How 'bout you go get yours?"

CHAPTER 40

Jess

"Listen, this does not define you. Whether you're admitted to this school has no bearing on your worth in this world."

Kit stared blankly ahead as I brushed her hair, her posture rigid with nerves.

I'd been second-guessing my decision to allow her to audition for the past two weeks. She'd been practicing harder than ever, so focused and serious and determined. While it made me proud, it also worried me. I couldn't help but dwell on the potential for devastation if she wasn't accepted. I wanted her to be a kid on summer vacation, yet I loved her dedication, and I wanted her to set goals and work toward them.

This was the torment that came with parenting. Always being torn in two, wanting to wrap my child in a warm, supportive blanket and shield her from failure or disappointment, then flip-flopping and pondering whether I should let her take risks, even while knowing that the end result could be painful.

"I've heard it all before, Mom," she said, her voice monotone. "Auditioning is an honor. Blah, blah, blah."

I tugged gently on the French braid I was working on. "It's the truth. We're going for the experience. Most kids spend years preparing, and you got a couple of weeks. That's my fault, not yours. You've worked hard and improved. This is just one day of your long, beautiful, successful life."

Her lips wobbled, but she kept her head high. "But I just want to get in."

"Of course you do. But someday, when you're an adult and have a little more perspective, you will realize that it doesn't actually matter if you get in. What matters is that you took this opportunity and worked your butt off. That you went in there with your head held high and a smile on your face."

I kept braiding, my chest aching, knowing that my words hadn't penetrated as deeply as I'd hoped. She was twelve, and after the changes and disappointments she'd been through, she wanted to hold on to hope.

Though the audition had consumed us for days and days, Vermont was still there, beckoning to me. The cottage was ready, and I'd met with the school principal during our trip. I hadn't made any solid plans regarding work, but I could help out on the farm until I found a social work position.

But since the moment I'd returned from visiting my siblings, none of it had felt urgent. Because all the positives that came along with moving were now being weighed against all the possibilities here. We still had a lot to explore. Like this audition and our new friendships. And Brian.

When I'd agreed to today and had told Kit, the girls and I had talked and decided we would take a little more time before making a final decision about moving. Given that it was mid-July, the clock was ticking, yet the pressure lessened every day.

"I just want to get in," she repeated, this time with a sigh.

I squeezed her shoulders and spun the chair around so we were eye to eye. "There are other schools, and there's always next year. Remember what Grandpa used to tell me when I was a kid? What are the only two things we can control in this life?"

"Our attitude and effort," she grumbled.

I dipped my chin. "Correct. We can't control what the committee decides, but you can control your attitude and your effort and be proud of yourself."

She looked up at me, her big brown eyes welling with tears. "Can we snuggle for a minute?"

With a smile, I pulled her in close, and as I tucked her beneath my chin, I closed my eyes and inhaled. God, this age was so hard. Some days she was a tiny adult, and on others she was my sweet chubby baby again.

"I love you," I said into her hair. "And I'm so proud of you." I held her tighter, savoring this moment and sending a silent prayer to the universe that today would go well.

My phone buzzed on the counter, breaking the silence, and as Kit stepped away to find Greta, I held it up and found a message from Brian.

Brian: Work emergency. I'll meet you in the city.

Annoyance flashed through me. Work emergency? What could be more important than Kit's audition?

I closed my eyes. The apprehension and concern that had been gnawing at my stomach had now been joined by a familiar pang of disappointment. Kenneth had done this all the time. He'd promise he'd show up, tell me it was on his calendar and everything, and then bail at the last minute.

Because work had always been more important.

I forced myself to breathe. Brian wasn't Kenneth. And we still hadn't officially defined what we were doing. He wasn't Kit's dad. He didn't owe us anything.

By the time I reminded myself of that, it was too late. The doubts had started to pile up. Had I jumped in too quickly? Was I falling back into old patterns? Being too positive, too sunny? Had I not been cautious enough? Had I set my children up for heartbreak?

Groaning, I tossed my phone into my purse, then focused on getting out the door. I'd deal with these concerns later. I couldn't let my baggage muck up Kit's special day. Lately, compartmentalization had become difficult, but I slapped a smile on my face and tossed a handful of snacks into my purse.

As the girls and I headed to the train, my gut churned, but I forced myself to smile and stay positive.

My confusion about Brian only amplified the sick feeling. Had I been so lust-drunk that I'd failed to see the bigger picture? Had I let my guard down and exposed my kids to more pain?

My mind continued to spin as we walked from the train to the school.

What had I been thinking? Brian had been honest about being a workaholic. In the last few months, I'd often found him in the office when I stopped by to get the girls, and sometimes, when he walked us out, he headed right back in to get more work done.

My mother had always said, "When people show you who they really are, listen."

And here I was, disappointed and overwhelmed, with no one but myself to blame. It wasn't his fault. This was who he was. I'd been the one wearing rose-colored glasses.

But for now, I had to put that out of my mind and focus on Kit.

This was her big day. My only job was to make sure she felt supported and loved no matter the outcome.

We stood outside the impressive brick building, all three of us taking it in. It was almost as wide as the block, with corbeled cornices and arches around the massive windows. It was beautiful.

Beside me, Kit suddenly radiated excitement rather than anxiety. This was her place. I could feel it. And I thought she could too.

I squeezed her hand, and she looked up at me with a smile.

"I can do this," she said as we walked toward the entrance.

"I know you can."

CHAPTER 41
Brian

Despite having a resident parking pass, finding a spot had been hell. I'd raced into the city after meeting Cliff, crying and thinking and spiraling the whole way. I hadn't realized how much time had passed until I finally pulled into a spot and checked my phone.

Shit. I'd missed my window to meet up with them.

I slumped in the driver's seat and squeezed my eyes shut, willing my thoughts to settle. I wanted to be there for Jess and Kit, but I couldn't risk interrupting. So I'd sit here and wait, sending all the good vibes and positive thoughts I could into that impressive brick building.

The school was gorgeous. And walkable from my brownstone. I didn't want to put pressure on Jess, but it seemed perfect.

Could I do it? Be the partner she deserved and a positive role model to her kids?

A year ago, I would have said no, but my whole world had changed the day Terry had forced Cal and Sully and me to move to Jersey. I'd stood on a solid foundation for decades, certain that I was following the correct life path.

For almost two hours, I ran through every scenario in my mind. Then I sat with my feelings, like Dr. Johnson had taught me to do. And I made a plan.

What I found as I took a step back and looked at my life was what I already knew: Jersey had changed me. Therapy had changed me. My conversation with Cliff had changed me.

There was only one thing I wanted now. A family. Specifically this family.

Movement caught my eye as I was mulling over how to convince the girls to stop by the apartment in Jersey without giving away the surprise. When I looked up, Jess was stepping through the wrought-iron gates, followed by a smiling Greta. Trailing farther behind was Kit, whose shoulders were slumped and whose lips were pulled down in a frown.

My stomach sank. Oh God. Had things gone badly?

I jumped out of the car and jogged over to them.

"Brian?" Kit's face lit up. She ran for me, and I opened my arms and scooped her up.

"I'm sorry I was late," I said as I set her on her feet and crouched, since she'd yet to release me. "Did you knock 'em dead?"

She nodded into my chest. "I think so. But now I'm not sure."

Greta darted over and joined our hug, giving me a big squeeze.

Jess appeared next, wearing a smile that didn't reach her eyes. "I could hear her from the hall. She was amazing."

"Proud of you, kiddo," I said, still looking at Jess.

She'd been an anxious mess for days, but now, she looked completely wiped out.

The kids, on the other hand, were already chattering, telling me about their day.

"They have math and science," Kit explained. "But I'd get to study music theory too. I thought I wouldn't do that until college." She turned and asked Jess for her phone. "And they have performances and show-cases all year long."

Once Jess had unlocked her screen and handed the device to her daughter, Kit and Greta babbled even faster, Kit scrolling through Jess's phone, showing me photos of the theater and the classrooms.

"So impressive," I said, peering up at Jess again.

Her eyes were distant, her skin wan, putting me on guard. What was going on? Did she know something the girls didn't?

"I just hope they accept me."

I kneeled and put my hands on Kit's tiny shoulders. "Whether or not they accept you doesn't change a thing. You worked hard and went in there and did your best."

She rolled her eyes. "You sound like my mom."

"So wise and supportive and awesome, then?" I asked with a wink.

With a huff, she skirted around me and headed down the sidewalk.

I dusted off my pants and stepped up in front of Jess. I wanted to hold her, to kiss her, but her body language told me it wouldn't be welcome. So I settled for ducking so we were eye to eye.

"You okay?"

She nodded, her gaze darting to the side. "Tired and stressed."

My gut clenched, but I ignored the sensation. This wasn't about me. Today was about Kit and Jess. "Do you want a ride back? I had to drive here, and we've got a little something planned back at the building."

She shook her head. "Can you just take us home? It's been a long day."

"But—" I snapped my mouth shut.

The look on her face told me she wasn't just tired, but I wasn't a mind reader. I had no idea what was going on.

"You didn't make it on time." She said it softly, disappointment rolling off her.

My gut plummeted. The last thing I ever wanted was to let her down.

"I got a call as I was getting ready to leave," I explained. "Cliff Phillips is on hospice. They think it's the end."

She gasped, her eyes going wide. "My God, I'm so sorry, Brian. I know how much you care about him."

"He wanted to see me." I scratched at the back of my head, ducking so she wouldn't see the tears in my eyes. "So I drove over there. I didn't stay long, but I didn't realize it would take so long to get to the city and find parking."

"It's okay," she murmured. "I understand."

"It's not." I gritted my teeth. "I promise I wanted to be there for Kit, but he needed me. I care about all my clients, but this one is hitting me hard." Emotion rose in my chest, but I swallowed it down. "I've worked with him since my early days at the firm."

She pressed her lips together, surveying me, her eyes misty. "When you've lost people like we have, every loss is harder than the last."

Our eyes met for a moment and stayed. It was palpable, the grief she carried. Not only for her parents but for the loss of her marriage.

More than anything, I wished I could take it all away. Pack it up in a backpack and lug it around for her.

The whole way home, the girls happily sang Lake Paige songs in the back seat, but Jess was silent, her focus fixed out the window.

When we pulled up to the studio, Kit and Greta bolted, as if they'd been cooped up for hours. They darted inside, leaving Jess and me sitting awkwardly as my car idled on the street.

Every instinct in my body was telling me to leave her alone, to give her space. Retreat.

Even so, I leaned in a fraction. "Are you sure I can't persuade you to come over? I think the fam has some things planned."

Jess shook her head, focus fixed on her hands in her lap.

"Can I come in, then?" I asked, tipping her chin up. "I'd love to talk more about today."

When she finally looked at me, her eyes were teary.

"Later," she said. "I need to feed the girls and get myself together."

I nodded. Though I was crestfallen, I kept my face even. She was having a hard enough time. The last thing I wanted was to make her feel worse. "I'll swing by with Dammit on our evening walk. Tell Kit great job again for me."

She nodded, though her gaze was distant, her mind elsewhere.

"I love you," I said softly as she reached for the door handle.

She turned back toward me, a tear cresting her lashes. "I love you too. And that's the problem."

My heart lurched. "Problem?"

"Yeah, Brian. It's a problem." She let out a shaky breath. "I'm a mess.

A screwup. And I'm worried that not only am I dragging my kids down, but I'll drag you down too eventually."

Part of my brain lit up. There was no stopping it. She'd just told me she loved me. But the more logical parts were terrified. How could she think so terribly of herself?

"We were doing fine. Rebuilding. Scraping by. We had a plan. And then you came along. And now everything is different."

"Yes," I said, my frustration growing. "Different because you're not alone anymore. Different because I've got your back and I love you and your kids."

Her tears were flowing in earnest now, the sight making my heart crack in two. Shit. I was only making things worse.

"I'm sorry," I croaked. "I screwed up today—"

"No. You didn't. You were with your dying friend." She splayed a hand over her chest. "I'm the problem. You got held up, and I spiraled. It all came back. All the Kenneth shit, all the feelings of being worthless and overlooked."

I wiped a tear from her cheek with my thumb. "I'm so sorry. But being triggered like that is natural. This is new territory for both of us. But I want to work through it with you."

"You do?" She sniffled. "Because this is the real me. I'm not some sunflower-in-human-form dream girl. I'm moody and have stretch marks, and sometimes my insecurities get the best of me."

I pulled her close and kissed her head. "You are my dream girl, and I love all those things about you. I've spent two decades in a fog, going through the motions. Doing what was expected of me and never stopping to think about what I wanted."

"What do you want?"

That was easy. "You. I want partnership and adventure. I want to wake up next to you every morning. I want to watch Kit and Greta grow up."

With my hands on her cheeks, I kissed her on the mouth. Her lips were salty with tears, but they tugged up in the tiniest of smiles.

"I want Munchkin Mondays and dance party Wednesdays. I want to make magic in the mundane moments of our lives together."

She sucked in a breath, her chest stuttering. "I want that too."

"Good."

"But I just need a minute."

Ice flooded my veins. What did that mean?

"I've got a lot to process," she whispered. "If Kit gets in, I have to find a way to pay tuition. And I'll have to break it to my family that we aren't moving to Vermont. I need to think about what our lives are gonna look like if that happens. If it doesn't, I'll have a devastated girl who's gonna need all my attention."

I nodded, willing myself to remain calm. "I want to be a part of your lives. I don't care where that is."

I'd move to Vermont in a heartbeat. I'd trade in my Tom Ford for LL Bean and learn how to tap a tree.

She didn't seem to get it. I was all-in.

But before I could verbalize that, she was opening the door and climbing out.

"I just need a few days," she said with a soft smile. "I'll call you."

Without turning back, she went inside, leaving me confused and heartsick at the same time.

CHAPTER 42
Jess

I was a mess. A certified messy mess. A snotty-nosed, red-faced, dirty-haired mess. I'd been avoiding everyone but my girls and all my responsibilities as I went round and round in circles, obsessing over what to do.

Kit spoke of nothing but music school, and Greta was cranky because we hadn't been over to see Murphy and T. J. But I just needed some space to sort myself out.

I loved Brian. I was madly in love with him.

And I was so mad about it.

For years, I'd worked to become a strong, independent woman. Not a lovesick teenager. And I had my kids to think about. Bringing someone into their lives was a big deal.

Then there was Vermont. With every day that passed, that dream grew more distant.

I'd take the weekend to get my shit together. That's what I told myself.

My girls had other ideas.

"Mom, we want to go over to play with T. J. and Murphy," Kit said from the doorway to my bedroom.

Greta popped up beside her. "We miss Brian."

They were both fully dressed and wearing shoes. Considering that getting them to put their shoes on was one of my biggest daily challenges, this was highly suspect.

"And we think you do too," Kit said. "So let's go see him."

I looked at my kids, so grown and self-possessed, and my chest ached.

But I exhaled and shook my head. "We have things to do today."

"You've been scrolling Instagram since before we got up," Kit snapped. "And we all know it's because you're super-duper in love with Brian."

"And want to marry him," Greta added.

Kit took a step into the room. "So instead of being all moody about it, go tell him."

They watched me, heads tilted in the same way, expressions full of expectation. Damn. Suddenly, I missed the toddler days. Sure, I'd had to chase them down streets and they used me as their personal napkin, but at least they didn't weaponize logic against me.

"Girls." I patted the mattress beside me.

Greta bounced over and sat next to me. Kit, on the other hand, glared at me for another moment before she finally shuffled to my other side.

"I care a lot about Brian," I said. "But you two are my first priority." I put my arms around them and pulled them close. "Being your mom is my most important job."

"You're talking like you can't do both," Kit said far too wisely. "And that's just silly. You're always telling us you want us to live big, messy, exciting lives."

"And to follow our passions," Greta added.

I pinched the bridge of my nose, simultaneously thrilled that they actually listened to me and annoyed that they listened to those parts so particularly well.

"Let's walk over," Kit chided. "Please. Talk to Brian. The two of you can work out all your adult stuff."

"And kiss each other!" Greta's eruption was followed by retching noises.

"And we can hang with our friends," Kit said. "Lo promised me she'd do my nails."

"And T. J. just got the *Up* Lego set," Greta added. "It's the house with all the balloons, and I wanna help build it."

With one more squeeze, I released them, then I took a calming breath. God, how badly was I spiraling if I was getting called out by my kids?

Standing, I reached up into a deep stretch. "Okay. Give me a few minutes to get dressed and we'll walk over and say hi."

The July air was already sticky with humidity, making me regret the decision to leave my hair down. I had no doubt it was a frizzy mess by the time we made it to the law office and Brian's apartment.

The hair situation wasn't the only thing I was regretting as I followed the girls up the back stairs.

Sloane answered, with Tia in her arms. She hugged the girls and ushered them inside, but as I stopped at the threshold, her smile faltered.

"He's downstairs in his office," she said, raising one eyebrow. Even in leggings, with a newborn in her arms, she was intimidating as hell. "It's about time you came over."

I nodded, biting my bottom lip, and thumbed behind me. "I'll just..."

"Yeah, you should," she said firmly as she closed the door between us.

My heart sank as I stomped down the steps. Dammit. Now my friends were pissed at me. Couldn't a woman have a crisis in peace?

The door that led into the office was unlocked as usual, but most of the lights were off. Probably because it was a Saturday morning. Cal and Sully were probably upstairs with their kids. Lo too. The thought made me sad, because I had no doubt that Brian had been toiling away for hours at this point.

Sure enough, the light in his office was on, casting a glow into the dark hallway. I approached cautiously and knocked gently.

He looked up from his computer, his eyes widening. "Jess?"

"Hi." I waved awkwardly. "You busy?"

"Never too busy for you."

My heart skipped a beat. God, why was he so perfect?

"I'm just getting all the Phillips stuff together."

Only then did it hit me that he'd probably lost a friend in the last forty-eight hours, and I hadn't even checked on him.

I swallowed past the lump in my throat and stepped into his office. "Did he pass?"

Brian nodded, lowering his face a fraction. "Yesterday. Funeral is Monday. I want to make sure things go smoothly with the estate."

Of course he did. Because he was endlessly devoted to his people.

He stood, running a hand through his messy hair, his eyes red rimmed and his beard a little unruly.

I wanted to jump into his arms and never let go. But I'd been the one to pull back. I'd been the one to freak out. So I had to be the one to apologize.

"I'm so sorry," I blurted. "With everything going on, I panicked and needed some time to process." My voice wavered. "I didn't mean to push you away."

He walked around the desk and pulled me into his arms. "It's okay to need space."

"No," I argued into his chest. "I was shitty to you, and you've only ever been amazing to me. Sloane is pissed at me."

Arching back, he smirked and tucked a strand of hair behind my ear. "She's overprotective of me, and I may have been a bit grumpy the past two days."

"Grumpy?" I asked with mock surprise. "You?"

He shook his head and perched on his desk, looking me over from head to toe. "But I do want to talk to you." Eyes locked on mine, he exhaled slowly. "If I made you feel pressured, I'm sorry. I can move slower, and I'm sorry I upset you."

"You didn't upset me," I said, stepping between his knees. "I'm upset with myself. Things have changed so quickly, and I'm struggling to keep up. I really thought that I'd healed from Kenneth, but I have more work to do."

"We're both works in progress," he said, angling forward to kiss me gently.

Instinctively, I closed my eyes and clutched his shirt. His kiss soothed me, healed me, left me wanting more.

"I want to stand by your side through the triumphs and the challenges," he urged. "I want to support you in any way you want. But I've got to know what's going on. Please let me in."

I laid my head against his chest, gathering the courage to unload all the ridiculous thoughts in my head.

"I'm so torn," I started. "I want everything. I want my kids to run barefoot around the farm, and I want Kit to go to music school. I want movie nights with my Jersey family and a job that I enjoy. I want you, so much, but at the same time, I can't lose the version of myself I've fought so hard to become. It's selfish. I'm selfish. I probably sound like a spoiled brat."

He wiped away my tears with the pads of his thumbs. "You don't sound like a brat. It's okay to want things, Jess. There are a lot of things I want too."

I sniffled, and he gave me a smile.

"I want it all with you too. You and the girls and my friends and my clients. For me, it's all interconnected." He swallowed audibly. "Cliff was family. Some of my clients are. I deal with extremely personal, sensitive matters for them, so lines get blurred. And while you and the girls and the rest of our Jersey family will always be top priority, my work also matters to me. I want to do it all too."

He huffed out a weighted breath, and his eyes welled.

"Cliff was my friend," he said. A tear rolled down his cheek, followed by another, until he was crying in earnest. "I cared about him. I've known him and his family since Terry hired me straight out of law school. And he trusted me with his legacy and his business. That's a big deal. It's a responsibility I take seriously. But I've realized that I'm so much more than my job.

"I'm sorry Kenneth was such a shitty husband and father." He wiped at his cheeks. "I'm sorry he chose his job and money over you girls. But that was his choice. It has nothing to do with who you are."

I was sobbing now. How did this man see all my deepest wounds and still want me?

"Look at me." He tilted my chin up and held my gaze, his eyes burning with intensity. "I choose you and Kit and Greta. Every day, I will choose you. For so long, I didn't think I could have it all. That I even deserved it. But then I found you again and realized genuine happiness was worth fighting for. I'll make mistakes and get things wrong, but I'll work my ass off to make it right and to put you and the kids first."

My heart panged. How could I not be madly in love with this man? I'd been so angry for falling hard and fast, but what choice did I have?

"I choose you too," I said softly, wrapping my arms around his torso. "I'm scared as hell, but this is right. I know it in my bones."

We remained like that, wrapped in one another's arms, and I embraced the connection and allowed his love to sink into me, all the way to my soul. This sensation was the kind of thing most people dreamed about. It was a once-in-a-lifetime kind of love. Sure, it would be challenging, but there was no use fighting this.

"I'm scared too," he murmured against the top of my head. "But if anyone can do it, it's us."

"That's very positive of you."

"What can I say? You're rubbing off on me. I'm becoming a full-blown optimist."

I palmed his cheeks and pulled him down for another kiss, this one far less gentle. He cupped my chin and teased my lips open, and as he explored my mouth, I melted into him.

"Wait," he said, pulling back.

Ugh. Things were just getting good, and there was a perfectly good lock on his office door.

"I want to show you something." He sidestepped me and pulled what looked like rolled-up paper from the shelf behind his desk.

"What is that?"

"This," he said with a wink, "is having it all." With care, he unrolled the papers and laid them on his desk.

I tilted my head, trying to decipher the design. "Are those blueprints?"

He nodded, a grin taking over his entire face. "I spoke to Josh. Negotiated a land deal."

Confusion swirled in my mind, like all the bed rotting I'd done these last couple of days had affected my processing skills. "What are you talking about?"

"Your barn." He traced his fingers over the design. "You, Jessica Lawrence Mosely, now own this lovely piece of property in Maplewood, Vermont. And these are the plans for your barndominium conversion. Multiple bedrooms, a screened-in porch, with a music room for Kit, a his-and-hers home office, and a small yoga studio."

My breath caught and my knees wobbled. This was something out of my wildest fantasies.

"How did you do this?"

"I'm a lawyer, remember?" He'd quickly reverted back to the confident man who was so good in the courtroom. "Paperwork and contracts are kind of my thing. So this is a gift. To you and the girls. You can make any changes you want. Do whatever you want. But it's yours."

My heart pounded wildly, and blood rushed in my ears. Was he saying what I think he was saying?

"I love you. I love Kit and Greta. And I love Vermont. So we're gonna build your barndominium on the farm. A little house where we can spend the summers. That way the kids can have the Vermont childhood you've dreamed of."

I shook my head, not understanding. "But what about your work?"

"I've already filed my application to the Vermont bar. It will take a few months to get licensed, but I'll work remotely from the farm in the summers and come back to the city when necessary. Cal and Sully are on board. Also." He tapped the blueprint. "You'll see the design has two large guestrooms to accommodate the visitors we'll likely have."

I traced my fingers over the walls and the roof. My mother's barn, turned into a home for us and the girls.

"Cal is already planning an annual firm retreat. And Lo's already had to talk him out of a maple syrup–drinking competition."

I let out a laugh. That was classic Cal.

"Why?" I asked, more tears welling in my eyes. "Why are you doing this?"

He put his arm around me and pulled me close. "Because I love you. And Vermont and the farm are part of who you are. You and the kids deserve everything. This way"—he nodded at the plans—"we can have it all together. School in the city, summers on the farm, ski weekends in the winter. We can even drive up for the Maple Festival every spring."

I had melted into a puddle. That sounded perfect.

"I just have one request."

"Anything," I said, still marveling at the massive porch that looked out at the maple groves.

"I want to get married on the farm too."

I froze, my brain going offline for a moment. When it rebooted, I squeaked, "Get married?"

"Yes. Not now. I'll wait till you're ready. But I want to marry you, Jess. And I want to do it here." He placed his fingers on the plans. "In a place that's special to you, where we know your parents will be looking down on us. Where we can be surrounded by family and friends and however many goats Josh has collected by then."

I gave him a soft smile. "I'm not ready yet."

I wasn't sure when I'd be. Marriage had been the furthest thing from my mind until he mentioned it. But I could see it. Someday.

He dipped his chin. "I know."

"But when I am, I'm gonna marry the shit out of you, Brian Machon."

EPILOGUE
Brian

One month later

"To one hell of a year," I said, raising my glass. We were in the parking lot behind the building, grilling and celebrating the official end of our Jersey City residency. We'd decided to go out in style with a parking lot party befitting this great state, and today was the perfect day. The afternoon had been almost scorching, but as we eased closer to evening, the temperature had cooled considerably.

"Started as a kick in the arse," Sully said.

"But ended bloody great." Cal held up his beer in a toast.

"It feels like we're a band at the end of a world tour," I mused.

"Or we're a group of best mates starting the rest of our lives," Cal offered.

Sully punched him. "Trust you to be the emotional one."

"My girl's not complaining." Cal pulled Lo away from where she'd been talking to Jess and kissed her square on the mouth.

Cheeks pink, she pushed away from him and walked away.

They were in the process of looking at apartments close to Murphy's school in the city with enough natural light to support all Cal's plants.

Sloane and Sully had been interviewing nannies for Tia and getting their penthouse baby proofed. Sloane's maternity leave was ending soon, and when it did, she'd be returning to Murphy and Machon.

Thank fuck. We'd all been eager to get her back.

As the party went on, I manned the grill with pride.

The two folding tables we'd set up were surrounded by folding chairs and a few desk chairs we'd rolled out from the office. Jess had decorated with streamers and paper lanterns, and the kids were playing cornhole while music pulsed around us.

Madame E was mixing her famous margaritas, which seemed dangerous, while we grilled burgers and Sloane sliced an enormous watermelon.

It was perfect. The perfect celebration of our imperfect little family.

"Looking good, grill master," Jess teased as she approached with a package of buns. "You've got a grill at the brownstone, right?"

"I've got a grill, a smoker, and a pizza oven. Don't worry. I'll make sure you're well fed."

She put an arm around my waist and squeezed. We were still discussing when she and the girls should move in, but since Kit had been offered a spot at music school beginning next month, I had a feeling I would wear her down soon.

"Stop flirting and throw the hot dogs on." She stepped back. "I'll round up the kids."

By the time we'd gotten everyone seated, it was getting dark. Madame E had made a third pitcher of margaritas, and the alcohol had made us all nostalgic and silly.

"To Murphy and Machon." We all raised our glasses.

"We survived," Sully said.

"We didn't just survive," Cal added. "We crushed it. Aces all around."

He wasn't wrong about that. What had felt like a punishment in the beginning had turned into the greatest opportunity of my life.

And between Terry and Cliff, I'd found the courage to finally seize it.

Jess sat beside me, smiling and giggling while Lo gave a dramatic reenactment of the day she found the maggots in the photocopier.

She was so joyful, even on the hard days. We'd slowly been figuring out our next steps while keeping up with yoga classes and Monday morning walks with the cat in search of Munchkins.

Madame E surveyed the table, her eyes a little glassy from the tequila. "I am seeing so many things right now." She waggled a finger at Lo, who pretended to ignore her. Not wanting to be in her crosshairs. "You." She squeezed Murphy's cheek. "Keep practicing your soccer. And you'll finally lose that tooth on Thursday."

He touched his lip and frowned. I'd heard nothing about a wiggly tooth, which led me to believe he hadn't noticed it was loose yet.

"Madame E?" Cal asked, bouncing like a little boy. "What do you think? Is Lola gonna make an honest man out of me?"

Lo ignored him, sipping her margarita.

Sully put his free arm around Sloane, the other cradling a sleeping Tia. "Don't want to brag, but when I asked Sloane to marry me, she actually said yes."

"Both times," Sloane added with a smirk.

Cal glared at his brother. "She will say yes one of these times. I just have to keep coming up with bigger and better proposals."

Murphy giggled. "Sure, Dad."

Madame E smiled. "Callahan, don't forget that when we read your cards, I told you there were good things coming. Now make sure to sell your Porsche like I told you to. Get something roomier for future family members."

Cal's face broke out into a massive grin, and Lo drained her margarita.

The conversation turned to plans for the school year, how we were going to bring the walkie-talkies to the Manhattan office, and our trip to Vermont in two weeks to meet with the team set to work on our new barn house.

We'd been having so much fun, making plans and sketching out our dream home together. Unsurprisingly, Jess wasn't fussy. She thought every idea was amazing. We'd decided on a large porch so we could sit on rocking chairs together and look out at the forest.

It was simple, but the idea that I'd found this, the person I wanted to spend the rest of my life with, felt momentous.

There was magic here. This group of people and the circumstances that had thrown us all together. As I eyed Madame E, who was twirling the massive rings on her fingers, I couldn't help but believe. That woman knew things, and I had no doubt that she'd been working with Terry to make sure we all got our shit together.

"I went over Terry's will while Tia napped the other day," Sloane said. "I'd forgotten that you're allowed to sell this building now that the year is up."

The three of us looked at one another.

On the one hand, it was a valuable piece of property. And now that we were headed back to the city, we had little use for it.

"The memories," Cal said.

"This was Tia's first home," Sully said, cradling the baby against his chest.

"And my first home with Murphy," Cal added.

"And the site of so many plant murders," Lo mused.

I stifled a laugh.

Cal turned and looked at her, his eyes full of love. "I still can't believe you kept replacing the plants."

"And the fish."

"But not the cat."

"That's because Fuzzy is irreplaceable," Kit piped in, giving me a big grin.

The girls had sat me down again to have another negotiation. And one of their terms was that they wanted the cat. It was a small price to pay in the grand scheme, but part of me had really been looking forward to getting away from the beast.

Lo had reasoned that since they were looking for an apartment and I had an actual yard at my house, Fuzzy would be happier with me. He hadn't had a yard yet, and he'd become very set in his routine, requiring two long walks each day, so that argument was bogus, but I'd been too deliriously happy lately to put up much of a fight.

Being with Jess, planning our future, and seizing every moment had left me vulnerable. If the girls asked for a pet giraffe, I'd probably say yes. At this point, all they'd demanded, other than Fuzzy, was just bunk beds, a foosball table, and a promise to see Lake Paige every time she went on tour.

"We could find tenants for the first two floors," Sully suggested.

"Sebastian and I will miss you all," Madame E said. "But you were terrible neighbors."

We all laughed.

She closed her eyes. "Oh my. Have I got the tenant for you."

I looked to Sully, then Cal, then Lo.

"Don't worry. She won't be here until October. Long story. Lots of drama. Ooh, look at the time."

She jumped up, smoothing the skirt of her orange floral dress. "I have to head to Harry's for a nightcap." With a wink, she headed back inside.

"Do we even want to guess what that meant?" Sloane asked.

I leaned back, putting my arm around Jess. She relaxed against me, dropping her head to my shoulder. It felt incredible being surrounded by my people, with the knowledge that our future was full of so much more to look forward to.

My life was different. I was different. The closed-off workaholic who had moved in here one year ago had gotten his ass kicked and had learned there was a better way to live. I'd taken risks and put myself on the line, and I'd won the love of my life and two amazing kids in the process.

I still had a lot to learn, but one thing was certain: New Jersey was a magical fucking place.

Acknowledgments

Thank you for reading my Dad Com! I hope you have had as much reading these books as we had writing them. As you know, this series was a labor of love that I shared with my two besties, Brittanee and Jenni. The life of an author is a lonely one, and I'm so blessed to be able to share this journey with my dear friends.

Like all my books, it would not have been possible without the support of several talented and dedicated people.

Morgan Leigh, I asked for help, and you jumped in with both feet, quickly becoming the MVP in my life and the person who keeps me organized and on track. I treasure your friendship and your positive attitude. No one is more willing and more capable of learning new things than you are, and I am pinching myself that I get to call you mine.

Erica Walsh, thank you for being my friend and cheerleader for all these years. From cover design to finding photos and editing blurbs, you are truly in my corner every single day. We have cried and laughed and yelled together over the past four years, and I am a better person and writer because of you.

Beth, thank you for your thorough editing. I am amazed by your patience, professionalism, and kindness. Your careful work has helped bring these characters to life, and I am truly in your debt.

To my oldest friend, the indomitable Caroline, thank you for igniting my love of romance by introducing me to Jane Austen (and Colin Firth in a wet shirt) at the tender age of fifteen. My entire romantic worldview has been shaped by our shared love of happy endings and your friendship for these last twenty-seven (!!!) years is a true gift.

Becca, thank you for your professionalism and excitement about this series. You and the Author Agency have been such wonderful partners throughout this process.

Catherine, getting to know you has been one of the highlights of my year. Thank you for your marketing expertise, your passion for books, and your invaluable TikTok wisdom.

To my hype teams, thank you from the bottom of my heart for loving these books and this crazy world I've created. Most days, I pinch myself that I'm surrounded by such an amazing group of positive, kickass people.

Thank you to my family for being hilarious, loving, and silly. To my children, G & T, you push me, challenge me, and surprise me every day. Being your mom is my life's greatest adventure. Thank you for never going easy on me. To G, my mini-me, you are my #1 fan and I can't wait to share my author journey with you as you grow. And T, thank you for kicking ass in first grade, so I had the mental and physical energy to write this book.

And finally, I'd like to thank Taylor Alison Swift. For getting me through not only the production of this book, but through all of my life's challenges for the past decade. You have taught me, and countless others, how to harness my creativity and, most importantly, how to invest in my potential. Your work has made me a better mom, writer, entrepreneur, and person. Thank you.

Also by Daphne Elliot

LOVEWELL

The Lovewell Lumberjacks Series

Wood You Be Mine?

Wood You Marry Me?

Wood You Rather?

Wood Riddance

The Maine Lumberjacks Series

Caught in the Axe

Pain in the Axe

Axe-identally Married

Axe Backwards

Axe-ing for Trouble

THE MOM COMS

Mother Hater

THE DAD COMS

Bonus Daddy

Also by Daphne Elliot

About the Author

In High School, Daphne Elliot was voted "most likely to become a romance novelist." After spending the last decade as a corporate lawyer, she has finally embraced her destiny. Her small town steamy novels are filled with flirty banter, sexy hijinks, and lots and lots of heart.